THE GIRLS OF LAZY DAISY'S

The modern young man, who knows nothing but that barbarous straitjacket called the brassière, can have no idea of the intimate delights of the Edwardian corset, especially when it supported a delicious pair of bubbies that needed no such aid. A gorgeous young girl like Kitten, whose breasts achieved the impossible – in that they were large in volume, firm in outline, soft in texture and voluptuously perfect in relation to her many other charms – a stunning young lass like that, I say, could turn those few frilly inches at the top of her corset into a pleasure garden where a man might lose himself for hours . . .

Also by Faye Rossignol

Sweet Fanny
Sweet Fanny's Diary
Lord Hornington's Academy Of Love
A Victorian Lover Of Women
ffrench Pleasures
The ffrench House
Pearl Of The Hareem
Pearl Of The Desert

Smiler's
Memoirs

The Girls of
Lazy Daisy's

Faye Rossignol

HEADLINE

First published in 1993
by HEADLINE BOOK PUBLISHING PLC

10 9 8 7 6 5 4 3 2 1

ISBN 0 7472 4036 1

Typeset by
Letterpart Limited, Reigate, Surrey

Printed and bound in Great Britain by
HarperCollins Manufacturing, Glasgow

HEADLINE BOOK PUBLISHING PLC
Headline House
79 Great Titchfield Street
London W1P 7FN

The Girls of
Lazy Daisy's

If Rachel Cohen had not opened her blouse and sported her divine young breasts at me from the window of her bedroom in the middle of that hot afternoon in the July of 1897, the whole of my life might have taken a different course. But then where does one stop with that sort of speculation? If I hadn't fallen out of the tree a moment later . . . if she hadn't laughed her head off at me . . . if I'd been able to banish the memory of those two adorable bubbies . . . if I could only have got some sleep that night instead of setting forth on the insanely dangerous expedition across the roof of our house, onto the roof of hers, and down the drainpipe to her bedroom . . . if, if, if!

But all those things did happen (or didn't, as the case may be) – and undoubtedly *somewhere* in that fateful sequence, my life changed course and I ended up where I am today. Just think! But for that unforgettable, peeping-Tom moment, I might now, at the ripe old age of sixty, be nothing better than my father was – a moderately success-ful provincial stockbroker with a few 'spicy' memories to chuckle over in his old age. Instead, I'm a rich profes-sional gambler (retired) with the happiest memories of more than hrmph-errm thousand women of every race and perfume, most of whom smiled that old vertical smile for me, some once, some many times. (Actually, I retired from gambling – except for horse racing – when I reached the age of thirty, which was almost forty years ago now, so my pursuit of Woman and her darling commodity was my full-time occupation for most of my adult life. Yet I was

1

never a mere cunny-chaser, interested only in adding to the score. I loved most of them in my shallow, decent way. If I'd been as rich and wise as Solomon the Lawgiver, I'd have given out a law to let me marry the lot of them – and I'd have cherished them, too, to the height and depth and breadth of my powers.)

Anyway, to get back to Rachel of the sporting bubbies. If there was a moment when you could say my life made a sharp lurch cunnywards, it was an hour before midnight on that same day. At that precise moment, when I was an hour short of my twentieth birthday, I stood on the edge of our roof, gazing in the moonlight at the five feet of certain death that separated me from the edge of Rachel's roof. 'What the blazes d'you think you're doing?' I asked myself. I usually borrowed my father's vocabulary for my own rhetorical questions – he being a highly rhetorical man. Fortunately I already knew the answer: 'I'm risking my life,' I riposted. 'And for what?' I pressed. 'Just because she lifted her blouse and showed you her bubbies this afternoon, it doesn't mean she's going to lift her nightie for you now. She'll probably scream. Your reputation will be in shreds, and, worst of all, your allowance will be stopped forthwith.'

Iron Jack inserted himself into the conversation at that moment. He's the fellow that's caused me most of the troubles in my life; but, to his credit, I'll add that he's made up for them hrmph-errm-thousand-fold in pleasures. On that particular night he burst hotly out of my pyjama fly, thrust aside the folds of my dressing-gown, and fluttered in the cool night breeze in the most appealing manner. It was his way of saying, 'Listen, Freddy, I'm twenty years old tomorrow. Don't think I'm not grateful to your right hand – we've had some wonderful moments together these last five years. In fact, we've had six thousand four hundred and seventy-eight wonderful moments together. But that only strengthens my argument. Don't you think it's high time you promoted me to the Senior League? Look at me! I'm almost snapping in two at the mere thought of slipping myself inside Rachel Cohen's soft, warm, and no doubt virgin cunny . . .'

Brave talk, of course, but one of us had to think ahead. Suppose Rachel *didn't* scream blue murder? Suppose she did lift her nightie and spread the Gentleman's Relish, just for me and Iron Jack? Neither of us would have the first idea what to do with her, or it, or It. And nor would Rachel, probably. She'd only just turned nineteen. True, I was a great deal older – a day short of twenty, as I said – but I'd never so much as seen Old Mossyface. I knew there was a sort of slit-like arrangement down there because someone drew it in indelible ink on the Venus At Her Toilette (a reproduction, appropriately enough) in the Passmore-Edwards Museum and the janitor hadn't been able to erase it entirely. But that, as I reminded myself, is no substitute for experience in the flesh, if you see what I mean.

I decided I would have to have a word with my Uncle Tommy. As I turned about and made my disconsolate way back off the roof, poor Iron Jack was so frustrated he started spermspouting into my hand (his old pal) as I tried to tuck him away. The shame of it – just think if he'd shot himself off like that the moment Rachel Cohen lifted her nightie!

That was the way I put it to my Uncle Tommy the following morning, straight after church. He was only four years my senior ('nearly five,' he would say) and, though he'd been rather cool toward me in my childhood, he had developed quite a *passionate* liking for me by the time I was rising fourteen. Many a free afternoon we spent together in the woods and fields and wild places north of Leeds, our native city, tickling cocks, dreaming of girls, and seeing how far and how much we could shoot. The

'Uncle' handle was a standing joke between us, though he was, indeed, my mother's sister's youngest son. (My own three brothers, all older than me, have always been utter prigs and I shall not mention them again.)

Tommy had 'lost his cherry,' as the lady in question called it, on his coming of age. His father earned his undying gratitude – and my unbounded admiration – by taking him to Lazy Daisy's; there he passed the night in the arms of a filly called Lucy, who showed him ten dozen ways to enjoy an oyster. It was months before I heard the last of that – or wanted to; Iron Jack and I enjoyed many a second-hand romp with young Lucy for years after that seminal occasion. Also Polly, and Fifi, and Susie, and Sandra, and the dozens of other fillies he enjoyed over the years that followed. (We called them 'fillies' because, as he said, they spent twelve hours a day getting filled.)

Now, I put it to Tommy, it was time for me to lose my cherry. At first he was most dubious. He'd lost his at the age of twenty-one, which thus became the right and proper age for such an event; he thought twenty very risky. I pointed out that it was nothing like so risky as going into action with a weapon of unknown calibre and performance. 'You had a wise father to pick your time for you,' I added. 'Nature herself seems to have picked mine for me.'

I could see him wavering so I added, 'You'd never be able to give me a better present for my birthday.'

And so, after dinner that evening, we took our acetylene lamps and moth traps and went bicycling off up the Moor Allerton road. Our homes in Roundhay Park were only a mile or so north of Lazy Daisy's in Lidgett Park, but Tommy never took the direct road; we turned south after half a mile, rode beyond our destination, changed back into evening dress behind a hedge, and so strolled into Lidgett Park from the south. This filled us with all the cocky assurance of two young men who knew they couldn't possibly be recognized. And thus it was that I gained my first view of the inside of Lazy Daisy's.

It is impossible for anyone in these 'Utility' years of the 1940s to imagine the sheer opulence of an Edwardian brothel (or sporting house, as we more often called it), even in a provincial suburb like Lidgett Park. The house has gone now – indeed, the whole street has gone, in one of Leeds's many road 'improvement' schemes – so there's no point in naming it. (Though how anyone can call it an improvement to knock down a house where thousands of men tasted the joys of heaven and dozens of fillies grew rich beyond their dreams and replace it by a motor-racing circuit is beyond me.)

The house was an original Georgian manor whose grounds had been sold off for speculative development in the 1850s. It had served briefly as a reformatory, then, in the 1860s, as an hôtel before Daisy McGovern, the original Lazy Daisy (who died before ever I visited the place) bought it. The visitor drove up the carriage sweep and strode between Corinthian pillars to massive oak doors, painted white; each had a six-inch porthole at head height. He knocked and a curtain drew back behind one of the portholes while he was inspected. If he passed muster, he was admitted to a world of soft lights, lovely fillies, music, gaiety, palm trees, thick carpets, cut glass, and plush furniture; he wandered among them in a trance, his nostrils thrilled by incense and other heady perfumes. At least, I did on that first occasion.

In the grand hall, immediately before us, a magnificent central staircase rose to a halfway landing, where it divided into two imposingly curved stairs, one each side. My eyes nearly popped out of my head (and Iron Jack out of my waistband) to see an almost naked young filly leading an elderly gentleman in full evening dress up one of them. (To me in those days, elderly meant 'over thirty.') Despite this distraction, I was vaguely aware of a dining room to our right, matched by a drawing room to our left – with just a glimpse of the ballroom beyond. The place seemed to be filled with near-naked fillies, though in fact there were probably no more than ten in sight at that hour; but it is amazing how even one nude can fill a room (or an artist's canvas) in a way that eight fully clad women cannot.

When I say near-naked, I mean most of them wore silk stockings to just above the knee; their dark, rich colours – black, ultramarine, viridian green, or deep crimson – were highly stimulating among the sombre black of all those gentlemen in evening-dress trousers. One or two wore stockings to near the tops of their thighs, held up by brightly coloured suspenders hanging from tightly laced corsets, which did nothing to hide the lady's bush beneath and a great deal to support the local dairy industry above. Corseted or not, all wore a long, diaphanous garment, which, if it had not been almost perfectly transparent, could have been called a coat; some of these garments closed prettily round the neck in a froth of lace, others in a black velvet band.

A filly who was invited to dine with a gentleman put on a housecoat, which revealed much less while somehow managing to suggest much more. Many a gentleman used Lazy Daisy's more as a dining club than as a sporting house, though he paid as much to savour a lady's company at his table as he would have done to enjoy her favours in her bed.

'I'm looking for Maisie,' Tommy said to the maid on the door – who told him she had been in the dining room for the past hour and a half and would probably be available again soon.

'We'll wait then,' Tommy said to me. 'She's worth waiting for.'

To fill in the time I asked him why the smell of incense was so heavy.

He grinned. 'Work it out for yourself, young 'un. Eighteen fillies on parade each day. Six customers each. About four hundred pokes a time . . . must come to over forty-thousand pokes a day. Hot male gristle thrusts into foaming female gluepot and emerges reeking of her juices – forty thousand times each day, and more. The place would smell like a brothel if they didn't burn the old resin!'

The young woman whom Tommy had been seeking on my behalf emerged from the dining saloon at that moment – alone, we were glad to see. 'Maisie!' he called out jovially. 'Just the gel!' And, seizing her by the arm, he led her round in a leisurely stroll beneath the main stair. When they emerged the other side I saw her glance in my direction and then, turning back to him, pull a most reluctant face.

A brief but animated discussion followed and some money (two sovereigns, I later learned) changed hands. Then, as Tommy slipped off her housecoat, she turned to me wearing nothing but a broad smile of welcome and some black stockings. Even so, her earlier response had made it clear to me that I was probably the last of all the males in the house that night with whom she would have chosen to earn that standard fee.

That, I must admit, was a bit of a slap in the face; all the way there I had buoyed up my spirit by imagining the fillies' delight to see a fresh, young face among all those leathery, bloodshot, debauched old countenances.

My misgivings increased as she murmured, 'Come on, then, Freddy – let's show you what all those years of waiting were for, eh? I just hope you'll think it was worth it!' And, taking me by the hand, she led me up the stairs.

My spirit was now about as low as could be. I *knew* I was going to make the most awful ass of myself; only one reflection kept me going: 'You had far better make an ass of yourself with this Maisie filly, whom you need never see again, than with Rachel Cohen.' It kept me going but it did nothing to reduce my state of desperate funk.

A fully clothed woman walking upstairs ahead of me is still one of the most erotically stirring sights I know. In those days when women wore bustles, it was sensational; those poor, deprived gentlemen who have seen them only in still photographs have no idea of the delights they offered. The bustle was a cage of wicker that rested against a girl's derrière and the backs of her thighs; when she walked upstairs, she naturally bent one thigh in front of her and stretched the other behind – and that was the *only* natural thing about it; from there on sheer artistry took over. The thigh that was stretched wiggled the bustle rather violently toward the thigh that was bent; at her next step, that thigh wiggled it equally violently back again. The effect was electrifying, for it turned even the most sedate stroll upstairs into a bottom-wiggling display that a modern young man has to travel to Hawaii to comprehend. (The fact that it wasn't her bottom doing the wiggling but only a cage of wicker didn't matter – certainly not to a horrified youth of twenty.)

Well, the thing I want to say is that Maisie, even when deprived of the assistance of a bustle, as she was on that night, could nonetheless have taught those hula-hula girls new tricks! The naked cheeks of her superlative young derrière, wriggling before me as only she knew how, made the bustle redundant, me sweat, and the world swim around me. I knew then that I'd never last the paid-up hour.

An hour! Already it seemed like a life-sentence to hard labour. Here was an experienced young woman of, I guessed, twenty-three, who had Done It with hundreds of men probably, among whom there would be lovers of the highest calibre, and here was me, twenty by the skin of my teeth, who'd never Done It with anyone. If she had turned and said to me, 'I'll let you off if you'll sit in a cold bath all night,' I'd have worshiped her as my deliverer.

What she actually turned to me and said was, 'Normally we'd go in here, to Madame's boudoir, where'd you'd pay her this' – she held up Tommy's two guineas and smiled. 'But you're in such a state, poor thing, she'd probably tell you to come back when you're more composed. So I'll just slip in and smooth things over.'

While I waited, I had a chance to take my bearings. Madame's boudoir was over the entrance portico; in fact, its Corinthian columns supported her balcony. There were two rooms each side, which I later learned were bedrooms. Down each side of the staircase was an arcaded corridor, leading to the back of the house – and, I presumed, more bedrooms. Two doors led off each corridor; all showed a line of light beneath them, so I took them to be bedroom doors as well. Somehow the sight, or thought, of all those bedrooms was a great comfort to me; in the most immediate way it brought home the fact that this was something like a *factory* – a place where the ancient act of frigging had become an industrial system. The experience that, to me, would be unique, unforgettable, never to be repeated, would, for Maisie, be forgotten by tomorrow's dawn. As if to underline that conclusion, a couple came out of one of the bedrooms and descended the stair, arm in arm. The filly smiled at me but the man, who was elderly, did not even look my way. At the halfway landing a much younger man called out, 'Sally! I was looking all over for you!' He held out a hand and said to his senior, 'Will you permit me, sir?'

'By all means,' was the reply as he gave his erstwhile partner a brief peck on the cheek.

Sally then did a smart about-turn and, clinging tight to her new companion, fell in step with him all the way back up to my landing. Unseen by him she pulled a comic, slightly conspiratorial face at me, as if to say, 'Heigh-ho, here we go again!' As I smiled back I tried to imagine what it must be like for a girl, her hole still tingling from an hour or so of poking with one man, to turn about like that and go straight back for a further hour with another man at her fork.

Maisie came out of Madame's boudoir as they went in. She had towels over her arm. 'We'll go to one of the old servants' attics,' she said. 'They're not so overpowering as these grand chambers.'

As we passed the open door to the opulent room Sally and the old man had just vacated, she paused to let me look inside. It was the sort of room in which I'd always imagined the grand courtiers of Versailles used to tumble their gilded and powdered mistresses. 'Fancy it, do you?' she asked.

'No!' I gulped.

She took my hand and led me along the arcaded corridor to the last door on the right. This opened onto the old servants' stair, which now led up to what were called the Intimate Rooms on the top floor of the main house. I was later to learn that the servants at Lazy Daisy's – of which there were, of course, many – lived in the annexe, which was, in fact, a remnant of the much earlier manor house, most of which had been demolished to make room for the Georgian mansion. The fillies of the establishment slept there, too, unless a gentleman had paid for an 'all-nighter'; they had four six-bed dormitories divided into individual cubicles.

'You take that,' Maisie said, handing me a lighted oil lamp. 'I'll lead the way.'

The narrow stair forced me to walk behind her; its steepness brought the fold of her derrière above the level of my eyes. Yet she was so close I was forced to squint to make out the details.

'Ever see the likes of that?' she asked, pausing and arching her back to make her bottom jut pertly back.

'No,' I whispered, shivering violently.

'Rest the lantern on the step between your feet,' she advised. 'Or you'll set the whole place on fire! That's a good boy! Now, let your eyes drink their fill.'

Her delicate fingers stole behind and coyly parted the tufts of her bush. 'Tell me what you see,' she said.

'Something I've . . . I mean, the most beautiful . . . I can't think of any words,' I finished lamely.

'It's a smile,' she said simply. 'Can you see that? Two lips parting in a smile?'

'Ye-es!' I murmured ecstatically.

'It's a smile of welcome, Freddy. It's a welcome for you. There's two dozen girls like me in this House, and we all keep a smile of welcome like that, all warm and snug between our legs – just for you. Think of all those smiles when you're feeling lonely, eh?'

And she walked on, leaving me to take up the lantern and follow her into the dimly lighted corridor above. She walked the full length of it and paused before the last door on the left – the room immediately above the deluxe chamber we had briefly glimpsed below. 'This is quite snug,' she said, 'yet not too small.'

In area it was little over half the size of the room below, but that, of course, was still very large for a servant's room. The mention of 'attics' made me think of poky rooms with sloping ceilings; but here they were all level. They were, however, a mere eight feet high, which made it impossible to leave the gas mantles burning all the time. Even their little pilot lights left a discernible (though quite homely) fug on the air. The first thing Maisie did was go round and turn them all up. 'I suppose we want as much light as possible for *this*,' she said, and again I detected a certain irritability in her demeanour. 'Incandescence may beget incandescence, eh!'

'I suppose you're doing this all the time,' I volunteered in a conciliatory tone.

'I've never done it before,' she replied vehemently.

After the soft illumination in the rest of the house the five incandescent mantles were almost painfully bright; as I stood there blinking she said, 'D'you want to learn how to do it in your clothes or what?'

I slipped off my jacket and looked about for somewhere to put it. She took it from me and went to hang it in one of the cupboards. Then she approached me, naked but for her dark green silk stockings, and murmured. 'We have a whole hour. So just relax. There's no need to hurry – with anything. Your waistcoat?' Then, in a more suggestive voice, it was, 'And trousers?'

I had never heard the word on a woman's lips before – apart from my mother's when she said things like, 'We must go into Neal's and get you measured for longer trousers.' Except for practical occasions like that, strictly *en famille*, it was not a word for use in polite society to hear it on Maisie's lips sent me into an erotic spin.

I must have taken them off, and she must have hung them out of sight, for the next thing I remember is standing there with Iron Jack thrusting like a flagstaff out of the opening in my shirt – and remember, shirts in those days were like the modern tunic shirt and short underpants all in one. 'Well!' she exclaimed in a slightly surprised (and, I flatter myself, more-than-slightly-admiring) tone, 'you're man enough in *that* department!' I was especially proud of him that day for I had spent an hour that afternoon carefully clipping away the hairs around the back of my balls, round my bumhole, and all around the base of Iron Jack himself.

She approached me and, taking him in her hand, said, 'A real red-hot poker! Let's go over to the basin and give it a good wash.'

She squeezed it gently and I started giving *her* a good wash – all up her arm and on the side of her right breast; and then, when she realized what was happening and capped it with her hand, I filled that with a good measure of hot starch, too. She just stood there, staring me balefully in the eyes as if to say, 'You traitor – how could you!'

I shrugged apologetically and tried a smile.

She smiled wanly back. 'If I washed your fellow now, would that happen again?' she asked.

I nodded glumly. 'Probably.'

Her eyebrows shot up with interest and I saw she had meant the question sarcastically. 'Really?' she asked brightly.

''Fraid so,' I said. 'Perhaps if I wash it and you just tell me what to do?'

'Heavens!' She laughed. 'I suppose any man knows how to wash his own prick! We usually start that way more to get them really stiff than to get them clean.' She gave Iron Jack another squeeze, much more circumspect this time. 'You've no difficulty there, I see!'

'I did give it a jolly good scrub before I left home,' I told her.

'All right. Let's skip that, then. D'you think you've got another two shots in you?' She went to the basin and swilled her hand.

I nodded. Actually, I thought I had more but I didn't want to commit myself and find I hadn't.

'I'll take your word for it,' she said, returning to me. 'Let's go and lie on the bed and fire one of them as fast as you can. You're a bundle of nerves still and I can't help you learn anything while you're like that.'

She took what looked like a square of chocolate fudge from a little drawer in the bedside table and, handing it to me, said, 'Remember that secret smile I showed you on the stairs? See if you can part its lips and find a hole inside them. Then push that gently up into it.'

She lay on her back and, bending her legs at the knee, spread them wide. The smiling lips parted before I laid a finger on them and the hole gaped uninvitingly before my

13

disappointed gaze. After all my fevered and lascivious imaginings this – my first sight of Old Mossyface – was distressingly *ordinary*. That flesh was made to glow and tingle; it should look as if that were its purpose, somehow – especially in a filly who did, indeed, live principally for that service.

'Take your time,' she said. 'Have a good long look.'

Gingerly, gently, I inserted the lozenge and pushed it in as far as my finger would go. I looked up over her belly and saw her grinning mischievously at me. 'That's not very far,' she said. 'Haven't you got something a bit longer to poke it all the way up?'

Her humour, simple though it was, did have the desired affect of relaxing me. I chuckled and, feeling rather ape-like, crawled on knuckles and knees until my body was over hers. The moment she felt the head of Iron Jack dock itself between her lips down there, she gave an athletic twist of her hips and engulfed him entirely.

I must say, that first moment when the soft, warm, succulent flesh of a woman's cunny closes around your tool is quite unforgettable. Iron Jack has gone nosing into thousands of them since then, but the sensation of Maisie's hole as it closed hot and tight around him that night has not been lost in that welter of experience.

She gave a sigh of satisfaction (that we had got so far without further mishap, I suppose) and threw her legs about me, digging her heels into my buttocks and encouraging me to begin. It was one action in which I needed no tutoring, for the stomach-and-sheet method (with a last-minute diversion into a paper tissue) had become my favourite ever since I got my own bedroom.

On my fifth thrust I began spending again – this time deep into her. She hugged me tight and said 'Well done!'

A moment later she said, 'My goodness – you're still stiff as a ramrod!'

'I know,' I told her.

'Want to try again?' she asked.

For reply I started poking away once more, as leisurely as before. This time I made it last almost three minutes; each thrust and each withdrawal was so thrilling I wanted to try and remember it as distinct from all the others. I almost passed out from the joy of spending right up inside her hole once again – although there was little enough seed left to spend.

When I got my breath back after the last sweet throb had died away, she burst into laughter, as if she had been holding it back until then. 'You still haven't gone limp!' she exclaimed incredulously.

'I know,' I said.

She laughed even louder. 'Is that all you can say? I know some men who'd pay a thousand guineas to have a blood transfusion from you!' She ran her fingernails up and down my spine. 'Well, what can I say, young Freddy, except . . . want to try *again*?'

I kissed her ear and whispered, 'Please.'

'Like to try a different position?'

She tried to wriggle me out of her but I clamped myself tight as a limpet. 'No,' I replied. 'I still want to feel . . . these.' I put my hands around her bubbies, which were adorably soft and sensual to my palms.

Again I poked her with slow, deep strokes, relishing every little movement. Iron Jack became like an exquisitely sensitive finger exploring every part of her vagina, discovering its smooth runs, its wrinkles and creases . . . the tender parts that moved in sympathy with his thrust and pluck, the taut reaches that strained against him like an ardent lover, doubling his bliss at their less yielding contact.

It was a long, ecstatic while before I spent for the fourth time, yet when I looked at the clock I saw only twenty minutes had gone by since we entered the room.

This time she heaved me off her and, sitting up cross-legged, took Iron Jack between her fingers and stared at him in disbelief.

'All right,' she said resignedly at last. 'You've got even me curious by now. Have another go on me!' And she turned on her belly, tucked a pillow underneath her and moved her legs slightly apart. I found the little half-glimpse of her cleft far more stimulating than the earlier open display and mounted her from behind with a will.

I think a woman's cunny is actually made for rodding in that position – from behind. There is an area of small but stimulating corrugations on the front wall, an inch or so inside her; properly explored and taken at the right speed, they can lift the scalp off a man. After much joyful experimentation I discovered it at last with Maisie. It was a dry spending for, of course, I had pumped my last little pearl of starch some while back, but it was more joyous than any that had gone before. The fourth one had actually been slightly painful but now I was into what a runner calls 'second wind' and was ready for any amount more.

'My God, I don't *believe* this!' Maisie exclaimed as she turned over and stared yet again at Iron Jack. 'Does that thing ever rest?'

'Six goes is not unusual,' I offered apologetically, for she sounded quite angry. 'Don't blame yourself. It's not your fault.'

She stared blankly at me and then gave me a playful punch. 'Artful dodger!' she exclaimed. 'You mean you've been with women before!'

'No, no!' I exclaimed.

She frowned. 'What d'you mean about six goes . . . oh! I see.' She raised her eyebrows and made a tossing-off gesture with her hands.

'God no!' I was horrified. 'That's called masturbation! I'd never do that. It makes a man go blind, toothless, and feeble-witted.'

'Oh yes?' she replied, heavily ironical. 'What are we talking about, then – sheep?'

'I call it natural copulation without a partner.' I lay face down on the sheet and demonstrated. 'That's not masturbation.' (Of course, I did masturbate, often – five or six times every night – but I was too ashamed of it to admit as much to her.)

She slipped off the bed and knelt beside me, watching in fascination. 'In all my time in this game,' she said, 'and all the men I've known – I've never seen that! What's it like?'

I stopped and gave her the same mischievous grin with which she had earlier favoured me. 'Nothing like the real thing.'

She had the grace to laugh. 'I walked into that! All right – have one more go. How d'you want it this time?'

'Could we do it standing?' I asked. 'I've seen couples doing it in alleyways like that. Well, not exactly seen, you know. But I've often wondered what it's like.'

With a game-for-anything grimace she went around and turned down all the gaslights until the room was bathed in a soft glow. Then she drew a curtain over one of the cupboard doors and leaned against it with her legs slightly parted. And the copulation I enjoyed with her then was the best of all. The freedom that position gave me to explore her glorious body, to feel the weight of her breasts, to fondle her nipples, to run the backs of my fingernails down over her belly and hips, to dig my fingers into her splendidly curvaceous derrière and, surprisingly, feel her respond, to rake my nails up and down her back and hear her utter little whimpering noises – and finally to feel her shudder and almost fall apart when Iron Jack began throbbing away inside her for his sixth and last festivity. She was bathed in sweat by the time we got our breath back.

'That's torn it,' she said glumly.

'What?'

17

She shook her head as if to imply she could never explain it. All she said was, 'It's Sunday night.'

Perhaps there was a rule among the fillies, *not* to take any pleasure in Doing It on the sabbath? It was news to me that girls could take pleasure in Doing It at all.

Now at last I went to the washbasin and gave Iron Jack a good soaping. He was still fairly stiff as I tucked him away in my shirt. She reached out a hand, gave him another disbelieving squeeze, and murmured softly, 'Incredible!'

'That was the nicest, most enjoyable, most rewarding hour I ever spent in my life,' I told her.

'*Spent* is the word!' she retorted. Then, softly, 'It wasn't too bad for me, either – funnily enough.'

'I'll tell you one thing that surprised me. I didn't know girls can enjoy Doing It just as much as us men. I thought you Did It out of the kindness of your hearts.' I saw the disbelief in her eye and added, 'I mean, I know *you* do it for . . . reward. But I've always thought the girls out there Did It out of . . . wifely duty. That sort of rot. Yet right at the end there . . . I mean, you enjoyed it, too, didn't you?'

She gave me a sad, baffled look and then put her arms around my neck and kissed me hotly, just below my ear. 'Oh, Freddy!' she murmured. 'Where do I begin? There's so much I could tell you . . . so much. Could you come again next week?'

'I could come again *tomorrow*!' I laughed.

She pulled away a little and stared into my eyes, forcing me to take my reply seriously. 'Could you? Could you come every night this week? It'd cost a tenner – have you got that much?'

I nodded. 'Afternoons would be easier.'

'And even better for me, actually,' she replied. Again she stared into my eyes, this time sizing me up. 'Can I rely on it? If I were sure you'd come and see me every afternoon this week . . . oh, the things I could teach you!'

I returned the following afternoon at two o'clock, the hour at which Lazy Daisy's opened for business each day. It was the greatest shock to me to discover the fillies all dressed as demurely and as respectably as young ladies in the strictest finishing school. Some were seated in the ballroom, others in the salon, which was an anteroom to the ballroom, and they were doing just what those ladies would be doing at such an hour, too: tapestry and embroidery, painting water colours, filling scrap-books with pressed flowers or crests from headed notepapers, or catching up on their diaries and correspondence. The heady smell of incense was replaced by the pure and maidenly perfume of lavender.

Maisie sprang up the moment I entered and, taking me by the arm, bore me from the room – but not before I had time to observe a good deal of whispering and sniggering among the others. I looked back over my shoulder at a sea of smiling, forget-me-not faces, seventeen in number. Never mind their faces – I could not forget their seventeen vertical smiles. Oh, sweet seventeen! I remembered Maisie's words last night, how they kept those smiles all warm and snug and hidden between their thighs – and all for me! Their thighs! I sweated at the mere thought . . . seventeen pairs of soft, luscious, yielding thighs! Yet their very outlines could hardly be guessed at, private as they were beneath the acres of frothy lace and pleated organza that presently clothed them. Oh God, that was probably the day I first lost my soul to the cunny-haunted vision that has heaped me all my days!

'What did you tell them to make them all grin like that?' I asked as we started up the stairs.

She half-turned, put a finger on my nose and gave a gentle push. 'Nothing for your ears, young man!' She was wearing a bustle now – a tight, small one, for the large

19

bustles of my mother's time had passed quite out of fashion. But Maisie wearing even a small bustle would have sent the hula-hula dancers home in despair. I had to look away to avoid making an ass of myself (and a mess of my trousers) for the second day running.

'And why are all of you dressed like young finishing-school ladies?' I asked.

'We *are* young finishing-school ladies, as a matter of fact.' She laughed. 'But no, we always dress like this between two and six.'

'Why just between two and six?'

'The gentlemen who call between those hours prefer it – clergymen, retired civil servants, generals on half pay – that sort. Then between six and ten you'd find us looking like . . . what? Like rather advanced, bohemian ladies in an artistic salon. We wear flowing, loose garments that reveal little but let a gentleman get his hands inside and grope what he's thinking of buying. And between ten and two in the morning . . . well, you saw us last night. From high-buttoned virgin to naked whore in just a few hours! Our daily transformation.'

'You're not whores,' I protested as we reached the landing outside Madame's boudoir.

She turned and rubbed the backs of her knuckles down my cheek. 'Bless you, Freddy, but we are, you know. Don't ever forget it.' As she turned away she added under her breath, 'Hark who's talking!'

Madame's boudoir was long, narrow, and tall – and, unlike the rest of the house, was in the Gothic style. It suited Madame, who was also narrow and tall, and most respectably Gothic in her appearance. Her iron-grey hair was screwed up tight in a bun and she wore gold pince-nez, which she held up like lorgnettes to inspect me. 'So this is young Master Stamina!' she murmured in a fruity, headmistressy voice. 'Our junior Hercules!'

The Labour of Hercules in which he got fifty princesses

with child in a single night had been rather glossed over at my school, so I didn't know what she meant by that. I was flattered nonetheless, of course.

'This is Freddy, Madame,' Maisie said.

I held out my hand, which surprised her a little, though she shook it warmly enough. 'And what are you hoping to do in life, Freddy?' she asked.

'My father wishes me to be a lawyer, Madame. But I think I'd prefer to be a gambler. He, himself, is a stockbroker, which I consider a dishonest form of gambling. I'd prefer to take up the honest kind – horses, cards, and so on. I have a very good head for figures.'

She chuckled. 'Most of the men I meet have a good *eye* for figures – but that's not the same thing, is it!'

'They could go hand-in-hand,' I pointed out.

She reached across her table and patted my arm. 'You'll do, Freddy. I'll admit I had my doubts when I heard you hadn't yet come of age, but you'll do. You're welcome here at any time.' She took up the two five-pound notes I had laid on her desk. 'Especially when you come garnished like this! Now are you quite sure about it? You want to see Maisie here – every day this week?'

I slipped an arm around Maisie's waist and replied, 'I was never more sure of anything.' Maisie said nothing, but I got the feeling it was because she thought of several things to say and couldn't make up her mind which.

When we were back outside she asked, 'Same room as yesterday?'

'Of course.'

She prattled blithely on as we sauntered down the arcaded corridor. 'So you think you have a good head for figures, eh? Tell me, did you see all those ledgers in her boudoir?'

'Yes – what a lot! Both walls!'

'Those pages record every single transaction in this house from the very beginning. The tales they might tell!

So riddle me this. Lazy Daisy's has been a sporting house for the last thirty years. It's always had two dozen girls – and offered eighteen for service on any given day. We put up the shutters for the whole month of July and for a week around Christmas, but otherwise we're open every day of the year. On average a girl spreads the relish for half a dozen gentlemen each day she's on offer – and I don't suppose that's changed much over thirty years. And every one of those occasions is noted down in those ledgers. So how many friggings is that?'

Of course, I had felt the question coming – from the challenge in her opening remark – so I'd been doing the calculations while she spoke. 'Well,' I said at once, 'it adds up to approximately thirty-five thousand, three hundred and sixteen friggings each year . . .'

'*What*?' She was aghast.

I repeated the figure and added, 'And if what my Uncle Tommy told me last night is true – each man pokes a filly four hundred times – that's over fourteen million pokes a year.'

She laughed feebly. 'A woman once told me a bus conductor on a double-decker carries four tons of loose change upstairs by the end of each day – but it's a kindness not to tell him. Now I see what she meant! Should I even ask how many friggings it comes to over the thirty years?'

I was there already, of course. 'It's one million, fifty-nine thousand, four hundred and eighty.'

'I knew I shouldn't have asked! Over a million? Lord, how depressing!'

'Actually' – I gave her elbow a gentle squeeze – 'it'll be eighty-*one* with what we're about to do.'

She laughed. 'Don't you mean eighty-*six*?'

'No!' I protested – then, realizing that my vehemence sounded rather rude, added: 'I mean, don't think it wasn't fun last night. It was the best fun I've ever had, as I said at the time. But I did make a bit of a pig of myself, didn't I?

Like scoffing six helpings of dinner at one session. And that would be all right if you, Maisie, were the equivalent of fish and chips.' We were starting on the servants' stair now. I reached up and stroked a finger up and down her spine, luxuriating in the touch of silk on skin. 'But you, my dear, are *suprème de la volaille gourmet*. And I want to learn how to appreciate you properly – like a gourmet.'

She did not answer until we reached the stairhead. Then all she did was murmur, 'My, you *have* been doing your prep!' When we reached the room she closed the door behind us and went on, 'I thought the idea was you'd learn how to appreciate a *woman* properly?'

'That was yesterday. Today it's not just 'a woman,' any old woman – or any young one, either – it's *you*.'

She slipped her arms round my neck and kissed me, not quite on my lips. 'You're not falling in love with me, are you, Freddy?' she asked.

In a curious way I think she wanted me to say I was; but I remembered the seventeen other sweet smiles down there in the salon and had to admit I wasn't. 'If I had come up here with any of those other girls, I'd be saying the same thing to her. I'd want to appreciate *her* properly. I don't think there is such a thing as "a woman" in these circumstances – not if you're a fumbling and hopeless beginner like me!'

She kissed me properly this time, and from the look in her eyes I guessed it was to stop herself from saying what was on her mind. When she broke off she strolled over to the window to draw the curtain. But instead she just stood there, staring out at nothing. 'The trouble is,' she murmured, 'you want to appreciate me *as a woman*, don't you!'

'Of course.'

'Of course!' she echoed bleakly. 'And to make matters worse . . . damn it, that's what I want, too!' She turned and held out her arms to me. 'Come here.'

23

As I drew near she took my outstretched hands and executed a country-dance movement, putting me behind her but keeping my hands in front of her. Her arms were now crossed, so that when she drew them to her she folded my hands over her bubbies. It was a warm and wonderful feeling, and all I wanted to do was savour the moment and make it last. Like a gourmet.

'Talk to me,' she said. 'Tell me how you feel about *me*. Can you remember what I look like? My face? Tell me about my face. Make me like it again.'

'Don't you like it now?' I asked in surprise.

'I used to.'

'Oh, but you should. It's a beautiful face, especially your eyes. They've haunted me ever since last night. You can say anything you like with your eyes, Maisie.'

'You mean I can give anything away! Thank's for the tip. I must watch that.'

'No!' I hugged her bubbies tight and felt wonderfully grown-up – to be so casual about a 'hot' gesture like that (and not to be spermspouting like a yard bull into my pants, too!). 'Don't talk like that. Don't talk yourself down. When my hour was up last night, although I could probably have gone on for another couple of goes, what I really wanted was just to lie down beside you and look into your eyes and talk. You're the easiest woman to talk with I've ever known. Maybe it's the same with the others down there – I don't know yet. I mean, when I'm talking with a girl outside, I'm thinking all the time, does she or doesn't she? How far would she let me go? I'm on edge every minute, see, and it sort of colours – or *dis*colours! – all our conversation. But with you and the fillies downstairs, that isn't a question, is it? We already know the answer, both of us. So we can really talk, without feeling on edge all the time. D'you know what I mean?'

She leaned her head back against my neck and said, 'Have you thought all this since last night?'

24

I nodded and kissed her temple. 'I've been thinking of nothing else since last night.' I went on grazing at her temple, reflecting that there was really no square inch of a girl's skin that *isn't* provocative; every bit of her is capable of carrying some powerful sexual charge. Last night Maisie's body had been gently perfumed, but today she wore none that I could detect. Yet the natural aroma of her person was more titillating than anything that ever came out of a bottle. How could I possibly explain such things to her – the thrill she afforded me just by letting me breathe her own girlish fragrance, for instance? I could only talk in cyphers. 'Your lips have also haunted me,' I added.

She raised them toward me and gave me the most passionate kiss I'd ever had from a girl – not that I'd had many, of course, but passion like that needs no comparative. 'Well,' she said, with an oddly forlorn sigh as we broke, 'you did ask to know me as a woman! I don't know how you've done it.'

'Done what?'

'I'll tell you one day. I don't think it'd mean anything to you yet. D'you enjoy holding my bubbies like that?'

'I'd enjoy holding your big toes, Maisie – every part of you is thrilling to me, and . . . special.'

'Whew! Let's just stay with my bubbies for the moment. Would you like to see what you've been and gone and done to them?'

'What?' Now I was intrigued. What could I possibly have done to them – just holding them? Not even moving much – just enjoying their curvaceous softness and perfect size. And, of course, my own fantastically mature calm in the process.

'Undo the buttons down my back – starting with the hook at my waist.'

Her blouse was in the newly fashionable leg-o'-mutton style, with translucent arms. The shimmer of her flesh

25

through the material was highly rousing. When I reached
the button between her shoulder-blades, she said, 'That's
enough for the moment,' and then, taking the hem at the
front, lifted the blouse up and let it rest in a great, frothy
gathering on top of those magnificent bubbies.

She shuffled a half-turn to our left, which brought us
directly facing a long, oval mirror beside the washstand –
one of three in the room, which seemed to me (at that
time) rather excessive. My eyes goggled at her adorable
hemispheres and I saw at once that their appearance was
different from last night. Then her nipples had been
like . . . well, not to put too fine a point on it, like big,
soft, rosy warts; but now their pink outer ring was swollen
and had turned the colour of dark coral, and as for the
nipples at their centres – well, they were like the polished
tips of miniature artillery shells, except for their colour,
which was almost crimson. 'They're utterly gorgeous!' I
murmured.

She swallowed hard and said, 'D'you notice any difference from yesterday?'

'Can I touch them? They look so touchable.'

'I was hoping you'd ask!'

They felt exactly as they looked – swollen, fiery, and
exquisitely sensitive. The moment I started fondling them
she gave out a great, shivery sigh of pleasure and cried.
'Oh . . . o-oh . . . o-o-oh!' catching her breath and letting
it out in a tiny explosion at the beginning of each cry.

The pleasure it gave me to hear her gasp like that is
hard to describe. Of course, it was not so electrifying nor
so physically thrilling as actually spermspouting inside her
– and yet, for some strange reason, if I'd had to choose
between the two kinds of pleasure, I'd have picked the
sound of her experiencing that thrill over and above my
own. Apart from anything else, I found I could make it
last longer! Certainly she seemed able to go on and on.

'Actually,' I said after a while, 'I remember they felt

like this right at the end of our time last night, when we Did It standing up.'

She snatched the blouse down again and let out a *whooo*! – the sort of noise people make when some violent exertion comes to an end. 'You noticed that, did you?' she said.

'I meant to ask you at the time.'

'Well, I'm glad you didn't! I might have said something rather sharp. Listen, Freddy my dear, I don't think I need *tell* you anything. You seem observant enough to manage without. I'll just offer the occasional suggestion – the odd little hint – and leave you to get on with it. Shall we try that?'

'For instance?'

'For instance, undo the rest of those buttons and slip your fingers in round the sides of my ribs. Play games with my bubbies. Tease me gently. Tantalize me. You know what my nipples are yearning for your fingers to do. Make me beg.'

'Oh well,' I laughed, 'if that's what you call 'the odd little hint,' I'm certainly willing to try!'

I would never have imagined the sheer, godlike plea-sure to be gained from simply standing behind a girl, kissing her, running my lips up and down her neck, and then slipping my fingers inside her blouse and tantalizing *myself* – never mind her – for the feel of her swollen nipples and the reward of her ecstasy at my touch. It amazed me for quite another reason, too. Last night my own feelings had been all over the place. If I'd touched her bubbies like this – only twenty-four hours earlier – I'd have shot my bolt at once – wasted my sweetness on the desert air. Now, however, though I was roused to a high fever, I was nowhere near that same crisis.

What had changed? Mine was the same body – the same cells, the same nerves – surely they don't change much in so short a time. The only difference, then, was in my mind. When I told her that she had haunted me ever since last night, it was the truth; I had thought of nothing else in all those hours; I had gone over our encounter again and again, like an obsession. And that had wrought some change in me, so that I was now much more in control of my sexual body and my responses.

She broke into these thoughts with the suggestion that I should now start exploring southwards. This time, remembering my sarcasm at her 'odd little hint,' she was more cryptic: 'See if you can discover the South Pole,' was all she said.

And what a journey of discovery that proved to be! Woman's body is the most wonderful arrangement of matter in the entire universe. The way her trim little waist, so supple and firm, swells outward in one dainty curve after another, over her hips and the sides of her buttocks to the wide, hospitable firmness of her hip-bones . . . well, I've held thousands of them between my two hands down the years and yet it still brings me out in a sweat just to think of it!

And then there's the front of Woman, too – from the piquant jut of her bubbies to the dimpled hollow that marks the end of her rib-cage, to the subtle curve of her belly, to the delicate mossy tendrils that mark the fringes of her bush . . . oh what ineffable joy it is to set the fingertips a-wandering at liberty there!

On that memorable afternoon with Maisie, when I first began to explore the glory that is Woman, all this was sheerest novelty to me. And yet, somewhere in the deepest recesses of my mind, there lurked an ancestral memory that prepared me for each discovery in the fraction of a second before I made it. When my hot, exploring finger ascended her Mount of Venus, trading my feverish perspiration for hers, it was a place I had wandered in before, centuries ago. And when I found the very first dimple of her divine crevice, it was more like a homecoming than a pioneer landfall. Nothing within me wanted to sing – like the Ancient Mariner – *I am the first that ever burst into this silent c.!*

In any case Maisie's c. was far from silent! When my roving finger pushed on south and touched her – well, she had called it her South Pole, but anything *less* frigid would be impossible to imagine – she let out such a cry of rapture I thought she would pass out.

'Oh, oh – I want to *see* that,' I said in a voice I hardly recognized as my own.

'Yes!' she gasped and pulled herself away from me.

As we ambled to the bed, shrugging off our clothes on our way, I sniffed my finger and was astonished at the pungency of what I smelled there. *Fish!* is the usual shorthand description, and, indeed, that was my first thought, too; but a second sniff, and then a third, awakened subtler senses in my nostrils and told me what a rich, elusive, delicate brew it is that keeps those tender lips so receptive to the intruding horn.

Our clothes now lay promiscuously intertwined, just where we had shed them, littering the floor between the window and the bed.

'You're like a gorgeous butterfly stepping out of your chrysalis,' I joked. All she wore then was the little padding of her bustle, which was tied round her waist and the tops of her thighs with frilly scarlet ribbons.

'Does that smell put you off?' she asked.

I blushed.

'I saw you,' she explained, pointing to one of the long mirrors. 'You'll never catch a whore unawares in her room! What about that smell? Fishy, eh?'

I shook my head. 'It's not a *smell*, it's a spice, a fragrance. When I was standing behind you at the window just now, I was just inhaling the warm air rising off your skin, breathing the natural fragrance of your body . . . and it was the most exciting thing ever. And I thought, how can I possibly explain this to Maisie? She'll think I'm daft – and I'm sure you do. But it is delightful. And now I discover *this*!' I held up my finger. 'It's like . . . I don't know. It makes me feel hollow. It makes me shiver with longing for you. But I didn't even notice it yesterday!' I laughed. 'Mind you – yesterday I didn't know if I was on my head or my heels!'

'You didn't notice it yesterday, Freddy, because I took great pains to wash it all away – as I do several times every day.'

'But not today.'

She shook her head and grinned. 'Not for' – she checked the clock – 'another forty-two minutes.' She lay back on the bed. 'Come and undo this bustle.'

I knelt over her and tried gently to part her thighs, to lie between them and toy with the scarlet ribbons; I had the fancy to undo them with my teeth. But she teased me by pretending they held her thighs so tightly clamped she couldn't move them at all. So I just knelt there on hands and knees, relishing their brightness against the pale tint of her skin. And then I thought them so pretty and provocative that I determined to leave them laced – and to force her by other means to part her thighs and show me that strange 'South Pole,' which, like her natural aroma, had certainly not been there last night.

I leaned down and kissed the smooth skin between her navel and the top of her beaver. And there my eager nostrils caught a faint whiff of the musky spice that had so excited me earlier – perhaps trawled up by my finger in its delectable wanderings a little farther south.

So, a little farther south grazed my lips – and now it was unmistakable. Again it filled me with a strange excitement, such as one might feel upon approaching a wild creature in the dark; it was such a powerful, *animal* aroma. I pressed my lips gently into her moss and started exploring with the very tip of my tongue, taking the path my finger had pioneered. Again I exchanged moisture for moisture until my tongue sank into the dimple at the upper corner of that adorable smile. And oh, what nectar it tasted there! I darted my tongue in and out, ferrying her honey to my palate, relishing its most lascivious tang; already I knew that if I lived to be a hundred, the zest of that particular spice would never grow stale.

She gave a little moan and her limbs fell slack. It would have been easy work to part them with my hands but I was determined she would spread herself for me entirely unaided. So I pressed my fervent lips to the hot dint of her fork and thrust my tongue as far as I could into the aromatic depths of her cleft. I was, naturally, so ignorant of the nature of a girl's secret crevices that I could not possibly have intended the effect this simple gesture had on Maisie. By searching with the tip of my tongue for the entrée to paradise I accidentally brought the firm, fleshy root of my tongue into tight, slithering contact with her excited bulb of pleasure, which I so earnestly wished to behold.

The effect on her was, as I implied, quite stunning. She emitted a little shriek and spread her thighs so wide, and so suddenly, that she knocked my arms from under me. My letching mouth was now the sole support of every-thing above my knees, so the full weight of my torso now pressed my tongue down on her sizzling hotspot of ecstasy – which I was now even more desperate to glimpse.

But no – as if the pressure were not already enough, she gripped me by the hair and held me into her fork, moaning, 'Go on! Go on! Go on!'

I got my hands back under me and spread them over the tops of her thighs, so tight into her fork that my thumbs were able to find the opening into heaven and then slide daintily up and down the insides of her lips, furling them over and back again. And all the while my tongue explored that strange delicacy which lay half-hidden in the upper end of her cleft.

The sensitive tongue – what a keen and discriminating little explorer it is! The finger is a blundering scout by comparison. Try to explore the roof of your mouth with the tip of your most sensitive finger; see how much of a mental map it allows you to make. You could draw it on the back of a postage stamp. But try the same thing with the tip of your tongue, working over the same surface one small fraction of an inch at a time. You'd need a foolscap sheet to record it all!

It was the same with the soft folds and fleshy rilles of Maisie's quim, among whose aromatic pastures my tongue now wandered in delirious liberty. True, I had seen it all yesterday, but had been so repelled by the novelty of the vision that I remembered nothing beyond the slack gape of her hole itself. The outer lips, where my thumbs were still making their merry sport, were blubbery and full – which, as I have since noted, is almost always the case when they are much trafficked. But the inner ones were fine and sinewy – as my own lips feel from inside if I tighten their musculature and resist the thrust of my tongue. I found the entrance to her hole but I postponed the pleasure of exploring within it. Instead, I ran the tip of my tongue lightly upward over a smooth, fine-grained region with what felt like a little nostril in the centre. Now I could feel a distinct taper on the inner lips and a deepening of the furrow between them. And then suddenly I came upon some flesh, about the size of a kidney bean but of an oyster-like succulence; it was tender, soft, complicated, and mobile – or movable, anyway. And the *excitement* that passed through Maisie's body when my tongue curled around it and tested how movable it might be! I don't know how she bore it. She strained her fork wider yet and lifted her bottom (bustle and all!) clear off the sheet, as if she would never have enough of me there.

Yet I was minded still to tease her. So, though my tongue played all around that fascinating bud, half-hid at the junction of her inner lips, it rarely touched or pressed against it, except in passing. At the same time I moved my thumbs down and got both of them into her hole, no deeper than the top joint – whereupon I wriggled them, sometimes in unison, sometimes counter to each other. And Maisie went *wild* at that! She collapsed back on the bed and lay quite limp in between the spasms that shook her whole body beneath me.

And then at last her hands relaxed their grip – in fact, reversed it – and thrust my head away from her. 'No more,' she pleaded. 'You'll ruin me for the day. Oh, my God, Freddy, who taught you that!'

I just lay there, gazing happily at all that my tongue had just mapped in such intimate detail – especially that bean-sized winkle, all feverish and pink. 'What *is* that?' I asked, touching the flesh near it.

She inhaled deeply and let it out in a whoosh. 'Something most men don't even know about – thank heavens,' she replied. 'And it's something very few men have ever found in me, I can tell you!'

'Well, it's big enough not to miss,' I objected.

She laughed drily. 'It is now. But sometimes I've a job finding it myself. So there!'

'But what's it do? It's shrinking, by the way.'

'Knowing you, Freddy, it'll be back to full size before long! What's it do? It's a good question. It ruins many a maid, that's for sure. I frigged a missionary here one night last winter. He said the blackies cut it off their womenfolk to keep their minds on motherhood and *off* the pleasures of achieving that state. And I frigged a doctor once (there's a lot of education in this game, let me tell you!) and he said it's the only *pure* organ of pleasure in the human body. Yours has to double as a pisser, as well . . .'

'Don't you feel pleasure in here, then?' I wiggled a thumb in the mouth of her hole.

She gave a little start of delight. 'There's your answer! But it does double-duty, too – like your pisser-cum-joystick.'

I frowned, not understanding her drift.

She reached out and tweaked my nose. 'It's also for letting babies out – in case you'd forgotten *that* part of the business!'

'No, I hadn't. Well, only temporarily. Actually, I meant to ask you about that. You fillies must spend half your time getting rid of babies?'

Her fingers tousled my hair. 'Funnily enough, no. Remember those lozenges you thought were chocolate fudge? They help. But Madame says the best preventive is to have half a dozen lusty men each day give you a good squirting inside there. Those millions and millions of little tadpole things fight each other to death and none of them wins. Anyway, I was telling you why this doctor said he could prove women are just made for pleasure – their own, not men's. Because we're the only beings in the whole of creation, male or female, the *only* beings who've got that little rosebud of pure ecstasy tucked away down there.'

'Gosh!' I was impressed beyond measure. 'And so you spend six hours every day, just wallowing in it, eh?'

'Save us!' She gave a helpless laugh. 'I'd be dead by Wednesday! Haven't you twigged yet, my love? What you've done to me – what you did just now – is something no man has done for . . . I don't remember. Except for Mario, of course. He's my macquereau. But I mean no paying customer.'

'But why?'

'I wish I knew. Somehow you've slipped underneath my guard.'

'No – I mean why don't you let the pleasure rip?' I

laughed as an apt thought struck me: 'Gather ye rosebuds while ye may!'

She shrugged. 'That's what you'd do if you were a woman – one of us?'

I nodded.

'You wouldn't, you know – not if you really were a woman. That's the difference between us.' After a pause she added sadly, 'Perhaps that's why so many man hate us.'

'No!' I tried to assure her.

'They do. It's because we have the chance to lead in reality the sort of erotic life they can only experience in phantasy – frigging up to a dozen different partners a day. They'd give their eye teeth for that power – *and* getting paid for it. And we don't even enjoy it!'

'Don't you?' The declaration surprised me.

'Not in *that* way. I mean, I enjoy meeting lots of different men, talking with them – seeing a side of them they wouldn't dare reveal to anyone else. Even making them happy. I enjoy all that, of course. But not the sort of enjoyment *they* get out of it. Except for you!' She gave me a playful box on the ears. 'As I say, you've got under my guard somehow.'

I kissed her cunny and cushioned my head lightly on her bush, sniffing deeply. 'Sorry.'

'I'm not. It makes an interesting change. And, most important of all, I don't think you'd take advantage of it in the way most other men would.'

To be called a man by someone with experience of so many men was delightful; I said nothing in case I spoiled it.

'I mean,' she went on, 'you actually *like* women, don't you.'

I was baffled. 'I should think that applies to most men who come visiting here!'

'You'd be surprised! I told you just now – it's not so.'

'Why did you pull a face when Tommy picked you as the one to initiate me?' I asked.

'Oh, you noticed, did you? I'm sorry about that. Nothing to do with you, actually, but you must understand that in this trade it's usually the oldest woman in the house who gets asked to render that service to young cherries like you – the motherly type who won't embarrass you too much.'

'Well, I'm glad it was you, Maisie.'

She chuckled. 'Prove it! That's enough talk for today.'

And prove it I did. I only spermspouted into her once that day but, with her help, I made the poke last half an hour, trying all sorts of wonderful positions that even my lascivious imagination had failed to envision.

I thought about her on and off for the rest of the day. Her comment that she experienced no erotic pleasure with the other gentlemen who took her up to bed was greatly to my comfort.

I wondered if I was ready yet to have a go at seducing Rachel Cohen but decided to let Maisie be the judge of that.

And so my education continued all that week. Every day at two in the afternoon I irrupted briefly but blissfully among the eighteen demure young ladies of Lazy Daisy's, dreamed of the eighteen lascivious grins concealed between their thirty-six demurely clothed thighs, and swore I'd taste them all in the fullness of time. And every day Maisie whisked me upstairs for a brief exchange of banter with Madame before taking me to what I now thought of as *our* bedroom. And there her experienced fingers trembled as much as my ten tenderfoot thumbs as we peeled each other's bodies from the frustrating encumbrance of cotton and satin. And her nipples thrilled as vibrantly as mine to the loving touch of our increasingly familiar caresses. And her *coquille* (as she called it), revelled just as tumultuously to the gentle clench of my tongue as my *coque* (as I affected to call it) rioted in the hot, spicy grotto of her sex.

And now we did not spin it out to the full hour, because, to tell the truth, I enjoyed our verbal intercourse every bit as much as the carnal kind. On the Thursday afternoon of that same week – by which time I felt like an old hand at the game – I was emboldened to ask her what she had meant the previous Monday when she asked me, 'Who taught you to do that?' It had seemed an odd question to me because she surely knew I had enjoyed no other tutor but her.

'D'you remember what it was you did?' she asked.

'I was playing with your *coquille* – with my tongue.'

'But you weren't, you see! That was my point. You were playing *all round it*, but you hardly ever touched it. You drove me mad with desire and then transformed it into the purest ecstasy with the deftest and briefest of licks on the little rosebud itself. That's what I can never get Mario to understand. He goes at it with his tongue in exactly the same way as he'd frig himself with his own hand. But that's not how a woman's little *coquille* likes to be treated. When a woman frigs herself, she does this, and this, and this . . .' She demonstrated – her fingers darted, tickled, trembled, quivered, stroked in a dozen lascivious ways, never straying far from that unique little Veiled Lady of Rapture. But only rarely did she actually touch it, and then with the most exquisite daintiness.

'Whoo! See what I mean?' She pulled the lips of her quim over the swelling *coquille* – with the sort of virtuous, self-denying gesture she might have used in closing a box of chocolates after sampling only one or two. As for me, I was thrilled to think that girls lay alone in their beds making exactly the same pleasurable discoveries about their bodies as we fellows do about ours; I had never supposed they were so earthy and physical. I thought it was all sugary dreams and sighs of longing with them.

Maisie repeated the question: 'So – how did you know precisely what to do to inflame me so?'

Ruefully I confessed I had merely been trying to tease her, as I might have offered her a bonbon and snatched it away.

She smiled at that.

'When does this Mario person do those things to you?' I asked.

'Why? Are you jealous?'

'No – but curious.'

She pouted, but then said, 'No, you're quite right, really. Never be jealous, Freddy. Don't let any of us get her hooks into you for a long while yet. As for Mario, he does those things to me on Sunday night. We close at eleven, remember, and then our husbands, lovers, macqueraux . . . call them what you will . . .'

'Husbands?' I asked in amazement.

She just nodded and smiled. 'Funny old world, eh? Our *men*, by whatever name we know them, are admitted and we have a supper and a little dance, and then we all go to our beds – where we rediscover why the Good Lord gave us a smile at each end of the corset.' Under her breath she added, 'Which it's very easy to forget during the rest of the week – believe you me!'

'Every filly in the house? You all have men like that?'

'No only about half of us.'

'And the others?'

She grinned. 'Am I giving you ideas, Freddy? Don't you worry about the girls who don't have men. They have delightful ways of consoling each other – rest assured.'

Another thought struck me. 'These men – they don't pay, I suppose?'

She laughed. 'I can see I *am* giving you ideas! No, of course they don't pay.'

'But then why does Madame allow it? What does it benefit the house?'

She replied with a winsome, faraway smile. 'Ah, Freddy – you should join us for breakfast one Monday morning. I don't suppose there are many houses of pleasure where you'd hear so much singing, so many happy little tunes hummed beneath the breath on that particular day!'

When Friday came around – my last day as Maisie's most ardent pupil in the art of carnal gratification – I approached Lazy Daisy's with heavy heart. I did not begrudge the house one farthing of the tenner I had spent, but the fact remained that it was half of all my savings – at least, of those savings on which I could easily lay my hands. My further pleasures would have to be sought between the unbought thighs of girls like Rachel Cohen – with results far less predictable than the more-or-less guaranteed delights to be procured in a place like this. A rather desperate remedy occurred to me, involving the risk of all my remaining savings, and yet I saw no other way out.

However, I didn't wish to think about that now; it would spoil this climactic encounter of a week already rich in climaxes of many kinds! So I drew a deep breath, squared my shoulders, put on my bravest smile, and knocked at the door.

To my surprise Maisie answered in person; it was usually the job of one of the maids – those broad-beamed country wenches who made the beds between occupations, tidied the rooms, and giggled horribly if you asked them what *their* price was. (Actually, it was three pounds, but I didn't learn that until later.)

'My, my! You're eager!' I teased Maisie as she almost dragged me up the stairs.

'It's your big day,' she replied.

'My graduation!'

'You could call it that.'

'Aren't we going to say hallo to Madame?' I asked as she whisked me past the gothic boudoir.

'No need. Anyway, she's been called away.'

'From the house?'

'No, just to . . . one of the other rooms. A little matter of discipline.'

'What! Is one of the fillies in for a good swishing?' I joked – remembering what the word *discipline* had meant at my own school. Of course, I never for one moment supposed that such barbarities might be applied to the fair and gentle bodies of these damsels, too.

'That's right,' she replied evenly. 'And of course we never waste such a money-spinning chance as that.'

'What d'you mean?'

'I mean half a dozen gentlemen have paid a fiver each to watch the stripes being laid on. So Madame lays them on good and thick. It's quite a ritual – poor Sarah!'

I stopped, and strained my ears to listen – suspecting she was pulling my leg. She grinned and shook her head. 'Spare your efforts, Freddy. You won't hear a thing from here. It's all happening this very moment down in the wine cellars – the *old* wine cellars in the annexe. Anyway, you've other things to consider now.' She clapped her hands and rubbed them in pleasurable anticipation.

She continued as we ascended the servants' stair: 'Was Tommy telling the truth when he first spoke to me about you? D'you really intend to frig the little girl next door?'

'D'you think it unwise?' I asked, for her tone was rather inquisitorial.

'My dear! I don't even know the child.'

'No, but in general?'

'Well . . . there is that old saying about not shitting on your own doorstep. But, on the other hand' – she brightened – 'you've got to start somewhere. Which brings me neatly to this afternoon.'

We had now reached the corridor at the head of that stairway. She turned and stared intently at me. 'We've *all* got to start somewhere. Even I, old and broken in experience as I am – even I had to start somewhere.' She raised her knuckles gently to my cheeks in a gesture I had come to know and love. 'And I wish,' she went on poignantly, 'you had been the one to break me in to this game, dear Freddy.'

I gripped at the tender emotion that suddenly overwhelmed me. 'So do I, Maisie.'

'Do you?' she asked earnestly. 'Do you honestly?'

'Cross my heart and hope to die!'

'Oh, Freddy – you utter angel!'

'Why this fervour?' I laughed. 'Surely it's too late now?'

'But it isn't, you see. I mean – yes, it's too late for *me*. But, as you know – or perhaps you don't, but I'm telling you now – one or two girls move on from this house every month. And one or two join us to take their place. And sometimes they are virgins and we sell their First Night for a very high price. But more often they are not. Usually some rude swain has already stolen their jewel. So then the debut of a Ruin'd Maid is worth no more than any other encounter under this roof. Yet her dread of that ordeal is hardly less than if she were a virgin still. Can you imagine it, Freddy, dear? And if you can, what would you give to help such a pitiable female survive it and flourish thereafter?'

I stared at 'our' bedroom door, already more than half-guessing what lay beyond it – or stood beyond it, perhaps . . . pacing the floor and biting her nails and trying for the tenth time to use the chamber pot, to no purpose. 'Oh no,' I almost whispered.

'Oh yes!' she insisted gently. 'For one thing it will redeem the pledge you so lightly gave just now. But consider this, too, my dear: It will prepare you far better for the maidenly bashfulness of the little girl next door than any charade of innocence I might be able of offer you. The debutante beyond this door is in a sort of halfway stage, you see. She's not a virgin, but she's never opened her legs for money yet, either. And she's not exactly over the moon at the thought of it, I dare swear!'

I drew a deep breath to still my pounding heart. A small part of me was thrilled at the prospect Maisie had unfolded to my lascivious mind; but mostly I was terrified I'd make a hash of it and spoil the girl for ever. 'How often . . .?' I stammered. 'I mean, how did she happen to . . .?'

'The usual.' Maisie shrugged. 'I think it was her father's valet, as a matter of fact.'

'How old is she?'

'Seventeen. And a real good-looker – tall, slender, long-legged, juicy bubbies with big nipples, and the most sensational ginger hair you ever did see! You won't regret it, I promise!' She burst into laughter for I must have been drooling at the chops by then.

'Seriously,' I chided.

'Come and see for yourself.'

I closed my eyes and, praying to Venus and Eros – and any other god or goddess within earshot – let her lead me to it.

There is a profound truth in the phrase 'made for each other.' And there is a profound instinct in every man and woman that knows when a meeting of two such fortunates occurs. It may be the prelude to a lifetime love; it may last no longer than an hour in an hôtel bedroom (for men and women can be in love as briefly as that); but when it happens you know it beyond all doubt. It happened for me the moment I set eyes on the as-yet-nameless debutante; it happened for her, too, but she was much shyer at showing it.

She was everything Maisie had promised. For some reason, the drooling description had led me to expect I'd find her already naked – or in stockings, corsets, and dressing gown, perhaps, but nothing more. Instead she was fully clothed in a long, flowery summer frock – white gloves, shoes, and all. Her head was crowned with a wide-brimmed straw hat and, yes, even her parasol lay aslant the bedhead!

She was sitting on the bed, her feet just swinging clear of the floor – not because her legs were short but because the bed, like all pleasure beds the world over, was high. And she leaned back on slender arms, so girlish they seemed to bend the wrong way. But all that was mere impression, something vaguely glimpsed at the edge of my vision. It was the vision itself, the vision of her face, that held me rivetted.

Her hair, as Maisie had said, was ginger – bright, bright ginger – the most intense I had ever seen. And it fell luxuriantly from beneath her straw hat, tumbled over her shoulders, and spilled in rich profusion over her breasts and shoulders in thick, lustrous coils. The curls of it around her head accentuated the swanlike elegance of her neck; and, when she tilted her head back and let her hat fall to the bed, it revealed the sharpness of her pale, pixie ears. Indeed, all her skin – the skin of her face (the only flesh that was then exposed) was pale, and most daintily freckled. Her chin was firm and somewhat pointed, adding to the pixie quality I had already noted. But it was her eyes that held me most – two great limpid pools of blue-green entreaty. Begging me what? Oh tell me, fair nymph, and I shall give you all! Only tell me!

'Good afternoon, sir,' she said, barely above a whisper – a musical voice, but cracked with her anxiety.

How I found my own voice I do not know, but I located enough of it to reply, 'Please! Anything but "sir"! What is your name, pray?' I was suddenly ashamed I had not asked Maisie earlier.

'Kitty,' she replied.

But Maisie happened to draw the curtain at just that moment, so I misheard. And the name I misheard seemed so beautifully apt to me I almost wept. 'Kitten!' I exclaimed. 'But it's perfect! It suits you absolutely, dear young Kitten.'

She drew breath to correct me and then, thinking better of it, gave me the warmest smile that ever wrapped itself round the cockles of my heart.

'We don't want that glaring sun in here, do we,' Maisie was saying – deliberately breaking across the violins in my ears. 'Come on, *Kitten*! Stand up, girl – you're an independent woman now! This is Freddy, I told you about.'

I would have given the rest of my savings to know what else she had said, apart from my name!

When Kitten stood up, however, I even forgot that Maisie was in the room. I went so groggy at the knees that I had to grab the brass knob at the foot of the bed to maintain my balance. She was fully clothed yet her whole body exuded a warm, slinky sensuality that all but robbed me of my wits. All she did was stand up and take two hesitant paces toward me; but the sway of her lissome waist and the swing of her voluptuous hips was such that, had I the skill of a Leonardo, I could have taken out my sketchbook and – without a further glance at her – have sketched her every line and curve, every muscle and sinew.

Maisie, bless her, broke the reverie once more – by asking if we wished her to stay. I think she wanted to watch, not take part; she wanted to see her star pupil graduate. But I was too consumed with my lust for Kitten to realize it then. 'I wouldn't dream of it,' I assured her.

And Kitten gave another of her gamine smiles and said she'd be fine. Somehow she managed to imply the words, ' . . . now that I've set eyes on him,' without actually saying them.

Neither of us looked at Maisie as she went, so I don't

know what her expression was.

'Well, Kitten,' I said as soon as we were alone. I eased the cotton square I liked to wear round my neck on hot summer afternoons. 'I suppose Maisie told you that this time last week I'd hardly even kissed a girl. So I hope you don't expect to find me a two-million-horsepower, gas-fired Casanova today!'

She laughed, and it made me feel so weak I had to sit down – on the bed, of course. She sat beside me and, despite the awkwardness of her position, tried to kiss me on the cheek. But she was so nervous she bungled it and stood up hastily, turning her back on me so that I should not see her furious blushes.

Fortunately the shirt I wore that day was of the sporting kind so I was able to draw it off over my head in a flash. A moment later I was standing at her back, naked to the waist and wrapping my bare arms about her, folding her into my embrace.

'I don't really know anything,' she said miserably.

'I know lots,' I assured her. For the moment I did nothing to change my affectionate embrace into one more openly erotic. 'For instance, I know you're one of the most beautiful girls I've ever had the good fortune to meet. I know I feel privileged beyond all words merely to be able to *talk* to you. I know this must be a most horrid ordeal for you – and if you want simply to lie beside me on the bed and do no more than that – merely talk to me – for the whole hour, and then pretend to Madame that it really happened, I won't give you away . . .'

'Why?' she asked sharply. 'Don't I appeal to you in that way?'

Oh Woman! I love you. I love you. And love you. *But* . . .!

At that moment she put her hand to my arm – and gave a little start of surprise to find it naked.

She turned round and stared at me. I stood quite still,

watching her eyes run up and down my bare torso, enjoying the naughty little smile that twitched at the corners of her lips. But when she murmured, 'Oh, but you are beau-ti-ful!' – drawing out the word and lifting her hand to touch my arms and chest – I felt bathed in the kind of pleasure I had least expected to find in a house like Lazy Daisy's.

'There's more of me,' I said.

Her cheeks flushed as her eyes fell to my belt, where Iron Jack was pushing like a coiled spring.

'But it's hardly fair,' I added, 'for me to strip to the buff while you . . .' I plucked at her sleeve.

With a sly smile she took my hands and raised them to the bottom-most button of her blouse. 'Go on, then.' Our eyes met, our knees trembled, our entire bodies were in a flutter.

One button. I glimpsed the white satin of her corset.

Two buttons. I could begin to make out the taper from her ribs to her slender abdomen.

Three buttons – and three to go. I could see the bones in her stays. How slack they hung. There was no pressure of flesh against them at all; not an ounce of fat did she have that called for such confinement.

Four buttons. My heart skipped a beat as I caught my first glimpse of her pale bubbies, their voluptuous roundness shimmering through the frilly gossamer around the top of her corset.

Five buttons.

I left the sixth, which was at the pit of her neck, while, with two delicate fingers, I furled the pleats of her summery blouse aside, lifting each half up and laying it over the swelling tops of her adorable bosoms. They shivered like jellies at the pounding of her heart. But, as I could tell from the shrunken state of her nipples, there was more fear than lust behind that hammering.

For a moment I just stood there, staring at her in awe,

drinking in her loveliness as she had done with me – but with far more reason. Then, with a look of smiling reproach, she herself undid the last button. I eased the neckline off her shoulders but she it was who shrugged it off her altogether. I suppose it fell to the floor but I did not notice; my eyes were rivetted on those twin globes and the merry dance her movements provoked them to perform. The perfume of her body – a musky combination of vixen and cinnamon – was something I have never quite forgotten.

She noticed my response and repeated the movement; I neglected to breathe.

The modern young man, who knows nothing but that barbarous straitjacket called the brassière, can have no idea of the intimate delights of the Edwardian corset, especially when it supported ('sported' would be a better word) a delicious pair of bubbies that needed no such aid. (I never look at a brassière without thinking that all it lacks is an address label, a postage stamp, and a customs declaration – and I wish we could send them all to Outer Mongolia.) A gorgeous young girl like Kitten, whose breasts achieved the impossible – in that they were large in volume, firm in outline, soft in texture, and voluptuously perfect in their relationship to her many other charms – a stunning young lass like that, I say, could turn those few frilly inches at the top of her corset into a pleasure garden where a man might lose himself and his senses for hours.

Now, fixing my eyes on hers, I took her elbows between my fingers and gently raised her arms above her head. A few tresses of her long, fiery hair now spilled forward over her shoulders and down beside her bubbies, accentuating their provocative thrust over the gauze of her corset top. The nervous sweat from the red fuzz of her armpits had a spicy reek whose memory, even now, more than forty years on, makes this pen tremble between my fingers.

With the gentlest possible touch of my fingernails I

caressed her, beginning at her elbows, down over the pale, freckled skin of her arms, down into the red cauldron of her armpits. But her response was ticklish rather than lascivious, so I at once moved my fingernails behind her, to scratch them lazily and lovingly down the long angle of her shoulderblade.

Our lips were very close by now. She lifted her face and brushed her sweet mouth against mine. I had been preparing myself for a longer, more passionate kiss, but found this teasing little contact deliciously wanton. I paid her the same compliment, and soon our mouths were darting round each other like two butterflies in a forest glade. Almost unknown to me my hands had returned to the sides of her ribs and my thumbs were playing lightly over the skin around her nipples.

But how they had grown since last I saw them! They were as large and as taut as ever Maisie's had been. And when my thumbs made a little cradle beneath each and slowly lifted them, she gave out a gasp of astonishment and collapsed against me. Then her arms were entwined around my neck, and her hair was all about my face, and her lips were crushed tight to mine. And she writhed so hard against me that I could not fondle her bubbies at all. Indeed, I could hardly extract my hands from between us!

When I did, I flung my arms around her and, flattening my hands to the small of her back – a sensual curve beneath the satin of her corset – I pressed her ever harder to me.

She squirmed even more forcefully then, arching her back and grinding her hips in a way that puzzled me – until she achieved her object, which was to get the tips of my fingers inside the waistband of her skirt. Then she settled tight against me and let out a long, lecherous sigh. I, of course, needed no second bidding. I explored downward with my fingers, over the frills that garnished the bottom end of her corsets, too – and discovered with some surprise that, underneath her skirt and petticoats, she was wearing drawers.

Maisie, even in the demurest of her afternoon costumes, had always worn nothing beneath her skirts to impede the ardent intruder – and she had told me it was the same with all the other fillies, too. Some impetuous gentlemen, she explained, like to bend a girl over the bed, forward or back, as soon as the door closes behind them. Then they rip open their flies, throw up her skirts, and plug themselves into her at once. (Which, incidentally, is why a pleasure bed is made so high – as I mentioned earlier.)

I had not attempted such a thing with Maisie, but I must admit I had tossed myself off at the notion of taking a filly to her room and laying her fully clothed on her back across the edge of the bed; then I had lifted her boots (cherry red and highly polished, of course) to rest on my shoulders, one each side of my head, and hoisted Iron Jack into paradise at once. I imagined myself peering down at her, admiring her black silk stockings and the creamy white of her thighs, and all the curves of her hips and bottom, and the black delta of her bush, and the oyster folds of her quim as they writhed to the pull and thrust of my champion girl-measurer. For a moment I even contemplated doing it now with Kitten.

What stopped me was not shyness, nor the thought that a more conventional initiation would be kinder, but an odd suspicion that she was no longer kissing *me*, wriggling her voluptuous young body so firmly against *mine*. She had, I suspected, done her best to turn me into a duplicate of her father's valet – the cause of her present situation.

Of course, I could not allow that! My fingers found the hooks that held her skirt and, with a deft movement I had practised on Maisie all week, I slipped them out of their eyes. Her waist was so trim that no sudden release of pressure alerted her to what I had done. So that when I pulled myself an inch or so away from her, the dress fell and she gave a startled cry. All she now had on below the waist was a pair of peach-coloured silk stockings, her drawers – which I had felt but not yet seen – and a brief, cream-coloured petticoat that covered no lower than her knee.

She stared down at her fallen dress a moment before stepping out of it. Perhaps she saw it as a symbolic gesture, a crossing of the Rubicon, the moment she truly took up her new profession. At all events she gave me an arch grin and, echoing my earlier mock-complaint, said, 'But it's hardly fair, Freddy darling, for me to strip to the buff while you . . .' And she plucked at the waistband of my trousers.

Until then I had had some vague plan at the back of my mind to cope with this delicate business of removing my trousers and exposing Iron Jack to her gaze – alarmed, admiring, indifferent . . . whatever it might be. I should do it discreetly, while we were kissing, while her hands caressed me about the torso; I should be entirely naked before she even realized it. But now, with the possibility that she was taking every chance to turn me into her father's valet, I saw it had to be done as deliberately and frankly as possible. 'Go on, then!' I took her hands and guided them to the topmost button of my flies.

She swallowed heavily and stared up at me with those lethally lovely eyes. 'I never . . .' she faltered. 'Can I . . .?'

Her fingers were already exploring the bulge inside the cloth. 'I never saw that . . . thing there,' she managed to confess at last.

'Take your time,' I told her. 'And see here – we can take it easy, too.' I backed toward the bed and lay voluptuously across it – as if *I* were whoring myself to her.

My shoes were of the new patent kind with elastic sides – very flash in those days. I was able to wriggle them off without troubling her at all.

Propped back on my elbows, I spread my tightly trousered limbs wide while she, giggling naughtily, knelt between them. As part of the manoeuvre she had to lift her single remaining petticoat, which gave me a delirious glimpse of her drawers. I was delighted to see they were of the 'convenient' kind – open right through her fork (designed to enable a woman to use a public convenience without undoing them). Curly wisps of her foxy-red bush peeped charmingly out of the overlap, promising delights too dizzying to contemplate.

Then she leaned forward to get her hands at my buttons, and her drawers fell again. Now her bubbies jiggled enticingly over me; I longed to play with them again – though I desired even more to watch her expression when she clapped those adorable eyes on a man's jewels for the very first first time. How had she and the valet Done It? Only in the dark? Always from behind? I itched to ask her.

'You undo them,' she said. 'I'm scared.'

'Of what?'

'I don't want to hurt it.'

I chuckled 'You won't. I'll show you the sensitive bits once you've liberated it. Pretend you're unwrapping a present – it's a nice, warm, cuddly present all for you!'

Her hands stole toward it again – and yet again she snatched them back. 'I can't believe it,' she exclaimed. 'All my life this has been bad . . . naughty . . . shameful . . . scandalous – scream, run away in horror – all that sort of thing! And here I am – here we are – suddenly – talking about it like the most natural . . .' The words petered out. She shook her head and raised her hands in a gesture of hopelessness at her inability to find adequate words. 'I mean, I'm *not* screaming . . . I *don't* feel ashamed . . . it's actually' – she bit her lip like an errant schoolgirl – 'quite exciting!'

I canted myself onto one elbow and reached out my free hand to give hers a reassuring squeeze – and then, in the same movement, pulled it firmly forward to my flies once more.

Her lower lip vanished between her teeth; she knitted her brow in concentration; one by one her fingernails gouged the buttons out of their holes, but – unlike me with the buttons of her blouse – she did not fold my flies open until she had the last one undone.

Iron Jack was straining fiercely against the waistband of my underpants – or, to be precise, against the two buttons of my waistband. So frenzied was his thrust it splayed wide the front opening of that thin cotton undergarment, revealing his long, lust-bloated shaft to her curious gaze.

It seemed to fascinate Kitten. Her tongue darted out and wet her lower lip – which was full and sensuous. 'May I touch it?' she asked.

'That's on the menu,' I replied.

She giggled. I expected her to undo the last two buttons and watch him spring to attention; a thrill fluttered through me as I anticipated that moment. But instead she slipped her hand into the opening and grasped him gingerly with the very tips of her fingers. The sight of those elegant digits, so slender, so delicate, so wonderfully feminine, as they gently squeezed that unfamiliar flesh, so ardent and so tumid, almost undid me on the spot.

I moaned with pleasure. She dropped it like a hot coal. 'Sorry! Did that hurt?'

Half of me wanted to ask what on earth she and the valet had done; the rest of me knew it would be disastrous to mention his name or evoke memories of her former life in such a way. 'No,' I gasped, taking her hand and replacing it on my joystick. 'It was just so . . . exquisite.'

'Am I doing it right?'

'Don't think about it – doing it right, doing it wrong. I'll tell you when you're doing it wrong. And I'll tell you now, Kitten – you could teach even Maisie a thing or two about how to touch a man's . . .' I nodded toward the object of all this attention.

'Yes,' she said, 'what *do* we call it? Or him?'

'I call him Iron Jack.'

She gave a dismissive laugh. 'He's not like iron at all. Shall I tell you what he reminds me of? You know when a bullfrog puffs up his cheeks like two balloons?' She nodded down at what lurked in the gape of my underpants. 'That's what your thing's like – only you've got long sausage-balloons instead of round ones. See – you've got this swollen tube running up the middle . . .' She ran a gentle finger the full length of it and I almost swooned with rapture; when she saw the effect it had, she did it several times more before she concluded her explanation. 'And you've got these two long, swollen balloons, one each side.' She chuckled and gave him a million-volt squeeze. 'I wonder – does he go *quaark*! and deflate, like a real bullfrog?'

I gasped a warning: 'He goes squirt-squirt-squirt – like a real bull – and *then* he deflates.'

'Ah . . . yes. Of course.' She gently stroked the two swollen sides of Iron Jack with her fingertips, studying my reaction. 'Not quite so sensitive, there?' she asked.

I grinned. 'But it's still very, very pleasant. That's what's important – the mixing of the two – the very pleasant and the exquisitely sensitive.'

She licked her lips again. 'Which is his *most* sensitive bit?'

'If you undo those last two buttons, you'll see it.'

I almost shot myself when her fingers fumbled there, right on my randiest parts.

'Oh!' she squealed when Iron-Jack-in-the-Box leaped

free at last – and I realized it was a sight she had never seen before. More than ever I was consumed with curiosity to know what, if anything, she and that wretched servant *had* done to make her parents throw her out – and more than ever I steeled myself to say nothing.

I squeezed the muscles in my crutch – the ones that men usually employ to nip off a pee. She laughed like a child to see my tool wagging his great, swollen head like a drunken maypole. Then she took him between her fingers and began giving him tiny experimental squeezes all over, making careful note of my responses, and proving so apt a pupil that words became superfluous.

Then I showed her other things – how, if she ran a fingernail up and down the inside of my thigh (she had to pull my trousers and underpants right off me for that), the testicle on that side would rush excitedly indoors and the whole of my body would tremble with an excitement I could not control; I showed her where she could safely caress a man's balls and where even the tenderest touch would be unwelcome. And all the while I kept 'accidentally' thrusting Iron Jack near her face, longing for her to kiss him and take him between those adorable lips, yet never daring to ask her outright.

Maisie, true to her brief – which was to prepare me to seduce an innocent young girl – had not even mentioned the practice to me; but I knew such things went on in high-class houses like this because Tommy had told me of them.

At last, in desperation, I said, 'He's quite clean and sweet, you know. I washed him thoroughly before leaving home – and put on fresh-laundered linen.'

'So did I,' she said brightly. 'At least, I washed between my legs this morning and I put on fresh linen just after luncheon. I was going to wash my tra-la-la again but Maisie told me not to – not until after.' She pulled a greatly daring face and, in a voice slightly hushed, asked,

'D'you want to see my tra-la-la?'

My eyes had to answer for me; my voice was suddenly too unreliable.

She lay on her back and parted her legs slightly, copying the position in which I had lain earlier. I scuttled down the bed like a crab and ducked my head between her knees; she started to roll up her petticoat but I put out a hand to stop her. And then I slowly inched my way up to paradise.

Plunging my head into that feverish space beneath her petticoat was like trespassing into the lair of some gorgeous feral animal. The breath that rises off a redhead's quim is unique among the whole tribe of woman; it is the subtlest possible blend of aromatic perfumes – zesty and soporific at the same moment, spicy and yet oddly muted, too. Trap it beneath fresh-laundered linen on a hot summer's afternoon when the girl herself is beginning to melt with sexual passion and you have a formula to stun the mind and enslave the body for life. I was stunned and enslaved to my luscious Kitten from that hour.

Every moment was golden as I kissed and sniffed my way up her silk-stockinged thighs, while she eased them slowly, languorously, seductively wider with every inch of my advance. At last my lips and nostrils were poised above the overlap of her drawers, which the spreading of her limbs had brought within an ace of opening. I truly feared that some part of my mind would snap at the surfeit of pleasure it was being asked to accommodate. I wanted to tweak the linen hems apart and close them again, tantalizing myself with glimpses of the promised land – but I dared not. I ached to insinuate my tongue between the folds of material and dart its tip among the softer, hotter folds of flesh inside – and again I dared not. And all the while that perfume of her sex assailed my tortured senses, racking me with joy so intense it bordered on pain.

At last she broke the spell that held me in such thrall. She spread her thighs a fraction wider still – and there, filling my ecstatic gaze, was the fairest, shapeliest, cutest, prettiest quim in all the world. And I write that judgement as one who has since studied many thousands of those divine oracles at equally close quarters. The exclamation that escaped my lips shames me now for its banality, yet it delighted her beyond measure: 'Oh!' I murmured, 'what a little darling!'

But it was, indeed, a little darling of a quim. The two outer lips made perfect brackets – the shape of an African shield – to guard the inner pair, which had the form of a double ogee. The beautifully symmetrical convex curves below girded the neatest, sweetest little gullet you ever saw – tight and pearly pink, and puckered into tiny whorls of flesh that simply craved the touch of the exploring tongue; above, their curvature became, by imperceptible degrees, concave, rising like fingers in prayer to enfold a bud of pleasure that – I now felt absolutely sure – had never yet tingled to the hand or tongue of man. I closed my eyes and went down to claim that supreme honour for my own.

I recalled what Maisie had told me and took enormous care to lick and kiss and stab my tongue all round that joyous swelling, but never to touch it. For a while – and a disturbingly long while it was, too – she just lay there rigid, until I began to think she was paralyzed with disgust. But then her thighs began to quiver, and the muscles of her buttocks twitched, lifting that fragrant lotus toward me as if imploring me to tantalize no more. And from a thousand miles away I heard her sighing and panting. And I felt the writhing of her body as her head thrashed wildly from side to side. And I felt the bed shake where she pounded it with her fists.

And at last I yielded to the dumb entreaty of that gaping cleft and cradled my tongue around her supreme organ of pleasure – and to my astonishment found it twice as large as anything Maisie had ever produced for my delight. It was the size of a runner bean compared with Maisie's petit pois. And the ecstasy my tongue was able to conjure from it was commensurately greater, too.

Still, I did not linger there, outstaying my welcome, but returned to grazing the pastures all around. And so I continued, bringing her back to the boil and letting her erupt in a frenzy, a dozen times and more, before she reached down and gently eased my head away, begging me, 'No more! No more!'

The sight of her quim now, so transformed by the ecstasies I had induced, made me realize that my own climax was not too far away; the lovely, pale thing I had seen, so exquisitely fine and slender in all its curves and folds, was now engorged with pleasure and wore a blush so deep it was almost brown.

'Now!' I gasped, rising to my knees and wedging my thighs beneath hers. From that position it was easy to lift her heels up beside my head and settle Iron Jack deep in between the juicy folds of her labia – like a sausage in the well-buttered split of a long bun. I poked him back and forth a time or two, relishing the sight, especially the way her lips clung to Iron Jack and moved a little way with him in both directions.

'Y-e-s!' She spoke the word on a long-drawn-out sigh. Her eyes were closed and her mouth hung slackly agape. She moved both hands down into her fork and pressed the tip of Iron Jack hard against her bud of pleasure. And her breathing grew short and staccatto as she rose to yet another climax. When it hit her, I drew back a little farther than usual, until I felt the head of him sink into the softness of her vestibule; then I parted my thighs slightly, to change the angle of her hips and let him slide into her with the least possible fuss.

Words have not yet been coined to describe the pleasure that overwhelmed me as the warm, juicy walls of that sweet young girl's vagina closed around my fellow and clenched him tight. I hoped I had achieved it so skilfully that she hardly noticed the moment of her initiation. But I could not have been more wrong.

The moment I slipped deep inside her she opened her eyes wide and stared at me in utter bewilderment, as if to say, 'What on earth are you *doing*?' Then she let out a mighty gasp and went absolutely rigid – but only for the briefest moment. Then she clawed at my arms and shoulders, toppling me forward onto her at the same time as she threw her legs up around me and shivered all over, like a willow in a storm. Of course I started spermspouting at once – one mighty squirt after another, flushing hot and hard into the top of her shaft. She could feel it and almost passed out – we both almost passed out – in our joy.

After an age, when the sweat that bathed us began to feel chill, we stirred as if in agony. She took my lolling head between her hands and kissed me passionately before collapsing in torpor once again.

I rolled off her, drew up the sheet, and, stretching myself beside her, cradled her lissome young body in my arms.

'What was that you did?' she asked.

'What d'you mean?' I replied. 'Surely you've done it before?'

She shook her head.

'But I thought . . .'

'The first bit, yes, where you just slid up and down my tra-la-la. But not the . . . what you did after that. Did you *make* that hole inside me?'

I merely laughed, feeling sure she must be joking.

'It was . . . beautiful,' she murmured.

'D'you honestly mean no man has ever done that to you . . . I mean that you've known a man who slid his thing up and down your crevice but never went inside you? Surely you knew you had a hole inside there?'

'A little one, yes. I mean, I never realized it went in so

deep! You went right up here!'

My hand was already near her belly button; she moved it an inch or two to show me what she meant.

A dreadful premonition overcame me. I sat up and wriggled my way down the bed, throwing off the sheet and parting her legs once more. And there, as I feared, I saw streaks of the telltale crimson oozing out of her, mingled with the escaping seepage of my ejaculation.

'We must have a word with Madame,' I said, although I was still twenty minutes short of my paid-up hour.

We rose and dressed, helping each other from time to time; it was a loving rather than an erotic act. I felt most warm and tender toward Kitten, which, Maisie had told me, is not how most men feel toward a filly once she has milked their spermspouters dry.

At the door, on our way out, Kitten leaned her forehead against the jamb and gave out a little sigh. 'Wish me luck for the rest of this day, Freddy!' she murmured.

I felt a sudden pressure of tears behind my eyelids. At that moment I would have done anything to spare her the ordeal that lay ahead. If I had been a wealthy man, I would have bought her out of that house and kept her free of that life for ever – and what a foolish thing that would have been! As it was, I simply held her in my arms and hugged her tight and assured her that with a body like hers and her adorable smile and a dash of boldness, she'd fly it.

Madame was wonderful about it. At first, of course, she was angry – chiefly with herself for having failed to spot Kitten's maidenhead. But, as I pointed out, if she, with all her experience, had failed to spot it and I, with all my faculties concentrated on the tip of my hymen-splitter at his most sensitive moment, had been equally unsuccessful in detecting it, then a gentleman who had paid a substantial sum to enjoy its taking would have felt justifiably aggrieved. She laughed then and pinched my cheeks and said I had deserved it. And as for Kitten, she gave her some cream to rub inside her hole and said she needn't go back into the salon until tomorrow.

When Kitten had gone, Madame added to me, ' . . . though whether she'll be grateful in the end, I don't know. A new girl's feet hardly touch ground for the first week or so, whatever day she begins, but to begin on a *Saturday* . . .!' She fanned her face and smiled ominously.

While on the subject of maidenheads, I'd like to say I think they are largely mythical. Down the years I have helped a couple of dozen girls shake off the affliction of virginity and I have encountered only three undoubted hymeneal veils, all of them before the Great War. My experience with Kitten, back in 'Ninety-Seven, has proved far more typical. Nowadays, of course, when you think of the way girls ride bicycles and horses and sweat away in gymnasia and on the athletics field, it's no wonder the species *Hymen muliebris* is as good as extinct; but even then, in the days of my youth, it was a rare, shy creature, never worth all the poetry it inspired – to say nothing of the murders its premature taking has occasioned.

The ten pounds that remained of my savings were obviously going to peg out within the week unless I did something rather drastic. And that was the direction in which I next bent my effort.

For as long as I could remember I had been aware that our butler, Hellmore, was a racing man. He earned about four pounds a month (plus all his keep and uniforms, of course) but managed to double it most months with odd little 'flutters on the geegees,' as he called them. It was our secret. And it was he who inspired me to see that gambling could provide a lucrative living; all you needed to do was remove the element of risk.

Some do that by doping the horses or bribing the jockeys. But there is a better way. It relies on the fact that most gamblers are utter fools – and that Lady Luck is astute enough to let them win every now and then, just enough to confirm them in their folly. But Hellmore was a true betting man – that is, he did not believe in gambling. He spent at least two hours every day studying form and he never staked a penny unless the odds were wildly different from his own expectation of the horse's success. Inspired by him, I, too, had studied form from the age of fourteen. In fact, for the past eighteen months I had been betting phantom money on real horses and keeping a record of each transaction – in the doubtless vain hope of convincing my father it would provide as good a living as stockbroking, and with much less risk, any day.

I had started with a notional five shillings and had never bet more than half my winnings; if I had been betting in earnest, with real money, my five shillings would have grown over those eighteen months to over £325 – one hundred and thirty thousand percent! Nothing on the stockmarket could hold a candle to that.

However, the time for theoretical exercises was past; I now needed to earn serious money. There were none of these modern betting shops in those days. Gambling for cash was illegal, so the streets were full of bookies' 'runners,' who could take a slip of paper and half-a-crown out of your hand right under the very nose of the police. That was gambling for the poor. The rich gambler had an account with a 'turf accountant' and could gamble to whatever limit was a agreeable between them. Gambling on credit was perfectly legal, although the debt, either way, was not legally enforceable.

So, that Friday afternoon, after leaving Lazy Daisy's happy in the knowledge that Kitten was to be spared further service for one more day at least, I persuaded Hellmore to take my remaining ten pounds and open an account for me at Raglan and Tatterthwaite, Leeds's leading turf accountants – known by many, and with good reason, as 'Rags and Tatters.' Of course, gambling was most certainly *not* legal for youths under the age of twenty-one, but I intended to deal with them only by telephone and I had the knack, I flattered myself, of sounding older on that as-then-primitive instrument.

The following day – I shall never forget it – I called them, gave my account number, and bet five pounds in a three-horse accumulator. It says something of what I suffered that afternoon when I confess I cannot recall a single detail about the first two nags. All I know is that by the time the second of them won, my five pounds had turned into £312 – all of which fabulous fortune now rode on a ten-to-one outsider running in the last race of the day at Sudbury (of blessed memory) – a four-year-old filly called Fool's Gold. She had been badly handicapped at her previous three outings and her apparent form was nowhere near her true capability – as I hoped she would prove that afternoon in her first non-handicap race of the season.

She did, of course – or I should not be boasting of it here! But I sweated a gallon and bit my nails to the quick and died a thousand tormented deaths before the classified edition of the *Leeds Evening Argus* hit the streets – and I offer no prizes for guessing who bought the very first copy of that edition – nor who has it still, or the one vital results-from-Sudbury column, lovingly pressed in his scrap book. I swore I should never place bets in that way again – and nor have I. I reckon I have made a profit of well over a quarter of a million pounds on horseracing bets alone since then – an average of roughly five thousand a year – mostly on ten-pound bets. But my biggest single winning, after that first, was some way below a thousand pounds.

So there I was, twenty years old, and idle-rich at last. Richer by £3,427 [*almost £140,000 in our debased modern currency*]. It was, of course, far too much. I was almost as frightened at possessing it as I had earlier been about losing it. The bet had been illegal because of my age and I felt certain Rags and Tatters would do everything to slide out of it if ever they got wind of the truth. I realized I needed advice, and quickly, and the only person I could think of was Madame at Lazy Daisy's.

It was eight in the evening by the time I arrived. Of course, I had hopes of seeing Kitten and telling her she could take the rest of the weekend off – indeed, never work again if she'd prefer to be kept by me. But she was 'occupied,' as Madame wryly told me – adding, 'As I predicted, she's having a very busy day!'

I swallowed my chagrin and told Madame my tale. She didn't bat an eyelid. Nor, I think did she believe a word of it. She asked me the names of the three horses – of course they were engraved on my heart then, even though I have since forgotten two of them. Then she asked me to wait outside while she made a telephone call. Five minutes later I was readmitted – and believed. 'Well, Freddy, you do have a little problem,' she said. 'But I think I know the man to help you solve it. And by the greatest good fortune, he's here at this moment – with Maisie, in fact. He'll be down before long and if you give me another five minutes alone, with him this time, I think he'll do his best to help you.'

The man in question was Sidney Graustein, who changed his name to Greystoke when the Battenburgs made it fashionable to Anglicize German names during the Great War. Until he died – in a German air raid on Leeds in 1942 – he was my dearest friend and whoring companion. Between the wars we cut a swathe through the quimscape of Europe, from Oslo to Constantinople. But on that day our relationship was very much that of an amused patriarch to a jumped-up whippersnapper. Actually – as I often told him in later years – he had a nerve playing the patriarch in front of me. I won't call him a *bent* lawyer – money could never have bought him – but he had a warm heart for the underdog and could be persuaded to believe that a ten-times-convicted burglar happened to stray into a millionaire's mansion, having mistaken it for his own two-up-two-down, five miles away; in such a tale he could discover some innate probability which entirely escaped the more pedestrian minds of judges and the plodding sort of policemen.

He was also, by chance, in partnership with Harold Cohen – the father of Rachel, the little nymph whose exhibition had, in its roundabout way, led to my present interview with Graustein. 'Interview' is not quite the right word for what proved to be a gruelling cross-examination; he was a master of the forensic question and he had me bathed in sweat and my ambitions neatly dissected within twenty minutes. He was also a master of the art of summing-up – as he proved over the many years he served as recorder in Leeds – but never so effectively as he summed-up my situation on that evening.

'Freddy, old son,' he said, 'your father's got you over a barrel – or he will have if he finds out about your little windfall before you reach your twenty-first. So you've got to, one, keep him sweet; two, make sure he never does find out; and three – because I'm a belt-and-braces man – put your capital beyond anyone's reach, including your own, for the next twelve months. In short, put it all into trust. Invested safely in the funds, it should yield you close on one hundred and forty pounds a year – enough to pay for six visits a month to this delightful establishment – which is a course I thoroughly commend. Whatever you do, *don't* spend it on material things, or things that leave their mark (I'm thinking mainly of spirituous liquors, of course). Follow my advice and your parent need never suspect.'

I had already started building castles in the air, of course – a gig of my own, a swell's wardrobe, a box at the theatre . . . that sort of thing, any one of which would have given me away within weeks. Reluctantly I put them all aside, like toys I had grown out of.

One final act of true friendship remained.

'A little word of advice,' he said as we were on the verge of parting, 'given me by old Arbuthnot Ramsden when I was articled to him. The fillies in this house take a deliberate risk every time they open their legs and let one of us shoot off inside them. That's understood. Getting belly-up is an occupational hazard for them. But only a howling cad would expose the other females of his acquaintance to that same hazard.' He delved in his pocket and fished out what I at first took to be a dried jellyfish; when he put it to his lips and blew, I thought it was a collection of deflated balloons – though I had never seen a colourless balloon in my life.

'Lambs' bungs,' he said with a grin. 'Take half a dozen. That should keep you going for a day or two! Next week I'll take you down to meet old Charlie Hackett at the abattoir. He takes them from the slaughtered lambs and cures them for me.'

While he spoke he took the one he had inflated and held it up for my inspection. It was, of course, a perfect, natural condom, for a lamb's 'bung' is the appendix of a lamb's intestine – strong as catgut, thin as a rasher of wind, and, nine times out of ten, perfectly fashioned to sheathe the excited poker of the full-grown male. Once it soaks up a little of a woman's juice, it turns so soft and pliable you'd never know it was there. One way and another I've filled over six thousand of those providential prophylactics over the past forty-odd years. I've tried the very best of the rubber johnnies, but they are crude passion-killers in comparison with even a mediocre lamb's bung. I never pass a field full of sheep in springtime without gloating at the thought of pleasures to come. The way the little lambs all spring and leap for joy – it's as if something of that spirit survives their deaths and lingers in those heavenly membranes.

Before I left Lazy Daisy's I sought out Madame and asked how Kitten was getting along.

'Oh but she's having the time of her life,' she assured me.

I was crestfallen. I had thought of buying up all her remaining hours and saving her from her ordeal. 'How much would it cost to buy her out for the . . .' I began; but she cut me off.

'I'm afraid she's reserved right through until after midnight, Freddy.' She tilted her head sympathetically to one side.

'Ah,' I said glumly. 'That means until three in the morning.'

'No, no! I'm not quite so heartless. Her last reservation is at one – a lieutenant from the Young Turks.'

It was a regimental nickname I had not heard before but, not wishing to show my ignorance, I raised my eyebrows as if she had said he was from the Royal Dragoon Guards.

It was obviously the correct response, for she smiled, nodded, and said, 'Quite! The most important encounter of her day – she mustn't miss that!'

'May I come back at two, then, Madame?' I begged. 'Just to talk to her, you understand.'

She smiled again and said I might, though she obviously thought I'd be fast asleep by then.

I was utterly miserable as I wended my way home. I kept thinking of that gorgeous young girl with her full, ripe breasts, her pale, slender figure and her long, shapely thighs. And then I thought of all the misbegotten, foul, crapulous, gross, lewd old men who, for a mere two pounds, could buy the right to thrust their gamey gap-stoppers into her warm, sweet, tight, juicy centre of bliss – so pale, so tender, so frail, and oh-so-nearly virgin. I cringed as I imagined them pumping the fill of their lust hard into her belly. I envisioned her crushed beneath licentious old goats with fat, hairy bodies and slobbering lips. I conjured up a phantasm of her graceful fingers toying with the unmanly sceptre of some effete young milord – the fifteenth Baron Sagprick – and pretending to adore it. I saw her wrapping her delectable legs around the withered shanks of scrofulous dotards. I pictured her bending forward and wriggling her provocative young derrière beneath the mammoth paunch of some obese sluggard and slipping the hot lips of her cunny around his obscene pizzle. It was almost beyond bearing. Madame might smile and think she knew better, but I would rather die than fail to appear that night when the clock struck two and the officer from the Young Turks took his congé.

When I returned home my father asked what I'd been doing. Normally he never bothered his head with such things. I told him I'd been bug hunting and he said, 'Jolly good! Keep it up!'

Perhaps this is the place for me to explain a thing or two about my family and upbringing. We were not rich but we were well-to-do. We were probably at the lowest rung of the ladder at which fathers did not automatically push their sons into a career. One of my brothers had chosen the church, one had gone into the army, and one was on the Baltic Exchange in London. My father had no objection to these choices and so off they went; but he did not press them to it. If they had chosen, instead, to hunt, shoot, and fish – or, like me, to collect nocturnal moths (ha ha! – there was a man who sold mounted specimens in Briggate, in Leeds) – he would have accepted that, too. We of the upper-upper-middle-class were not brought up like the middle-middle-class to believe that everyone *must* work. There were probably a hundred thousand young men like me around the turn of the century, idle rich young men who did nothing and whom nobody expected to do anything.

Of course, what I really wanted to be – as already explained – was a professional gambler. The gambler and the whore are the two professionals whom you may dump in any city in the world who can start up in business within minutes of their arrival. But that particular career was, of course, out of the question. It would have to wait until I came of age – but at least I would now have the capital on which to start.

Before my father returned to the most serious business in his life – removing daisies from our lawn with a special knife I'd given him for Christmas – he passed on some splendid news: Poor Rachel next door had been put in quarantine because a girl at her school had gone down with measles. However, Rachel herself had not contracted the illness and was consequently bored to death. 'Since you've already had the measles,' he told me, 'you'd be in no danger, whether or not she has it. So why not slip next door and play bezique or something with her?'

'Bezique!' I exclaimed joyfully, as if I'd forgotten the game and was glad to be reminded of it; but even then I was thinking that his other suggestion – 'or something' – sounded more the ticket.

So I took a quick bath before popping next door.

Old man Cohen himself let me in, explaining first that Nannette, the French maid, was keeping Rachel amused, then that the rest of the servants had the evening off to attend a cricket match, adding finally that Mrs Cohen was on a protracted visit to one of her aunts. I was too young to recognize the guilt that almost always prompts copious explanations of this kind; I just assumed he was in rather a talkative mood. So I told him about meeting Graustein – though not, of course where or why!

'Ah, yes – the Law!' he sighed. It set him off on a new train of thought. 'You can be of great assistance, if you will, my boy,' he told me. 'I have no son, as you know. But I have a daughter with a mind as sharp as a gimlet.' He tapped his skull. 'And she has enough spare energy to bale out Otley Reservoir with a whelkshell. She leads poor Nannette a merry dance, I can tell you! She'll be the death of us unless we can harness her vigour. I pity any man who marries her in the belief he can keep her in the doll's house!'

'I'll help in any way I can, sir,' I told him. 'But, er, I don't quite see . . .'

'I want her to follow me into the practice, my boy. Become a lawyer. But I can't article her – the Law Society would have a fit. And I find I can't teach her myself because I tried that with her arithmetic. I can teach her well enough but as soon as I try to *test* her knowledge she loses her temper and throws the books at me. It's a longshot, I know, but she might *just* be willing to take a test from you. I could tell you the right answers beforehand. She thinks you're one of the very . . . well, I mustn't give you a swollen head. She thinks highly of you – nuff said! Go and talk with her now. The three of you can play whist.'

But, as I reached the halfway landing, he called up after me: 'Just tell Nannette I'd like a brief word with her, there's a good fellow.'

If anything could have taken my mind off the sexual humiliation poor Kitten was being forced to endure at that very moment, it was Rachel's smile. Rachel had the peculiar ability to stand at the side of a room and somehow become its centre. When she was around, people's eyes – men's and women's – sought her out. She was pretty, to be sure, yet not *dazzlingly* so. Her special attractiveness lay far deeper than that. Quite simply, she carried some personal electricity around with her; the very air about her became live when she stirred it.

She has that quality still, even now, when she is

approaching her sixtieth birthday – so it was no accident of
her youth and budding sexual allure. But that, of course,
is how I saw it then! I saw *everything* in those days in terms
of sexual energy. If I won ten pounds on a horse, it wasn't
just a couple of fivers; those two crisp white notes were
charged with the power to command five alluring fillies for
five delightful hours at Lazy Daisy's. When I pored over
law books getting ready to test Rachel (for, of course,
both of us leaped at her old man's suggestion like manna
from heaven!) I'd find myself turning to entries charged
with stimulation for my fancy, like *Unlawful Carnal
Knowledge . . . Incest . . . Rape . . . Keeping a Disor-
derly House* . . . and so on. The voice of a scullery maid,
singing over her potato peelings two doors away, could
burden me with half a ton of erotic enticement and leave
me melting with lust – and so, indeed, could quite
innocent words like, *split, mound, curve, suck, cul de
sac* . . . and so forth. In my cunny-haunted world, Iron
Jack spent hours each day, risen to the most ferocious
bone.

So when I timidly entered Rachel's room and saw her
wet, sensual lips break into a smile of welcome, I was
already in a fever. As I drew near her I ran an appreciative
eye over her white neck, her dimpled cheeks, her sparkling eyes, the ringlets of her jet-black hair and the
appealingly dainty ears they framed. And I remembered
those adorable bubbies she had flashed at me exactly
seven days earlier. And I went as weak at the knees as I
was lusty in the groin – for both of which reasons I had to
seat myself abruptly and without ceremony. I covered the
action by telling Nannette of her employer's request.

When the maid had withdrawn, Rachel brought me
down to earth with a thump. 'You've taken your time!'
she said.

I flushed pink – which then made it impossible for me to
pretend I had no idea what she was talking about.

'Been learning how to go about it?' she taunted.

When you sail into a rip tide, your wisest course is to turn and face it. I drew a deep breath and said, casually, 'Yes, as a matter of fact, I have.'

She opened her mouth to tease me further, then actually heard what I'd said; she left her lips agape while she stared at me. 'Really?' she asked at last.

'Yes.'

She recovered her aplomb and the teasing note returned. 'But why? I could have told you. I've read all about it in Papa's books.'

Deep in her merry eyes I saw a familiar mixture of fear and bravado and it was all I could do not to burst out laughing. This was a Rachel I knew so well. The day we, then aged seven and eight, went up onto Ilkley Moor and flew my first kite, she knew *exactly* how to do it; she'd never handled a kite in her life, but that was no deterrent. 'I got out Simon's old *Boy's Own* last night and read all about it,' she said – and with exactly the same sort of provocative solemnity she was employing on me now. Dear thing!

However, this reference to her father's books was of more immediate interest. 'His law books?' I asked. Perhaps I should think about a career in the law after all.

'No,' she replied scornfully. 'The ones he keeps out of sight in the plinth of the statue of Venus in the conservatory – the ones he's probably showing to Nannette this minute.'

Now it was my turn to gape.

She giggled. 'Where did *you* go to learn? Do move closer.'

When I obeyed she put her hand on my knee.

'D'you really not mind?' I asked.

'Why should I? I think it's jolly considerate of you. What did you find out? Who taught you? Was it one girl or lots? Oh, you men are so *lucky*!'

'Ah!' I pulled a rueful face, for I did not wish to answer such detailed questions. 'I wouldn't have bothered at all if I'd known about *you*.'

'What about me?'

'Well – your being so experienced et cetera.'

She chuckled and pulled a rueful face. 'But I'm not. Not really. You know me. All I've done, as I told you, is read a few books. I can't wait to try. Except . . .' She licked her lips and glanced anxiously at me.

'Except what?'

'Well, I'm also a little frightened. That's why I'm talking too much. D'you think we could . . .' She gulped heavily. 'I mean, not *quite* Do It tonight but almost – and then Do It properly tomorrow night? One of Papa's books says it's far more loving and beautiful to stretch things out like that, but another one says it's very harmful and damaging and unfair to the man. So that's why I'm *asking* you, really – not telling you. What d'you think?' She squeezed my knee again.

I leaned forward and put my lips near hers. 'I think I must be very privileged to know you, Rachel. Not only are you one of the most beautiful girls I've ever seen, you are also one of the most fascinating, too.'

'Only *one* of the most beautiful?' She pouted playfully.

I kissed the very tip of her nose. 'Well, certainly *the* most fascinating.'

'Ah! You may steal a kiss for that.'

I think one of her father's books had given her the idea that she might dole out one little reward after another and so lead me forward – from kissing to groping to fingering . . . and so on. But after I had been kissing her for about five seconds she changed her mind; she must have realized that we were engaged in something rather majestic, something that would change our whole perception of life and give us new goals to strive for. In that context such little games were absurd. It was as if, hand in hand, we had passed through some unseen barrier, going from a confined space into one that was infinite.

Rachel and I had played together since childhood; indeed, her four-year-old quim was the first I ever saw – when she climbed out of the sandpit to piddle in the flower bed. Later, until we were about ten, we had bathed naked under the garden hose many a time, so we were well acquainted with each other's bodies. Usually when unrelated boys and girls grow up so closely together, they feel too much like brother and sister to develop a sexual intimacy. Indeed, I think something of that sort happened for her and me between the ages of ten and fourteen; certainly we saw less of each other (in all senses of the phrase) during those years. Then, when a renewed intimacy sprang up between us, it was of a different character – full of excitement and electricity. Yet something of the innocent ease of our childhood returned, too. She would not have sported her breasts to any other fellow that Saturday afternoon, and I should not have talked so freely to any other young lady, nor kissed her so swiftly, either.

'Here!' she gasped when our lips broke contact at last. 'This won't do.' And she caught me by the wrist and drew me to the wall between the two windows. 'That's better.' She relaxed again. 'Anyone in your house with a good pair of binoculars can see into this bedroom.'

'Really?' I was surprised into a degree of naïvete that a moment's cool reflection would have spared me from displaying. 'How d'you know?' I asked.

She chuckled. 'Because I assume it works both ways, Freddy, dear!' And she pulled me fiercely to her. 'Hold me tight,' she urged. 'Really press me against the wall.'

'What if Nannette should return?'

The chuckle turned into a dismissive laugh. 'She won't be back for an hour. She and Papa have been at it like rabbits ever since Mama went to Aunt Hannah's. Nannette's getting married when she goes back to Dijon in

September and she intends to be an utterly faithful wife, so she's trying to get all the fun she can in the meantime.'

I goggled at her. 'Does she tell you all this?'

'Some of it. The rest is in her diary – the best bits. Don't look so shocked, Freddy. It's vulgar to gape so. Besides, that's what French maids are for, you know – to tell young girls half truths and then to put the other half in their diaries and leave them lying around.'

Her air of knowing superiority aggravated me slightly. Of course, I realized later that that was precisely her intention – to spur me on and make me bolder; she knew her worldly-wise tone would needle me – a chit of a girl who'd never Done It talking like that to a past master who'd spent an entire week learning the art. A moment later she was panting most pleasurably at her success – when my hands began to stray in places where no fellow's hand had strayed before. She was wearing a light cotton blouse and a simple summer dress with only one petticoat, so there was little bulk between us. When my hands fell to caress her buttocks, it was, indeed, her buttocks they felt and not a dozen layers of material over a vaguely protruding rump. I could feel their roundness and the cleft between them and the divine undercut below. And when I drew her tightly to me, my fingers dinted flesh, not linen. Yet linen slipped and glided over flesh in a most seductive manner.

In drawing her to me like that, mound met mound. Their mutual pressure was quite obviously a delight to her though it was somewhat painful to me because my flannels were constraining Iron Jack to peer one-eyed *down* my trouser leg – when all his natural inclination was to stand like a guardsman and drill. I withdrew slightly from her and thrust my hand into my pocket, pretending to search for something. But she was not for one moment deceived. 'Let me?' she begged coyly and, not waiting for a reply, slipped her fingertips down inside my belt.

There she paused and said, 'May I?'

I let out my breath in a rush and nodded, bending slightly forward to make it easier for her.

In one way I was sorry I had been to Lazy Daisy's. It would have been so charming if Rachel's had been the first female fingers since Nanny Gresham's to grasp Iron Jack like that. (Nanny G. used to put her hand up under my pinafore and toss me off – though it was to be ten years, when I was fourteen and she long dead, before I realized that was what she had done.) In every other way, though, I was glad that Maisie and Kitten had 'blown the husks' off me, as the saying goes, and had taught me some self-control into the bargain. Had it not been for them, I should have glued poor Rachel's fingers together with a spectacularly uncoordinated spermspouting the moment they touched Iron Jack.

Now, when she touched him, I ejaculated nothing more than a long sigh of contentment.

'Oh, Freddy,' she exclaimed, 'it's *huge*! Last time I saw it . . .' She chuckled and held the thumb and index finger of her free hand an inch apart.

'It's a faithful barometer of desire,' I told her. 'A woman may deceive a man that she lusts for him but no man may deceive a woman in that way.'

'No! But many's the man has deceived a maid *this* way.' She gave Iron Jack another delightful squeeze. Then she chuckled again: 'But it's so *exactly* what I imagined it would feel like! Can I see it? Oh, please let me see it! I'll show you mine after if you wish.'

My thumbs found her nipples through the thin cotton of her blouse; alas it unbuttoned (or buttoned *up*, as girls prefer to say) at the back. 'These are what I want to look at first, Rachel,' I murmured in her ear. 'It's only fair – they're what started it all.'

But she – while still clutching Iron Jack in the hand that was plunged inside my trousers – withdrew a little from me and covered her bubbies with her free arm. 'Please no,' she begged. 'Not my beauteous orbs!'

'Why ever not?' I asked.

'Because I know what'll happen if you do. I shan't be able to say no – and then it'll all be over and done with in one night. And that's not the way I've dreamed of Doing It with you all these months.'

'Months?' I echoed in surprise.

'Hah!' Her eyes raked the ceiling. 'That just proves there's no such thing as telepathy!' She gave my lad a squeeze and repeated her question. 'May I look?'

I slipped my belt out of its buckle and held the two ends apart, indicating that the rest was up to her.

Fascinated, she applied her dainty fingers to my fly buttons. Her eyes stared without blinking, her little pink tongue darted out and wet her lips as she undid first one button, then two – the two topmost. Then she paused, though her fingers were trembling with excitement. 'Oh, I want it to last and last,' she said.

I raked my fingertips into and out of the hair at the back of her head. 'We could both make ourselves more comfortable,' I pointed out.

'How?'

'If I go and sit on the edge of the chaise longue and you kneel between my feet.' I chucked her under the chin and added, 'Or isn't that how you've dreamed of it all these months?'

'Beast!' She raised her hands to my head and pulled me down to kiss her. Then she murmured, 'That's exactly how I dreamed of it but I didn't like to suggest such a thing. Maybe there is a kind of telepathy after all.'

We moved across the room to the chaise longue, where I seated myself at the very end and spread my flannels wide; she knelt between them and sat on her heels, resting her elbows across the tops of my thighs. With the same delicate movements as earlier, though now with far greater control, she loosened the remaining buttons. The shirt I wore that day was of the conventional pattern of the period, with two short legs that one stepped into before putting it on. It was shirt and underpants combined, in fact. Iron Jack now reared across my belly like a gristly ramrod, straining at the thin material. Hesitantly Rachel ran her gentle fingertips up and down the length of him.

'Lie back,' she said, 'so I can kiss it properly.'

I almost had a fit. Yesterday I had spent the best part of half an hour trying to induce a virgin (as it turned out) to 'kiss it properly' – which she, though dedicating herself to the arts of venery, had signally failed to do; and today a second virgin (as I had to assume) was volunteering the service before I had even reached that stage where my conscience would forbid me to tempt her amateur innocence in that way.

I stretched back upon the chaise longue before conscience could awaken. She put her lips to Iron Jack – or, rather, to the cotton that shrouded him, and breathed out slowly, bathing him in the heat of her breath, which is, of course, body heat – which, in turn, is the one heat he absolutely dotes on. 'Where did you learn that?' I gasped when my scalp had returned to my skull.

'Lady Cuntibella did it to Lord Horniman in *Amore Alfresco*,' she informed me. 'And this, too.'

Her fingernails raked lightly over the taut skin of my belly, first on one side of that throbbing truncheon then on the other. I struggled to shed my flannels; she managed it with two deft tweaks that left them round my heels, where they fell away without my noticing – for I was by then straining all my efforts to avoid a premature disaster while her fingers slipped my shirt buttons from their holes and let the swollen shaft of Iron Jack leap free of his strait-jacket and pound the empty air.

'It's like the heat off a fire!' she whispered in an awestruck voice. The heat of her bated breath was like warm, elfin fingers dusting my flesh.

During the next ten minutes there were many uncomfortable echoes of a similar scene I had played only the day before with my darling Kitten. There was the same sort of childish joy at playing with a forbidden toy, the same questions about his most (and least) exquisitely sensitive part, the same giggles when some chance tickle sent me into a paroxysm of delight – and the same gusto in repeating the stimulus until I craved mercy. But then she went beyond anything Kitten had done – not, I think, because she was innately more licentious but simply because she had read things in books and Kitten hadn't.

Rachel was always the most ardent tourist. After the Great War, when she was widowed for the first time, I went with her to Italy. And I was most struck by the way she would devour her Baedeker in advance of every visit we made. She loved walking into a gallery and being able to say something like, 'Ah yes, here's the Mantegna. We must remember to look at the Ucello in Gallery Twelve. They say there are great similarities in the handling of the paint.' By way of contrast, I took Kitten to the Walker Art Gallery in Liverpool once. She was a well educated girl of good class but her parents had frowned on all kinds of Art as inherently corrupting, so she didn't know Whistler from Hogarth. She just wandered among the canvasses exclaiming 'Oh!' and 'Just look!' and 'How beautiful!' Doubtless Rachel learned more and 'got on' faster, but I believe Kitten had more true enjoyment and ended up with a profounder understanding of what art is really about.

And it was exactly the same with their quite different approaches to sexual fulfilment.

Not that I was in a mood (or condition) to be so nicely analytical on that particular evening, for Rachel now did all those things I had longed for Kitten to try the day before. She made me drag cushions to prop up my head so that she could watch my expression. Then, grinning wickedly at me all the while, she grasped Iron Jack round the base, the way a carpenter holds the handle of a hammer, and lifted him toward her lips. She opened her mouth in a snarl, as if she was about to bite off his head. And for a moment I was truly afraid that, in her ignorance – or under the influence of some absurd book in her father's collection – that was precisely what she intended.

For what seemed an eternity she held Iron Jack in suspension between her pearly teeth; I thought of a lion tamer putting his head into the lion's gaping jaw. I drew breath to protest. I raised a hand to ward her off. And then I became aware of the most subtly delicious sensation imaginable. At first it was so gentle I thought I must be imagining it, but then I saw it with my own eyes, too. She was running the very tip of her tongue up and down the groove on the underside of my old man – the deep and almost unbearably sensitive groove between the furious purple of my knob and the ivory pallor of my swollen shaft.

I almost collapsed with the pleasure of it. She was doing it every bit as gently as I later intended to tongue her own little bud of pleasure – not that I was in the slightest hurry to progress to that stage yet. And all the while she watched my face like a hawk, searching not just for the increase or decrease in my rapture but for the subtler changes in its quality, too.

Slowly, tantalizing me every step of the way, she closed her gaping jaws about old Iron Jack's head – not to bite him but to enclose him in the furnace of her mouth and furl her tongue under and round him like an amorous boa constrictor.

As I write about it now, more than forty years on, I can see what an extraordinary thing it was for us to be doing within the first *ten minutes* of a sexual relationship with a well-bred virgin of nineteen! Especially when one reflects that Rachel had never even seen, much less handled, a man's erection previously. But that was Rachel for you; to her it would not have seemed odd at all. She wanted to see what an erect penis looked like before she'd let it inside her – was that unnatural? (This is how she'd have argued the matter.) And when you look at something like that at close quarters, of course you handle it, too. What's unusual about that? And when you've read in books that licking the thing and sucking it can drive a man into a frenzy of bliss – and since the giving of pleasure and the taking of pleasure is the very essence of the business – well, isn't that just one small step further?

And, put like that, who's to disagree?

Not I – not now – and *certainly* not then! I just lay there in a half-swoon of ecstasy, fighting on the one hand to stave off a sticky climax while, at the same time, luxuriating in sensations that were both novel and shattering to me.

There is nothing that even the most inventive young lad can do with his fingers and lubricating creams and jellies to simulate the hot enclosure of a girl's mouth and the gently muscular suppleness of her tongue. I had tossed myself off with loaves of warm bread, the invaginated necks of quart milk bottles liberally wiped with petroleum jelly, a melon raised to blood heat on the conservatory stove, and two rubber hot water bottles smeared with cocoa butter – but nothing had prepared me for the voluptuous excitement of Rachel's mouth. Especially after the first five minutes, when she forgot her father's books and began experimenting with licks and sucks of her own devising.

At last, and with what great reluctance the reader may imagine, I had to beg her to desist. 'Or else . . .' I added ominously.

'Oh!' she exclaimed, 'but I wanted to see the 'or else' bit – when the mighty Captain Standish throbs uncontrollably and pours out his copious libation upon the altar of Eros. What does it look like?'

'I haven't the faintest idea,' I replied.

'You've never watched it yourself?'

I had, in fact – when I turned fourteen and Tommy took me into a haybarn on the Harewood Estate and we tickled cocks together. I had been astonished to see a little pearl of white, milky fluid come welling up and fill the eye of Old One-Eye. And again last year on a very hot night when I had lain on my back in bed, without nightshirt or covering, and had made myself come accidentally, just by caressing my nipples, and I had seen great gobbets of my milt come flying through the air and landing like splatters of paperhanging paste on my face and chest. But I didn't want to explain all that now.

'I'm usually a million miles away in paradise when it happens,' I said.

'Oh, Freddy? Mmmm?' She whined and begged me with her eyes.

'You want to *see* it happen?' I asked, feeling a strange excitement stirring within me.

She nodded delightedly. 'What do I do?'

'Just carry on the way you were. Suck up and down. Try and pretend you're a snake swallowing a mongoose – swallow as much as you can and then pull sharply away from it. Open your mouth and breathe in sharply – chill him with a sudden blast of cold air. Then breathe out all over him – hot and cold, hot and cold. Furl your tongue round him as if you were in a toffee-apple-licking contest . . .'

'You won't vanish off into paradise in the middle of all this, and pour your libations to Eros in my mouth, will you? I want to see it.'

I promised and she began again. This time, knowing I was going all the way – and feeling the pressure of 'my libation' already filling my balls – the sensation was exquisite and radiantly joyous. There was an inevitability about my climax that I had never known before. I felt it coming almost two minutes before it arrived, whereas usually I was lucky to have ten seconds' notice. As a result I experienced a curious detatchment – curious because although part of me was able to observe the sequence of events quite coolly, the rest of me, liberated from that cool observer within, abandoned itself to the most hedonistic and primitive enjoyment of the act.

As the pressure mounted and the sharp tingle in Iron Jack's frenulum turned into a broad, hot thrill that spread like fire through my every vein and sinew, I groped for her hand and showed her how to grip his shaft and work the loose skin up and down over the part she was sucking and licking with such consummate skill.

Then as the fires gathered together again, focussing on that sensitive pipe which runs all the way up the Old Man's underbelly, I took her other hand in mine – in *my* other hand, that is – and held her fingers loosely ready near the crown. 'Watch!' I croaked, to warn her to take her lips away.

It is an odd fact to record but I would probably have been ashamed (in those early days) to stage such an exhibition for Kitten, and even for Maisie and the other fillies at Lazy Daisy's, even though I knew that the more experienced of them were gulping away at a 'libating' cock at least once a day; yet I felt a wonderful sense of pride that Rachel had asked me to do this for her. I can only compare it to that equally wonderful moment when Tommy and I lanced small cuts in our forearms and mingled our spilled blood in the boyhood rituals of blood-brotherhood. And now this new ritual of sexual kinship forged the same sort of mystical bond between Rachel and me. She was asking me to confide my body's innermost carnal secret, and I shared it without hesitation.

And copiously, too, for a moment later my left hand,

grasping her right, was unconsciously showing her how to squeeze and let go, squeeze and let go, a fraction of a second before each mighty gusher of semen shot impetuously skywards – or would have done if my other hand was not holding her fingers over it like an umbrella. It was a shock to me how hot it felt; I usually toss myself off into an old handkerchief or something and never felt it until after the twentieth little dry thrill, by which time it's cold and dank.

She watched it happen with the most intense and absorbed fascination I have ever seen in a girl's face. When it was halfway over I removed my hands and let her continue as I had shown her, quite unaided. The spontaneous squeezing and letting go, now owing nothing to me, restored the intensity of my climax and even (somehow) made the old spermspouter gush more copiously than ever.

At last, when each little kick brought forth no more than a seeping ooze of white fluid, no thicker than coconut milk, she let out one long sigh of repletion – in which I joined. When I next opened my eyes and looked at her I saw tears brimming on the edge of her lids. 'I think that was one of the most beautiful things I have ever seen,' she whispered. 'Thank you, *darling* Freddy. What shall I do with this?'

I peered down and saw her holding her left hand like a cup. I sat up on my elbows and, looking into it now, realized it was half-full of my libation – a mixture of thin starchy sap and thick, semolina-like lumps.

'There's a handkerchief in my flannels,' I suggested. ' I took it out clean this evening.'

'Is it poison?' she asked, peering intently at my tribute to Eros. 'What's it taste like?'

'I have no idea,' I assured her.

'You're not very curious about your own body, are you,' she chided and, raising the 'cup' to her chin, dipped the very tip of her tongue into it – followed by chef-like smacking noises of tongue and palate. 'It's very sweet,' she said judiciously. 'But there's a second flavour there, too. Oh, I know what it's like. My aunt makes a sort of health-giving drink out of mushrooms. It's like that with a bit of sugar added – sort of mushroomy and sweet. Try.'

She held out her cupped hand, where my milt was congealing into a kind of thick, uniform starch – all my millions of unborn, never-to-be-born sons and daughters! With a sickly, cannibalistic smile I did as Rachel had done – and was surprised to find it tasted much less interesting than she had made it sound. I love mushrooms, especially with scrambled egg on toast, but detected no such flavour there. And as for *sweet*, well, it was no sweeter than that disappointing little hint of nectar you can garner from a dozen dismembered honeysuckle flowers; if ever a plant was misnamed, it is the honeysuckle – or perhaps 'vegetable oyster,' which neither looks nor tastes even vaguely like either the marine bivalve or the female pudendum. Big disappointment. And the flavour of my own milt was another. To me it was just bland.

I kicked my flannels within reach and was able to get out my handkerchief and put an end to this persiflage. I was just about to suggest a reversal of our positions, and rôles, when her sharp ears caught the sound of a distant door slamming. I have never dressed so fast. By the time Nannette returned, Rachel and I were sitting opposite each other while I dealt a hand for bezique.

The maid said she didn't want to interrupt but we both protested we'd had enough of the game and insisted she should join us for three-handed whist.

I have read in certain types of salacious literature of the appearance of young girls 'after an exhaustive, diligent, and leisurely poking.' Their eye is bright, their cheeks shine, and their skin is said to glow contentedly all over. I am often tempted to a tiny smile of unbelief. *Tell it to the marines*, I think – until I remember Nannette's appearance on that evening. If ever a lively young wench enjoyed a thoroughly good poke and returned to society with the evidence of it stamped on every visible inch of her skin and showing in every gesture she made, it was Nannette on that evening. If *that* had been going on ever since Mrs Cohen left, small wonder that Rachel had been almost beside herself in her longing to cross the same Rubicon!

We parted an hour or so later on a whispered promise from me to return the following night at eleven; she for her part promised her bedroom window would not be fastened. 'And I want to hear all about the place where you learned and the girls that taught you,' she added brightly.

I was in bed and fast asleep by ten that night, but I put my alarm clock beneath a tea cosy and hid it under a blanket near the head of my bed; it was set for twenty past one. However, when it faithfully awakened me at that ghastly hour I felt so exhausted I almost turned over and went straight back to sleep. I forced myself to rise, nonetheless, and I put on my cross-country running togs before climbing out of my bedroom window into a warm, silvery night. By ten minutes to two, when I trotted up the drive to Lazy Daisy's, I felt on top of the world again.

My appearance in that strange attire boggled the yawning maid who answered my knock, but Madame understood the reason for it at once and laughed heartily. 'How very ingenious, Freddy,' she cried. 'The earlier your parents discover your absence tomorrow morning, the *greater* is your merit in their sight!'

There were about eight girls still free at that hour, all quite delightful in their nakedness. I saw them wetting their lips to make them seem more sensual before they turned to me with their eyes all wide; they leaned forward to make their bubbies tremble enticingly – and I must confess I was sorely enticed. I did not know it then but Maisie had told them about the number of times I had shot her between wind and water on that first afternoon, and it had stirred their competitive spirit. They all wanted to lead me upstairs and try to make me exceed that tally. In silken murmurs and husky whispers they told me how good they would be to me and hinted at the many 'special' things we could do together.

Madame rescued me and took me to her boudoir. It was only then that I realized I had no actual cash about me – a sign, I suppose, of how uncommercial were my feelings toward Kitten, even at that early stage. I explained my predicament to Madame and asked her if my credit was good until Sidney Graustein had sorted out my *embarras de richesse*.

She peered deep into my eyes and said, 'Do you intend to actually *screw* Kitten tonight?'

Until that moment the question had not crossed my mind; but now, the more I thought about it, the more I realized there was only one possible answer. 'No,' I said, slightly surprised. 'How did you know that?'

She smiled. 'I don't believe you would have, anyway – not when it came to the point.' She strained an ear toward the ceiling and said, 'Here she comes.'

I had heard nothing, but she knew the creak of every floorboard in that old house and the closing of every door.

When we returned to the landing outside her boudoir I heard military boots on the old servants' stair; until then I had forgotten that her last partner for the night (apart from me, of course) was an officer of the Young Turks – a regiment I still had not identified.

'Cherish her, Freddy,' Madame said quietly at my side. 'What happened between you and her is not so common that either of you can afford to let it blow away on the breeze.'

Did she know what I was going to see the moment

Kitten and the last customer on her first day as a pro came strolling through that doorway? If ever there was a sight to make a callow youth of twenty feel only half his age (and a quarter of his experience) that was it.

I saw an officer in his mid-twenties, tall, handsome beyond bearing, languid, monocled, aristocratic. Desperately I reminded myself that I was, at least, worth £3,427 – only to reflect that this peacock in his pride probably enjoyed an annual income four times that size. Further observation only added to my woe. He was wearing full mess undress, sword and all, which showed off his trim, athletic body to perfection. On one arm he carried the plumed tricorn of the Duke of Leeds Light Infantry, and on the other, laughing at his jokes and hugging him as if she would seduce him all over again, was my darling Kitten. She wore nothing but her high-heeled boots, black stockings, and the skimpiest black corset imaginable. But what pierced my heart to the core was the glow on her skin, the shine on her cheeks, and the happy gleam in her eye. I recognized it the quicker because it was the very look I had seen in Nannette less than six hours earlier. It was obvious to all the world – but most of all to me – that this dashing lord of creation had spent the past hour screwing the tail off my darling Kitten. And, equally plainly, my darling Kitten's sexy little tail had tingled in giddy delirium through every blissful moment. How I restrained myself from dashing forward, seizing his sword, and cutting him off at the knees I do not know.

He did not even glance at me – for which I was grateful. A moment later I was wishing Kitten had not glanced at me, either, for when she did her face *fell*! I prayed for the floorboards to open a crack and let me seep away between them. I shrank back toward Madame's boudoir and I believe I would have scaled down the rainwater pipes and run all the way back home if Madame herself had not put a finger to my spine and prodded me forward. 'It's only because she doesn't know the good tidings you bring her,' she said.

'What? Oh, my winnings.'

'No, you chump! Well . . . that, too, of course. But, believe me, the best news for her will be . . . what you told me just now. You just watch her face when she realizes that!'

I am as sure that Madame is now in heaven as I am that most of the Almighty's more obvious supporters here on earth are not and never will be.

Kitten came springing lightly back upstairs. Her lovely bubbies bounced so seductively in and out of the cradle of her corset that I almost reversed my resolution on the spot. 'Hello, Freddy!' she cried enthusiastically. 'Couldn't gweet ya pwoperly on the way down. Unpwofessional, don't ya know. What!'

I saw that she was parodying her last lover, trying to reassure me. Even so, it grated.

'Well,' she went on, 'are you going to take me straight upstairs – I hope! I've learned lots of wonderful things we could do together.'

The banter and the smile were oddly impersonal; the promise in her eyes was indistinguishable from the promises of the other young fillies below. My heart sank as it dawned on me that my chances of ever discovering her true feelings about me were in danger of drowning under the fast-rising tide of her professionalism. I also knew that if I lost my resolve and actually screwed her tonight, just like any other customer, I would lose her forever. I drew a deep breath and prayed for strength. No saint ever prayed harder nor with more sincerity; no sinner was ever more aware of his own frailty in the face of such stupendous temptation. Outwardly, though, I was cheerful. I slipped my arm around Kitten's corseted waist and bade Madame a grateful goodnight.

'Have you paid already?' Kitten asked.

'I had a little windfall win on the geegees today but couldn't collect it because I'm still in nappies. Madame knows of it, though. I've opened an account here now.'

She stopped in her tracks and pulled me to face her. 'Really?' she asked excitedly.

I nodded.

'And will you . . . I mean, will we . . .' She gave up trying to frame a question she thought might embarrass me – because she already thought of me as a customer rather than as a friend, and it was a point of honour among the girls that a customer should feel absolutely free in making a choice among them. They did not try to commandeer the gentlemen.

But then I wondered if Kitten wasn't now indulging in a little self-protective pessimism? Perhaps she genuinely wanted me as a friend, yet did not wish to risk the disappointment of watching a friend turn into a mere customer. It was a small hope, but the only one on offer.

'I hope so,' I told her, and left it as vague as that.

The moment we were in her room she flung her arms around my neck and kissed me with every semblance of passion. 'Oh, Freddy,' she sighed, 'I'm so glad it's you and not . . . any of those others!'

'Been a hard day?' I suggested.

After a pause she replied, 'It's been an *interesting* day.' She giggled and left my embrace to skip over to the dressing table. There she picked up an open hatbox, which she held out for me to see. It was full of coins and notes.

'Tips,' she said. 'I haven't even counted it yet.'

We sat cross-legged on the carpet, facing each other with the hatbox between us. It came to twelve pounds, fifteen shillings, and a few odd pence [*over £500 in today's currency*]. 'All because of Little Darling,' she chortled.

Then, on an impulse, she rose and stretched one leg over the box, showing off its contents to her quim. 'Look!'

89

she cried. 'Clever Little Darling! Look what the nice men gave you today.'

But I, staring in fascination at 'Little Darling,' could see that the nice men had given her a great deal more. The beautiful, pale, delicate labia I had seen only yesterday were all red and swollen with the prolonged and repeated excitation they had suffered since then.

She went on talking to Little Darling as if to a favourite child: 'And there's *another* ten pounds waiting for you downstairs in Madame's treasury! You clever, clever thing!'

'Ten pounds!' I said aghast.

'I've earned it!' she said touchily as she rose to put the hatbox back on her dressing table.

'I believe you! It's not the sum of money, darling, but what it implies. Ten men!'

'Eleven counting you.'

'Yes, but I was yesterday.'

'No, silly. I mean now.'

I went to her and took her in my arms again, hugging her tight and pressing my head against hers – wishing that my thoughts and feelings could somehow spill directly from my mind into hers. 'Dear Kitten,' I murmured. 'Did you really think that's what I came back here for tonight?'

She drew her head back as far as I'd let her. 'Didn't you?' Her eyes flickered between my left and my right eye, as if each might reveal a different truth.

'No! I just didn't want you to be alone. Not after your first day and all that. We're just going to lie in bed and relax and talk – that's all.'

'Oh, darling!' She kissed me again – and then drew her head back once more, this time eyeing me with a cheeky grin. 'Still – now you're here, you could change your mind?'

I shook my head. 'Do you honestly want to give me pleasure, Kitten? The greatest possible pleasure?'

'It's what I'm here for, kind sir.'

'Then take off all your clothes and . . .'

'That'll be something new!' she interrupted. 'Believe it or not, I haven't been stripped naked once, all day!'

'We'll both take off all our clothes. And climb into nightshirts, which I believe are kept in that cupboard over there – or they were when Maisie showed me. And we'll get into bed. And I'll just hold you in my arms. And you can tell me all about it.'

She held her ground and stared at me; there was still an uncertain glint in her eyes. 'Honestly?'

I nodded.

She reached down and felt Iron Jack, who was living up to his name, I'm afraid.

'Someone down there doesn't agree!'

'He doesn't know any better – but I do. And I mean to be his master – with a little friendly help from you!'

She eyed me suspiciously. 'Are you getting a bit of a soft spot for me, Freddy?'

I gave her a rueful smile. 'Everywhere except where your hand is at this moment.'

She laughed and let go of me down there; but still she bit her lip anxiously. 'It's supposed to be a very bad thing,' she said. 'Never fall for a customer – that's what the other girls tell me.'

'You're not my customer,' I pointed out with a smile as I took her in my arms again.

She smiled, too. 'I wasn't referring to *you* falling for *me*.'

'Ah.'

She slipped once again from my embrace and went back to the dressing table. This time she opened a drawer and took out her handbag, from which she drew a small object wrapped in tissue paper. 'D'you recognize those?' she asked, handing it to me.

I unfolded the paper and found two sovereigns. I tried

to be funny. 'I've heard of things like these,' I told her. 'They possess almost magical powers to open the legs of young girls, I believe.'

But she remained serious. 'Those are the actual coins you paid for me to open my legs yesterday. You gave her ten at the start of the week, remember? Those were the last two. Fortunately, I asked Madame for them before she'd put them in the cash box among all the rest. I'm going to keep them, Freddy. I'm never going to spend them.'

Too choked for words, I rewrapped the coins and handed then to her. She put them back in the bag and returned it to the drawer. 'D'you really want us to sleep together without doing anything?' she asked.

'Only if you want me here at all,' I told her.

She raised her arms and almost collapsed on me. 'Oh, Freddy! I owe you everything, you know.'

I laughed. 'I don't see that at all.'

'Come on. I'll race you into our nightshirts and then I'll tell you. Oh, such a day I've had of it! I'm bursting to tell someone and I'm sure the girls in the dorm would hiss me to shut up before I'd even begun.'

'So, I'm better than a brick wall,' I said dryly.

'You're better than anyone, so you can stop trying to provoke me with self-pity!'

'Better even than . . .?' I began – meaning to refer to the lordly Young Turk.

'Who?' she asked innocently, though I could see she knew damned well.

'Never mind.'

Twenty minutes later, after we had washed and brushed our teeth, and I had combed and brushed her glorious hair, I insisted on rubbing some of that soothing salve into the ravaged lips of her abused little quim. A wary look crept into her eyes at once but I was proud of the way my spermspouter stayed limp all through the operation.

When I lifted my nightshirt to show her, she was convinced of my sincerity at last. A moment later we lay side by side in the dim glow of the lamp, and she did, indeed, tell me all.

'I said I owe you everything,' she began. 'First, I owe you my very name – Kitten. I suppose you know my real name is Kitty?'

'No! You said Kitten yesterday.'

'You thought I did. I almost corrected you then, but when you said it was the perfect name for me, something inside me leaped up and cried, *Yes – he's right!* It's the perfect name to *hide behind*! I was talking about it with Valerie last night – she sleeps next to me in the dorm – and she said we've all got to hide our real selves at this game. Mind you, I think everyone does – no matter what their game in life may be. The men I've met today – I tell you!' She shook her head and sighed at the impossibility of conveying the full measure of her astonishment.

'Yes, who were they?' I asked. 'I've driven myself mad, imagining you having to submit to the foul embraces of the most odious characters.'

She chuckled and, turning to me, kissed me briefly on the ear. 'Bless you, love! No, thank heavens, they were all extremely pleasant men.'

'But going to seed, perhaps?' I tried.

'No. Mostly in the prime of life, I'd say.'

'A bit fat, maybe?'

'A paunch here and there,' she allowed. 'But I like a man with a little importance – men of that age, anyway. I'll tell you, if you're really interested. My first gentleman was the Lord Mayor of Harrogate – Reginald something. He made a beeline for me the minute we opened. Two o'clock on the dot! And immediately after him was Arthur, who's Somebody Very Important in the police. In fact, he's the one who's protecting Madame and us girls from the attentions of the law. Madame warned me to be

especially nice to him! He had me and Valerie together –
that was *very* interesting, I may tell you! Then came a
twenty-minute break before I was covered by Bertam,
who's a High Court judge.' She gave a little shudder but
said no more about him. 'Next was Augustus – a dean of
the cathedral. He wanted me to dress like a nun, a
Catholic nun, although he's a Protestant. Could you
imagine! Then there was a man who called himself Pindar
– that can't be his real name, can it? He's a university
professor. Then a barrister called George – followed
immediately by his friend Michael, who was also a barrister. Then a *big* businessman – if I told you his name and
the mills he owns, you'd gasp. And also there was a man
who owns a large hôtel in the city centre – you'd know his
name, too. Whew!' She wiped imaginary beads of perspiration off her brow, but the gleam in her eye – insofar as I
could read it in the gentle lamplight – was one of pride at
her achievement. 'Anyway, the point I'm really making is
that there you have all those *big* important men who
spend all their days solemnly putting the world to rights –
and yet I bet all their friends would be just amazed out of
their skins to see how they behave when they're alone
with girls like us. That's what I mean when I say everyone's hiding their real selves when they go about their
profession. It isn't only girls like us. How did we get on to
this? Oh yes – you calling me Kitten! It's the perfect
personality for me to hide behind, you see. Whenever I've
been in doubt about what to do today, I've just thought to
myself, *Behave like a little kitten!* And the men have
absolutely *loved* it!'

'As your hatbox proves.'

'Yes. And I owe it all to you, for that inspired suggestion! Also to the other name you gave me: Little Darling!
That's what you called my tra-la-la when you first saw it,
d'you remember?'

'How does that help?' I asked.

94

'Well . . .' She buried her face in the pit of my neck. 'You're going to laugh at me now.'

'I promise not to.'

She was still reluctant. 'When I say it out loud I know it's going to sound mad. Anyway, the thing is, you see – when I bring a man up here to screw me – or to screw my tra-la-la – I stop thinking my tra-la-la is part of *me*. D'you follow? I think of it – I mean *her* – I think of her as Little Darling, who's a very close friend, a twin sister, perhaps, but not *quite* me. Oh, I *said* it would sound idiotic.'

I gave her a squeeze. 'To me it sounds the most sensible thing on earth, Kitten. How does she feel now, by the way? Is that salve beginning to work? By the look of her she must have had a pretty hard time of it . . .'

'*Hard* is the *mot juste*!' she joked. Then, after a thoughtful pause, she added, 'If you really want to know, Little Darling has felt absolutely numb all day.'

'Ten men!' I sighed in sympathy. Then, as offhandedly as possible, I added, 'Though, oddly enough, you mentioned only nine just now.'

She punched my arm, playfully but still quite hard. 'You've been waiting to talk about *him* ever since you saw him, haven't you!' she accused me with jovial vehemence.

'Ever since I saw *you*,' I corrected her. 'Clinging to his arm – the way you looked. The glow in your eyes . . .'

She stopped my words with a kiss. When I relaxed, she pulled away and said, 'You're not jealous, are you, Freddy?'

I sighed. 'A teeny bit, I suppose.' At that moment, with him gone and her lying at peace in my arms, I could pooh-pooh my earlier feelings about the man.

'Because jealousy on your part would make life under this roof fairly impossible for me – considering my new choice of profession!'

'Well, I see that, of course.'

'I hope so. Listen – let's clear this up now.' She

withdrew from my embrace and, turning on her stomach, propped herself up on her elbows. 'No man will ever again give me quite the same sort of thrill . . . no, it was much more than a thrill. It was the deepest, profoundest, most wonderful pleasure I've ever known – or ever will know – that experience with you yesterday afternoon. No man will ever give me so much pleasure again – not even you, perhaps, though I'd love you to go on trying! And as often as possible, please. But that doesn't mean to say other men aren't going to take me some *little* way down the same road from time to time. Surely you see that?'

'Especially if they look like Adonis and wear the uniform of the Young Turks!'

Her face jerked toward mine and I could just see the whites of her startled eyes. 'You know about the Young Turks? Has Madame already told you?'

'Isn't it the nickname of the Duke of Leeds Light Infantry? That was his uniform.'

She laughed. 'No! The Young Turks is a private club, here in Leeds. It's a house in Headingley, all decked out like a Turkish Hareem. The members are all young army officers under the age of thirty-five, and they have to be below the rank of major. They formed it about ten years ago when they realized how fed up they were with the formality and stuffiness of the typical officers' mess. At the Young Turks they can take their jackets off, loosen their ties, gamble, play billiards, smoke where they like, swear . . . and, every Wednesday and Sunday evening, enjoy the favours of two fillies from Lazy Daisy's!'

'But today's Saturday.'

'Wait! Madame obviously hasn't told you. They don't come here. What happens is that every Wednesday and every Sunday, at twenty to four precisely, a private carriage draws up outside this house and two freshly bathed and perfumed young flowers step into it. And it conveys them – and their most valuable Commodities, which are well-buttered against the exertions ahead – to Headingley. And there, for the next six hours, they do them mighty pleasure – as many young officers as may be present. At around eleven of the evening the same carriage returns two wilting but (some girls whisper) blissful blossoms to the fold, where, unless the trade is excessively brisk, they are excused further service for the night. Lieutenant the Honourable Wellesley O'Toole de North, or Tooley to his friends, is their present HRO – Horizontal Refreshments Officer. He was merely ensuring that the newest young filly at Lazy Daisy's was up to standard before she is whisked to Headingley. You know how meticulous the army is in some things!'

'You mean' – I gulped heavily – '*you* are to be one of those two young "flowers" tomorrow – I mean later today?'

She turned and lay on her back, stretching out luxuriously and heaving a long sigh: 'Y-e-e-s! It seems Tooley thinks I'll do very nicely.'

'And,' I asked miserably, 'you really did enjoy, er, Doing It with him?'

'Oh, Freddy!' She threw herself half on top of me and gave me a passionate kiss. 'He was an oasis in a howling desert. Yesterday night in the dorm, when I started telling Valerie, who sleeps next to me – when I started telling her of the unbelievably sweet sensations I had felt with you . . . well, actually, if you must know, I told her I didn't believe I could possibly go through that same experience ten times in a day with ten different men!' She gave a dry little laugh. 'That was only twenty-four hours ago, too – I already live in a different world!'

'Well, to tell you the truth, I was wondering about that. But Maisie said it doesn't happen with every man. Of course, after you've been doing it for five years . . .'

She cut across me. 'It doesn't happen with *any* man, Freddy. That's what Valerie told me. You can imagine my relief. She said it was very good I'd experienced the real thing with you because I should try to counterfeit it with the customers – make them think they're wonderful lovers who can thrill even girls like us. Anyway, I still didn't believe her, not quite. I thought she might just be trying to comfort me. So I was terribly nervous when Reginald took me upstairs straight away.'

'You and Little Darling,' I pointed out.

She grinned. 'Quite right. Anyway, I was so worried about not letting him get me all hotted up and amorous, I didn't pay enough attention to him – and he shot his load in the handbasin while I was soaping his carrot.'

'Is that what you girls call it?'

'It's what *I* call it. They do look so like them, don't they! I shall never be able to peel carrots again! Anyway, I thought I was staring disaster in the face. My first go with a customer and he shoots his sticky before he's got half his clothes off! He was very sad, I can tell you!'

'So what did you do?'

'Just what I told you. I thought to myself, *Be like a little kitten!* So I led him to the bed – he was grumbling all the way, saying I was wasting my time and nothing would come of it – a real moaning minnie. And then I took all his clothes off, and me just in my stockings. And when I saw his little carrot – well, little *radish* was more like it! – I began to think he was right. Nothing would come of it. And he had such a big one before, when it was stiff. Anyway, I laid him on his back and crawled on top of him and I just sort of wriggled and squirmed my body all over him – for a long time, I can tell you. And he went on saying it was no good, and in the end I was just about ready to agree with him when I noticed he'd stopped talking. Then I noticed he was breathing shorter and with a sort of shiver in him. And *then!* I could have sung the Hallelujah Chorus! I felt his plaything start to tickle the insides of my thighs! He was still only three-quarters stiff but getting harder all the time – with a sort of pulse, pumping it up – like when you pump a bicycle inner tube. Anyway, I nipped it tight between my thighs and did extra-vigorous wriggles and *wham!*' She raised a fist and shook it toward the ceiling, like one pugilist threatening another. 'The Eddystone Lighthouse! Then I just sort of slid Little Darling down over him and then I sat up and did all the work for him – while he just lay there, chortling like a baby, saying he'd never have believed it. And then after about twenty minutes he shot himself off again, right up inside me this time.'

'So he didn't go the full hour,' I said.

She chortled. 'He jolly well did! I made sure of that. I told him he wasn't going to cheat me out of thirty minutes of fun. And he just gawped at me as if to say was I mad! But I . . . well, I did some things Valerie told me about last night, and . . .'

'What sort of things?'

She hesitated and then said, 'I don't like to say it.'

'All right,' I told her. 'You can show me some time.'

'This!' She took my hand, pulled my thumb stiff, and sucked at it.

'Like I did to you,' I pointed out.

'Well, it had the same effect on him – it drove him wild. He was stiff again in no time. He said I was a miracle and he'd never got stiff twice before let alone three times, and now he'd give me all the fun I wanted. So I just lay there and he poked me happily for another twenty minutes and shot himself off again – what Valerie calls a dry-bob. He gave me a thirty-shilling tip when he left.'

'And was it fun?'

After a pause she said, 'Not in the way he meant it. But it *was* fun in another way.'

'What way?'

She seemed to need to touch me before she could reply. She laid her head on my chest and, stroking me gently with one hand behind my ear, said, 'I'm not especially proud of myself for feeling like this, Freddy. Will you think less of me if I'm completely honest with you?'

'No. Not the smallest bit.'

'I believe you, but I wish I could be absolutely, utterly, completely sure. Will you be equally honest with me?'

'I'll try.' My heart dropped a beat.

'If we become lovers, you and I – do you realize you won't be able to come in and pick me out of the salon. I couldn't ever bring you up here like any other customer.'

I hadn't, in fact, thought about it, but the moment she spoke I saw the truth of it. 'Yes,' I said wanly. 'Actually, I have sort of half-formed some other plans.'

She giggled. 'So have I. D'you want to tell me yours yet?'

'Not really, Kitten. Do you?'

'No, so let's leave that aside. Anyway, that wasn't my real test of your honesty. That comes next. What I'd like you to tell me, absolutely frankly, now, is this: If you and I became lovers – real lovers – would you still want to come to Lazy Daisy's and go upstairs with the other girls?'

I sweated trying to think of a bright-sounding evasion but in the end I confessed it. 'Yes,' I sighed.

She let out the breath she'd been holding all that while and kissed my body through the nightshirt. She said nothing but I had an intuition that if I had given any other reply, it would have been the beginning of the end between us. I took a chance on that and went on to tell her about Rachel – not because I was excessively flushed with honesty that night but because I realized I would have to tell her anyway – about not being able to come to Lazy Daisy's the following night. (I also suspected that Rachel would not be satisfied with a single night and a 'see-you-next-Sunday' promise, but I didn't break that news just yet.)

Kitten was fascinated and not in the least jealous – an

object lesson for me which I resolved to study. She wanted to be told all about it, every little detail. I was amazed at her liveliness after the gruelling day she'd had but she was on the crest of a wave that night and would have found sleep impossible. I replied that I'd tell her all about Rachel on one condition – namely that, while I would not go out of my way to tell Rachel about her, if Rachel asked for details, I'd hold nothing back, either. She thought that fair enough. So then I related all that had passed between Rachel and me that evening, including the off-stage business between Nannette and old man Cohen.

'What an eye-opener!' Kitten said when I'd finished.

'Old Cohen certainly opened one of Nannette's eyes,' I replied. 'The blind one she keeps in her drawers!'

'Blind is the word,' Kitten replied, in a more serious vein than mine. '*I've* been blind all right. All this screwing that's going on all the time – everywhere – I mean, have *you* been aware of it before now, Freddy?'

''Fraid so,' I told her. 'In fact, until last week, I was painfully aware I wasn't getting my fair share of it.'

She laughed. 'Well, you've certainly made up for *that* deficiency since! But seriously, I had no idea. I thought that what I did with Thomas . . .'

'You father's valet?'

'Mm-hmm. I though that what we did was . . . oh, I don't know. I thought there'd be a national stink and questions asked in parliament if word of it ever got out!'

'What *did* you do, exactly, Kitten? I didn't like to ask on Friday, but he obviously never penetrated you.'

'No. Wasn't I the fool! I'll tell you all about it another time. But I was thinking about it a lot today, while all those men were screwing away inside me. That's the hardest bit, you know – keeping your mind on the job. But I was thinking that if I'd known three weeks ago what I know now, I need never have "sunk" to this level.'

I chuckled. 'You say "sunk" as if you didn't believe a bit of it.'

'I don't! I think life here is going to be a thousand times richer than ever it was at home. It's all right for you young men. You have all the freedom you could want. You have no idea of the stifling boredom, the unutterable stuffiness of our lives – "respectable" girls like me. Or like I was. Take my older sister, who's twenty and getting rather desperate to catch a husband. She lived in an absolute delirium for two weeks because she accidentally dropped a glove when coming out of church and a young army officer she's keen on picked it up and gave it to her. All he said was, "Yours, I believe, Miss Bossom?" but she never stopped talking about it – the kindly tone in his voice . . . the gentle light in his eyes . . . on and on and on until, if I'd met the gallant fellow in the street, I'd have drawn his sword and run him through.'

'I know that feeling very well,' I said heavily.

It was a second or two before she took my meaning. Then she punched me lightly and went on with her tale.

'Can you imagine how utterly stifling a life must be in which such a trivial incident can keep a young girl's spirit dancing among the clouds for two whole weeks! That was my life, too, Freddy. The high point of my last week at home came when I mounted half a dozen dried flowers in my herbarium – I hardly slept for the excitement! And that explains how Thomas was able to . . . well, mount *me*, if you like! As to what he and I did together – it was little enough, as I now realize. He got me into a doorway, where we kissed for a few minutes, and then he lifted my dress and stuck his carrot in between the lips of my tra-la-la and moved it slowly in and out. It was a blissful sensation even though he didn't get inside Little Darling. And that was what we were doing when my mother caught us. She threw a fainting fit on the spot, of course. Then I was dragged before my father, who asked if Thomas had

had carnal knowledge of me, and I said yes because I didn't know any better – I didn't even know what carnal knowledge meant except I know carnal means fleshly, so of course I said yes. And that was the end of that. Seventeen years of genteel rearing – pfft! Gone! He threw me out. He threw both of us out. If whipping at cart tails was still legal, he'd have done that, too.'

'I hope you don't mind my asking,' I said diffidently, 'but is your father, by any chance, Sir Charles Bossom of Hetherington Hall?'

'Who else!'

I did not wonder at her comments on his severity. Sir Charles was the greatest prig and prude in Yorkshire. He performed enormous works of charity, scattering the countryside with orphanages and rescue missions of every kind; but it was well known that the slightest breach of the moral law would shut a pauper out in the cold for ever. Such a respectable, scrupulous gentleman could quite easily throw his own seventeen-year-old daughter out of house and home after no deeper inquiry than that. Even so, though I already held the man in the deepest contempt, I was not prepared for what Kitten said next.

'He not only threw me out,' she said cheerfully, 'he also advised me to seek employment here at Lazy Daisy's! He said I'd find congenial females of my own class under this roof.'

'And have you?' I asked, struggling to appear as blasé as she was being.

'Yes, indeed! But not as he meant it. He meant females of a depraved, wanton, and abandoned class, of course. Actually, most of the girls here come from solid, middle-class families – as you've probably noticed. It was the first thing *I* noticed, anyway. I asked Valerie about it on my first night here – golly, that was almost a week ago now!'

It was news to me that Kitten had been at Lazy Daisy's a whole week but I saved my questions on that for another time. 'What did Valerie say?' I asked.

'It seems that Madame prefers us middle-class girls. Obviously we can talk to the customers better – and I've talked with some really interesting gentlemen today, about all sorts of things. You'd be surprised. I've never in my life been able to talk to men with such freedom, nor so naturally, as I have today. In the past twelve hours I've enjoyed more interesting conversations than in the whole of my previous life. But, more important even than that, Madame says that working-class girls find the work too boring! Only the money keeps them at it, and their mercenary attitude soon shows. But we middle-class girls know what *real* boredom is! Which is what I was saying, too. So there you are!'

Her reference to 'interesting conversations' reminded me of her earlier remark that she'd had an interesting day and lots of fun, though not of a sexual kind. I reminded her of it then and asked her what she had meant.

'O-o-oh!' She gave a long groan, as if she'd hoped I'd forgotten. 'It's what I said just now – I've had some really fascinating conversations today. That's all.'

Somehow I knew she was fobbing me off with the nearest convenient half-truth. Earlier in our conversation she had started something she did not now wish to finish. I decided to leave that, too, for another day.

She continued: 'When men pay for an hour with me, I expect them to honour their half of the bargain, too. That's why I kept Reginald at it for the full time – much to his delight. But there were several men today who finished after about forty minutes and who obviously meant it when they said they didn't want a second go. So I said, 'All right, then, just lie on the bed beside me and let's talk.' And they did.' She chuckled. 'It surprised some of them, I must say. And, d'you know, they were almost *grateful!* Imagine! Big, important, powerful men like that – grateful to a little kitten like me for wanting to lie on the bed and just *talk* with them! I don't think the other girls do much of that sort of thing.'

'And what did these fellows talk about?'

'Their wives, mostly. And their daughters. One or two of them talked about their daughters. 'Why is my darling Emily so sullen most of the time? Why is dear little Agatha always going down with little illnesses?' That sort of thing.'

'And did you tell them?'

'A bit. I gave them tiny hints at the truth. One can't do too much all at once. But I really enjoyed it, Freddy. Today, for the first time in my life, I really felt I was *someone*. I felt of value.'

I reached across and lightly stroked her cheek. 'You've absolutely fallen on your feet here, Kitten – haven't you!'

'Absolutely!' she echoed. 'I hope I'm going to be here for a long time.' After a pause she said – in a much more hesitant tone, 'Actually, darling, do you think I could ask you an *enormous* favour?'

'Anything. Consider it already granted.'

'You may not be so light-hearted when you hear! The thing is – could you manage *not* to come here for the next three or four days? I mean, I'll remember until my dying breath how glad I am to see you tonight. To care for someone as much as I care for you – and to have those feelings reciprocated, too – is wonderful beyond words. But it wasn't just Little Darling who took a bit of a battering today. My emotions are all very, you know, jangly, too. So I'd like a few days to settle into the work – and without too much emotion. I can't ask you to stay away a whole week – and I'd be miserable if you agreed to, anyway! But . . . is Wednesday too far off?'

I kissed the tip of her nose and said, 'Actually, I'll go now.'

'Why?' She was mortified. 'Because of what I said?'

'No. Because of what I am! If I woke up tomorrow

morning and found you beside me, not all the chains on earth would keep us apart.'

I got dressed before my resolve could weaken again; as I sat on the bed at her side, to pull on my running shoes, I said, 'I'll stay away until Wednesday, or, actually, until two o'clock on Thursday morning, on one condition.'

'What's that?'

'You must keep a diary of everything that happens on the days in between. Starting with today as well.'

Her laugh was slightly bewildered. 'What sort of diary?'

'Whatever seems important. When I talked with Maisie about the customers here, it was clear to me she no longer sees much difference among them. Hunchback, dwarf, octogenarian, young Adonis . . . they all coalesce into a sort of blur with her – a hairless ape waggling a great carrot in his hand as if it were Christmas. I'd hate you to go that way, too. I think you could become one of the *great* courtesans – the sort poets write about and people remember for centuries. But only if you can keep alive this spark that's been struck in you today. Writing a diary might help. Call it *Little Darling's Diary*, if you like.'

She swallowed heavily and said, 'You're rather a frightening man at times, Freddy. D'you think some Power might have caused our paths to meet at this particular moment in our lives?'

I guided her hand to my groin, where Iron Jack was threatening to burst through the thin cotton of my running shorts. 'It's some Power, right enough!' I quipped. 'The Power that rules the world!' More seriously, though, I feared my suggestion might be putting too much of a burden on her so early in her career, I modified it: 'Or you could simply get into the diary-keeping habit by making a daily list of each of your customers – his name, what he does, how old he is, the size of his carrot, what he likes to do with you, what he talks about . . . that sort of thing.'

'The size of his carrot!' she exclaimed in amazement.

'I think it would be interesting.'

'Who to? Not to me, I assure you.'

'To the men who may one day read your memoirs, perhaps? When Little Darling cannot earn much more, little pen and fingers may!'

That gave her pause for thought. 'Yes!' she said slowly. 'I think mere size *does* interest men. Three of them today waggled their carrots at me and asked if I didn't think them too big – wasn't I afraid they'd hurt me, and so on.'

'And did they?'

She yawned. 'The funny thing is there's not a great deal of difference in size once a man is good and stiff. There's a huge difference when they're limp but the big ones just get stiff without growing much and the tiddlers grow like balloons! And another thing – big or small, once they're hidden inside Little Darling, they all feel pretty much the same.'

She yawned again. I kissed her and left. The entire house was in silence by then; even Madame had gone to sleep.

Jealousy! What a terrible, corrosive serpent it is! And why, even when we know what hurt it will bring, do we clasp it to our bosom and feed it so assiduously? The image of Kitten, naked down to her corset and stockings, smiling her head off and slinking provocatively at 'Tooley's' side – and him in all his magnificence – seared deep into my soul. Throughout the vicar's interminable sermon that Sunday morning, I tortured myself with imaginings of what had gone on between the two of them in the privacy of the bedroom above. I played the scenes over and over, homing in on the most hurtful bits and repeating them with especial relish.

I imagined him having taken off nothing more than his sword, lying on the counterpane in full uniform, boots and all, while Kitten's delicate fingers toyed playfully with his flies, plucking them open one by one and making sure that each little fumble sent unbearable thrills and tickles down his hatefully majestic organ. And at last, when she fished it out in the open air – oh, what a magnificent specimen it was! White as alabaster in its formidable shaft and crowned by a bloated head of deep, ardent pink. And how beautifully sculpted it was, too, with a swollen ridge all round the glans to make any girl gasp when she felt it chafe the walls of her vagina.

All through the offertory hymn I pictured Kitten's audacious lips and spirited tongue giving Tooley's tool no peace – kissing it, licking it, treating it to little love bites . . . darting, flickering, drooling all over it – while he just lay there in the drowsy numbness of erotic stupor.

On our walk home from church across the fields I slashed viciously at all the thistleheads, wishing each one was Tooley's wonderful tool; but in my mind's eye I could see Kitten, now naked to her stockings, lying on top of him, wriggling her lithe young body and giving out gasps of pleasure as that perfect column of gristle nudged into the furrow of her exquisite Little Darling. My astral body, the tortured witness of each damnable moment, drew closer, closer . . . until those two passionate organs filled my entire field of vision. I could see every little hair on her blushing quim, every tiny vein on his throbbing tool. Still she had not plunged him deep inside her. Only that fervid crown, purple now with the swelling of his lust, nosed in and out of the heat of her most intimate nook; but I could see how the lamplight gleamed on the wetness it garnered there and I could hear the sticky little noises it made as she wriggled it in and out of her.

And all through Sunday lunch it continued – not unceasingly, of course, or I really should have gone mad. Indeed, I flatter myself that I kept up a pretty good outward appearance of a young fellow who could not wait to get on his bike and hunt a few rare butterflies over in

Wharfedale. But as soon as there was a lull in our family conversation – which was habitually inane – that abhorrent scene would come rushing back to me. Wriggle by wriggle, writhe by writhe, she introduced Tooley's sublime plaything deeper and deeper into Little Darling's orifice. I watched her break out in a sweat at the thrill she felt when his protruding glans skimmed over the sweetly ticklish surface of her love passage; I heard her cry out – little animal whimpers of pure joy in one unending stream – at the ecstasies he was giving her.

But worst of all was the moment of *his* final ecstasy, when I saw how the fleshy buttresses of that stout white column swelled with his semen and then fired off like a mighty cannon. And now it was as if my inner eye had developed supernatural powers, for I could somehow see his phallus *inside* her there, even though her writhing derrière remained as temptingly fleshy as ever. I saw the pulse of his orgasm pass right up that swollen column and I watched it ejaculate into the very top of her vagina. While she cried out for mercy in her ecstasy, he shot spurt after spurt into that fervid cul-de-sac; I could see the sticky, blobby white of it swirling around his purple knob and then come surging down to lubricate them both in the last frenzied spasms of their immaculate coupling.

That was the moment when I knew I had to go back to Lazy Daisy's that very afternoon and there, with my binoculars, endure my final moment of absolute torture – in the slim hope it would burn the jealousy out of me for ever.

It was half past three by the time I arrived, so I had not long to wait. I hid in the shrubbery near the top of the drive and tried to keep my mind off the affair by scanning the visible windows, seeking signs of fillies at their daily work. But the sun was too bright and the curtains resolutely drawn. Once I caught a brief glimpse of Maisie, with the mere shadow of a customer in the room behind her. It was the deluxe bedroom beside Madame's boudoir; Maisie stood at the window and gazed out, rather forlornly, for a moment before drawing the curtain. I pictured her going over to the bed, to suck and drool over the customer's tool – and I felt nothing beyond a minor erotic titillation. There was no doubt about it: Kitten was something special to me.

A moment later I almost burst into tears of frustration. The promised carriage went trundling past me down the drive and drew up in the sweep, slightly to one side of the front door. A filly named Virginie emerged, clothed in the very height of elegance in a pale cream dress with a blue sash about her tiny waist; she put up her parasol for the brief walk to the carriage. I knew her slightly for we had talked a couple of times in the salon. She was a fair-haired, blue-eyed French girl of about twenty, with large, soft breasts and, as I have just said, a wasp waist. Maisie had told me she was 'very sexy.' I had no very precise idea what that meant, but I intended to find out as soon as decently possible.

That, however, was of no comfort now, for Virginie was scarcely halfway to the carriage when the door opened again and out came Kitten. She was dressed like a princess in a long, flowing dress of white silk with a great crimson sash around her waist; she wore white kid gloves and was crowned with a broad-brimmed straw hat with a fetching upward sweep.

Virginie took a pace or two back toward her and they linked arms. Kitten said something and they broke into merry laughter. Last night Kitten had seemed to parody the suggestion that these two 'beautiful blossoms,' plucked fresh each Sunday from Lazy Daisy's garden, would return from Headingley, 'wilting but blissful'; but her attitude now was very different. I remembered her other jocular comments – about how their bodies were freshly bathed and perfumed, and how they rubbed plenty of cream into their young quims against the exertions of the Young Turks – but now those jests rang horribly true.

As they trod the few paces down the drive and climbed into the carriage, their every move and gesture suggested to me that here were two young girls setting off to meet an unknown number of dashing young officers and pass the next six hours with them in frisky sexual romps. And every part of them was already fluttering with the joy of anticipation – especially those well-lubricated smiles, now tingling in secret between their creamy thighs but soon to be spread wide to the world and pierced by . . .

I dropped my glasses and beat my brow in fury.

And of course, no sooner had the carriage gone by on its fateful journey, than I was back on my bicycle, following it discreetly all the way to Headingley – for now I simply had to know what this house that tortured my waking dreams was like. On the way I pondered the mystery of Time. *Twenty seconds ago*, I thought, *this spot where the tip of my nose now cleaves the air, this precise point in the universe, was filled with the warmth and softness of the most desirable nook in all creation!* In fact, Time was the only thing that kept my nose and that ambrosial nook apart. A mystery, indeed!

The Young Turks Club was rather grand. In fact, it was the mansion of some mid-century wool magnate before he got even grander ideas and moved out to an old country estate. I could see about two acres of mature garden to either side and stretching away to the back, but the façade of the house was only about twenty paces from the road, leaving room for nothing but an in-and-out carriage sweep and a narrow stretch of lawn, from which reared a phalanx of cedars of Lebanon. I stood panting in their shade and stared through the pierced brickwork of the high front wall. The main house was three storeys high, built in Venetian gothic style with romantic turrets and lots of poky little pointed-arch windows that gave little clue to the floor levels within. To a miserable observer half-concealed in the street they gave even less clue as to what was going on behind them.

I had arrived just in time to see the doors open and the two girls walk in; they faced a barrage of cheering from the dimly lighted hallway beyond. I hear its reverberations even now and can recall the chill that settled round my heart on that day. It came from two dozen lusty male throats at least – of that I soon convinced myself.

As they crossed the threshold I saw that the wide sashes they wore about their waists were tied in huge, ornate bows, which flounced enticingly on their lightly bustled derrières. In my very last glimpse of them, as they were swallowed by the gothic gloom, they both had their arms raised to unpin their hats – a gesture that would also have uplifted their proud bubbies into seductive prominence.

Two lovely girls, one of them in her early twenties, the other a mere seventeen, versus a small army of horny young men, who had doubtless been stoking up their randy cravings all this long, hot summer day . . . It did not bear thinking about – and yet I could not bear to think of anything else. And thus was I furnished with images to goad me all the way home. My mind's eye, now my most cursed faculty, furnished me with visions of hell. I saw officers' trembling hands delving for milky-soft breasts among folds of silk . . . officers' eager fingers playing a dainty tug-o'-war with sashes of blue and crimson . . . officers' greedy paws moulding themselves tightly around those two young nymphs' curvaceous bottoms as dresses of tulle and muslin fell away . . . and a whole forest of officers' cocks, superb in their proud virility, thrusting, poking, rodding, prodding, squirt-squirt-squirting . . . but why go on! By the time I arrived home I was ready to curl up and die.

My spirits had considerably recovered by that evening,

however, when I went next door to 'cheer up' Rachel, who was still languishing in quarantine. Old man Cohen was entertaining some in-laws to dinner, so Nannette was with us the whole time. Rachel and I behaved impeccably, not by a single word or gesture did we even hint at the stupendous experience we were going to enjoy together later that night. By nine o'clock, when Kitten was about to begin her final hour at spreading her thighs, giving the last of the Young Turks a warm hole to hide in, I was quite my old self again. I understood that if I could not sustain my anguish through so long a period as five whole hours, powerful and deep though it was, then she, even if she had entered that mansion with her entire body on fire with sexual frenzy, could hardly have sustained it through the same tedious span.

I realize it says little for my character that I grieved when I thought Kitten might *enjoy* being rogered lustily by the Young Turks yet I became much happier when I suspected she might find six hours of non-stop poking both tedious to her spirit and irritating to her quim. As St Augustine often said – a stiff prick hath no conscience.

A stiff prick hath an excellent nose, however, especially when it gets downwind of a ravenous quim. Rachel and I could have been blindfolded and lost, miles apart in the Great Grimpen Mire, yet we should have found each other nonetheless, for never was prick stiffer than mine nor quim more ravenous than hers. Fortunately the path between us could hardly have been simpler. Our roof was being repaired by slaters at that time and I was able to span the narrow gap between our houses with two of their ladders. And, to pour cream upon custard, I had a harvest moon to guide my feet.

So I had no excuse for descending onto the wrong balcony. Had I not done so, however, I might not have been so easy of mind during the hours I spent with Rachel that night.

As soon as I saw the plain deck chair I knew I had mistakenly lowered myself onto old Cohen's balcony, for Rachel's had a much grander chair of wickerwork and beads. The windows were tight shut, which I thought odd on such a warm night, but when I put my eye to a crack in the curtains I realized why. The long hours of enforced separation between Nannette and her employer that evening had obviously stoked the fire of their lust to an inferno – which was plainly going to take them hours to extinguish.

Cohen slept in an ancient four-poster bed, the frame of which he and his young French mistress were now putting to splendid use. They had thrown a broad sash of brocade over the cross-piece at the end – the kind of sash used for bell-pulls in the drawing-rooms of that period – and Cohen had lightly bound one end of it around her wrists. Even through my narrow peephole I could see how loosely it was tied; she could slip out at any moment she wished. But, equally obviously, escape was the last thing she desired at that particular moment. She was standing at the foot of the bed, facing it, undressed down to her corsets and stockings. Her arms, as I said, were lightly bound at the wrists and then drawn high above her head, so that she had to stand on tiptoe every now and then to relieve her shoulders. This had the effect of raising her voluptuous bubbies right out of the cradle of her corsets and exposing their defenceless nipples to the marauding fingers of her eager lover.

He stood behind her, sporting a ramrod so ardent that, even though he seemed notched deep within her, I could see the crimson tip of it sticking out beneath her belly as if she were a hermaphrodite and the thing were hers. He was thrusting it back and forth with a slowness that must have been driving them both mad, at the same time letting his fingertips flit lightly over her generous bosoms and their grossly swollen nipples. Every time she stood on tiptoe to ease her shoulders, the movement thrust her provocative and well-fleshed derrière into his groin. Then, giving her breasts some respite, he would grasp her lightly by the hips, withdraw almost fully from her, and push the tip of his tool against the button of her bumhole – being careful not to push inside her there. I noted that it drove Nannette wild with pleasure.

It had a similar effect on Iron Jack, too. He poked his head, all hot and imploring, out between the folds of my dressing gown, beating the air in time with my racing heart. Had he not pleaded with me so piteously, staring up with his one baleful eye, I could have stayed there all night. It would probably have cut short my amorous education by months. I was sad to bid farewell to that sweet chink in their curtains, but I resolved to return some other evening when Rachel was not so desperately hungry for a helping of gamecock and gravy.

I clambered briefly back to the roof and skittered along the parapet until I was over Rachel's balcony. She heard me even before I got my foot in the wistaria, whose contorted branches gave me an easy climb down to her. She was standing there, waiting for me – though, curiously enough, her opening words belied the fact.

'I can't wait,' she panted before I was even halfway down.

'Eh?' I let myself drop the remaining distance.

Her trembling fingers opened my dressing gown and she insinuated herself inside it before I had fairly turned round; she was utterly, delightfully, naked. 'Can't wait,' she repeated, wriggling and squirming her firm young body hard against mine. 'Do it now, quickly – as quick as you like. I'm ready to burst.'

My pyjama trousers fell around my ankles; she already had all my tunic buttons loose. Her hands were all over me; her fingernails like panther's talons in my back; her tongue and teeth made sensual havoc of my nipples; the heat of her breathing on my chest almost undid me entirely. I barely had time or enough presence of mind to fish out the first of the six bungs I had brought; how I worked it on over Iron Jack remains a mystery.

She already knew of such devices, having read of them in her father's *Casanova*, so she twigged its purpose at once. She gave out a contented gurgle and lifted her right thigh as high as it would go, circling me with her leg so that her calf rested on the jut of my buttocks.

'Go in!' she urged. 'Quick as you can and hard as you like.'

In that position Iron Jack would have had to be an octogenarian fumbler not to find the way up to heaven. And what a torrid heaven it was that night! A tropical storm of love juice poured down there between her thighs. Two or three lascivious kisses from those slavering nether lips got the bung so wet and slippery that all sensation of wearing it vanished; it turned into a second skin.

At that same moment she raised her other thigh and wrapped me in a nutcracker grip. In my mind's eye I saw the hungry parting of her labia, the virgin passage between them pouting in silent craving. You know how it is when you go past a steam engine in the dark, you can *feel* the heat pouring out of it? I had precisely that sensation now, with the heat of Rachel's desire. I seemed to feel it pouring out of her sex and bathing mine, thrilling me to the marrow. This moment of achievement, when a man's proud priap nudges apart the outer lips of a woman's receptacle and luxuriates briefly in their amorous warmth and softness, is the moment toward which the whole of human life, man's and woman's, is aimed. No matter how many times I experience it – even after a hundred nights in a row – the actual instant when Iron Jack's knob nuzzles at the steamy portals of paradise always feels unique.

That night with Rachel I wanted to spin it out over the

next thousand years; but her mood was quite the opposite. She gave a little wriggle with her hips and a moment later Iron Jack was as deep inside her mysteries as he was ever going to get. Her naughty wriggling did not stop. With her arms clamped tight about my neck and her thighs locked around my waist, she ground and gyrated her hips, purling and writhing her firm, soft body against mine. She never gave Iron Jack a moment's rest – though he did no work at all!

She was brimming over all the while, enjoying one climax after another. From the moment my cracksman began to slip himself in and out of the tender squeeze of her holey, she was lost to all reason – or so it seemed to me. She fought for every breath. She shivered uncontrollably. She showered me with a hundred impetuous kisses. And the sweat broke from her body at every pore. Yet the moment my lustful spermspouter gathered his strength for the first mighty bombardment, she sensed it and clung to me in the most amazing stillness. It had the strangest effect on me – and on her, too, I'm sure. After that frenzy of wriggling and squirming, the sudden calm induced a supernatural concentration on that one last point of moving contact. I have enjoyed more orgasms than I could possibly count since then; some of them have climaxed hours of amorous engagement with the most skilled and wanton women in the world. Yet that first stupendous eruption inside Rachel is one I shall remember to my dying hour.

Earlier that day I had imagined I could 'see' the imperious Tooley's tool rammed to the hilt of Kitten's dainty quim and gushing hot semen like a fumarole. Now that image came to me again, except that I was no longer the anguished voyeur of another's joys but an ecstatic witness of my own. My fingers were locked beneath Rachel's buttocks and struggling to maintain their clasp despite the outpouring of slippery, randy juices from her holey. My little fingers were just nudging against the base of Iron Jack, touching that tube where the semen gathers for its first and last great leap into the darkness of life. All this I could somehow see, not as if I were a Peeping Tom crouched down between my own knees, but actually from the present location of my head, pressed tight against Rachel's and fighting for breath in the warm July night.

So I needed very little extra imagination to 'see' my spermspouter, snug in his bung, and even snugger in the amorous clutch of Rachel's holey; and I saw him with preternatural clarity at that moment when he kicked with the ultimate joy of life and shot her full of his creamy tribute. I saw my milt come gushing out and swirl around up there even as I felt the sweet fever of it and its hot, thrilling pressure, drenching my knob.

And all the way through, to the last little squirt, she remained still and rigid. Somehow I knew that she, too, was picturing that scene, giving it the different colour of her own sensations. The myriad nerves in her most exquisitely sensitive passage detected every nuance of this stupendous new event inside her there, giving her all she needed to create that picture in her mind.

(In fact, this was no pretty fantasy on my part, for, in the days that followed, she confirmed it and we spent many a happy post-coital hour trying to describe our separate experiences of the other's sex. For me the hot, juicy walls of her vagina were the very wellspring of all delight; to feel the subtle pressure of their embrace was the be-all and end-all of my existence. Iron Jack did not know he was alive until that loving flesh held him in its passionate grip. She, of course, experienced the perfectly complimentary sensation. The walls of her vagina were, one assumes, in constant touch with each other, yet the contact gave rise to no sensation at all – and certainly produced no feelings of pleasure. But the moment a man thrust his hot, importunate gristle up there and pushed them apart . . . my, that was another thing!)

That first evening, as soon as sense and breath returned to our bodies, she slipped out of my dressing gown and, taking me by the wrist, dragged me into the relative dark of her bedroom. The vision of her eager derrière wagging invitingly before me in the golden light of that harvest moon is one I treasure still.

Once inside she drew the curtains back and the moonlight flooded in. She turned me into the full glare of it, just a couple of paces from the balcony door, and squatted before me for a close scrutiny of Iron Jack, or, rather, of the bung whose tough but limpid membranes had so perfectly separated the commonest pleasure in the world from its most frequent consequence. Iron Jack, after twenty-four hours of tortured continence, was stiff as a cannon still.

'Oh, but it's beautiful!' she murmured drawing the membrane lovingly off me and holding it up to the moonlight. 'I'd love to keep it and press it in my scrap book.'

'I think it might start to whiff after a bit,' I warned her.

She leaned forward and sniffed it. 'Eurgh! It smells of Miss Laycock.'

I frowned in bewilderment for I had not heard the term before. (All her erotic vocabulary came from her father's somewhat archaic library.)

'You know,' she explained. 'My holey of holeys!'

'It scents of *you*,' I assured her. 'And that is the most divine aroma in the universe, Rachel. One sniff of it would bring me across half the world to you.'

'Really? Gosh!' She giggled and, rising to her full height, threw her arms around my neck and kissed me. The pressure of her firm young bubbies against me gave Iron Jack a couple of tremors.

'Ooh!' she exclaimed. 'He's still kicking with the joys of

life, isn't he! How many times will he go the full distance, d'you think?'

I licked her ear lobe. 'Shall we try and find out?'

She gave another giggle and raced me to the bed. I shed my few remaining clothes on the way, keeping only the five residual lambs' bungs, which I laid carefully on her bedside table.

She counted each as I laid it down. 'Five more!' she exclaimed in awe. 'Can you really, Freddy?'

'I don't know,' I answered. 'But I came prepared for anything.'

'Can I put the next one on? I read about a lovely way to do it in *Sweet Sixteen, or Confessions of a Paris Vestal*.'

I straddled her, one knee in each of her armpits. Iron Jack rested for a brief, soulful moment on her chin. She kissed him and gave him a few delicate licks. 'That's what I'd like to be doing to you,' I murmured.

She looked up at me, half in disbelief. 'Is that really true what you said?' she asked. 'About the most divine aroma in the universe?'

Behind me, even as she spoke, I heard little sticky noises; she was already spreading wide her thighs, preparing to let me prove it. A moment later my face was drowning in the glorious aromatic wetness of her fork.

If Kitten's flavour had been vixeny, Rachel's was like a young game bird that had been hung to perfection. My first close-up whiff of her quim was slightly too strong for my comfort; but once the shock was past, it became the most stimulating and provocative savour imaginable – tangy, salty, and mysterious beyond words.

I garnered these impressions in passing, of course, while I concentrated on a tender little love affair between her *coquille* and the very tip of my tongue. The delicate folds of her quim were more complex – and vastly more sensitive – than either Maisie's or Kitten's. My tongue traced every little crimp and groove she possessed –

maddening her by its refusal to discover either her holey of holeys or her little rosebud of joy. But oh, how close he came to both! And oh, how she writhed and wriggled her wide-gaping fork, trying to trick my tongue into making that ultimate contact.

And when at last I relented – oh, what delirium it produced in her!

While shaving that evening, just before going up on the roof, I had taken the opportunity to study my tongue in the mirror. I was trying to see what shapes I could make it form – shapes that would be titillating to a girl's secret places. And I noticed in passing that my tongue kept on moving even without my trying; in fact, it was impossible to keep it absolutely still. Some part of it was forever heaving and swelling – though by the merest fraction of an inch. It occurred to me at once that if I pressed it gently against that amazing organ of female pleasure, which hides in the upper end of her vertical smile, and did my best to keep it absolutely still, those subtle but involuntary movements might have an interesting effect on whatever girl was smiling for me at the time.

Tonight it happened to be Rachel, and the effect it had on her was dynamite. She gave out one long, deep moan of pleasure and spread her thighs wider and wider yet; I could hear the sinews crack and feared she might injure herself. Then, not content with that, she raised her derrière off the bed and I felt her scrabbling to push a pillow beneath her there. I continued until my tongue ached with its attempts not to move.

Then I remembered another little trick I had discovered at my mirror that same evening. I have the gift of being able to stick out my tongue and turn it upside down *in both directions!* I believe it to be quite rare – at least, I have met only two other people who can do it, both of them women. Naturally, it is an accomplishment I tend to discuss far more frequently with women than with men, for the discussion usually occurs immediately after I perform this amiable little trick inside their vaginas; it begins with a gasp of mingled surprise and delight, followed by the words, 'What on earth did you *do* to me just then?'

And so it was with Rachel that night. When I saw the engorged lips of her quim parted like that in tender supplication, I could not resist the impulse to thrust my tongue as deep inside her as possible and twist it as fiercely as I could in both directions – left, right, left, right – as if I intended never to stop.

She jerked beneath me in a sudden spasm of rapture. Then she fought to get my head out of her fork and my tongue out of her holey. Clamping her thighs tight together, she asked, 'What in the name of all that's wonderful was *that?*'

I showed her, using her half-closed fist as a substitute hole. I wanted to go back down between her thighs and do it again – and again and again; but that was never Rachel's way. She always wanted to press ahead to something new. We could do it again another night. Now she giggled and remembered a trick she'd promised me earlier. She took one of the bungs, which were ready-rolled for easy action, and popped it in her mouth. I asked her what was the big idea but she just smiled and shook her head, and went on apparently chewing it. But all became clear when, after a minute or so, she wrestled me onto my back and bent her darling head over Iron Jack, taking the very tip of him between her lips and working the now thoroughly softened lamb's bung over his knob.

Then, bliss upon bliss, sucking and softening as she went, she took more and more of him inside her mouth while she continued to unfurl the tube of the bung over Iron Jack's column.

By that time we had got each other worked up to such a pitch of wanton desire that there was little point in trying for a long, languorous engagement. I rolled her on her back, with that handy pillow still placed beneath her well-fleshed derrière, and split her beard without ceremony.

'Try and make each poke different from all the rest,' she whispered before the thrill of feeling my gristle go all the way up inside took her breath away.

She later told me she had read something of the sort in *Tricks and Secrets of the Hareem*, by the Houri Nariyah. She certainly picked the perfect time to recall it, for nothing else could have prolonged our pleasure so beautifully that night. It forced me to concentrate on not-repeating myself, or *not*-repeating each movement of my knob inside her. It concentrated me – and her – on that delicious point of contact between us, specifically on the rim of my glans rubbing silkily against the walls of her vagina. It transformed what would have been a five-minute romp into one that lasted a good fifteen. And, believe me, fifteen minutes with Rachel was worth an hour with any other woman on earth.

And so we continued through that long, heavenly night. A distant church clock was striking two when her ever-agile quim sucked the last pearly drop from a throbbing Iron Jack into the sixth and final bung. After that it seemed safe to do without, for we had by then got our second wind and could think of nothing beyond getting back our breath before plunging once more into the old four-legged frolic. Dawn crept over the windowsill as I plugged her for the fourth and final dry-bob – my tenth of the entire night.

As I crawled back home across the roofs, I reflected happily that Kitten would by then be fast asleep. I forgave her whatever pleasure she might have snatched in the arms of the Young Turks. Even if that adorable little split of hers had rejoiced to open and receive each one of them, she could not have experienced one hundredth part of the pleasures Rachel and I had discovered in the night just gone.

At the time I was only dimly aware of the differences between my two partners in life's great game. Or, rather, my experience of females in general was so limited that I unconsciously believed each one of all those unknown thousands to be unique. And so they are, of course, in an absolute sense. I have gazed with loving eyes at thousands of quims and have never seen two precisely the same; so it would be impossible to find two women who matched each other in all those subtle and delightful strands of personality that make each one of them so good to know. And yet one can discern certain very general traits that large numbers of women hold in common. For instance, I think that in matters sexual, far more women are like Kitten than are like Rachel.

For Kitten, sex was never an end in itself; it was always a means to something else, usually something quite non-sexual, in fact. I don't mean she didn't enjoy it for its own sake. She did, and quite often, too – even with some of her customers. But that was not what kept her at it, long after the financial necessity had been removed. For her, each sexual encounter was a necessary preliminary to the *real* encounter, which was almost entirely verbal. She loved talking to people. Men fascinated her more than women because she understood them less. She had grown up without ever enjoying a real conversation with a man. In her childhood they had patronized her; then, as her nubile bits began to blossom, they had fought shy of her in different ways, some by teasing her, others by turning severe. At Lazy Daisy's, by contrast, no man ever dismissed her like that.

For Rachel, however, sex was always an end in itself. She was like me. She thought about it day and night and would go to any lengths to gain its satisfaction. And she

124

was entirely without shame in the pursuit of it. I don't mean to imply that Kitten *was* ashamed of her way of life. She was too happy at it and too pleased with the opportunities it brought her to feel at all negative; yet there was always a certain reticence about her, a kind of inner shyness that nothing could touch – even when she obliged her customers with the most *outré* pleasures.

Rachel, on the other hand, saw everything to do with sex as holy. She pored over her father's arcane library as if it were sacred writ; she adopted its vocabulary without a blush; and she wanted to try out everything she read about – usually with me as her willing and often astonished partner.

As I say, these differences between the two girls did not strike me so forcibly then, but they go far toward explaining how our lives unfolded and intertwined during that blissful summer and autumn of 'Ninety-Seven.

But I must not anticipate my tale any further.

The Monday night after our first marathon encounter found me back in Rachel's bed, ready – though not, I must admit, brimming over with eagerness – for one or two encores. I think I knew something of how Kitten's virgin quim must have felt after ten good rogerings the previous Saturday; how she then went on to pleasure her horde of Young Turks – and how her quim felt after *that* assault – I could not imagine. So I was really rather relieved when Rachel said, 'Just hold me in your arms, Freddy, dear, and talk to me of all sorts of lascivious things. And perhaps we'll do one quick knee-trembler before you go back home.'

No sooner was I settled – we were both quite naked – than she said, 'Oh dear, Captain Standish is all stiff again, I feel. Is it a terrible sacrifice I'm asking – not to give him his innings?'

I told her that he probably got stiff to no purpose twenty or thirty times every day, and if you added all the minutes up, it would amount to several hours – which put the 'sacrifice' in its proper perspective for her.

'What makes him go stiff so often, then?' she asked.

I replied that almost anything would do but that lecherous thoughts were the most usual cause.

'About me?'

'About you, and Emma, our scullery-maid, and *The Nude Bathers* by Ingres, and that nanny I once had with big bubbies . . .'

'Miss Wassermann – the German one who used to beat you on the botty?'

'She used to pin me down under those bubbies and beat me black and blue.'

'Who else? I'm sure there are dozens of others.'

'Two dozen, actually,' I replied. 'The darling girls at Lazy Daisy's.'

'Oh yes!' She pretended to have forgotten my earlier mention of the place. 'Tell me about it. Or . . . I wonder if you should? I have my own daydreams about places like that and you might ruin them.'

'*Day* dreams?' I asked slyly.

'Getting-off-to-sleep dreams. Stinky-finger dreams. Wake-up-in-the-small-hours-and-more-stinky-finger dreams. Satisfied?'

I laughed. 'I hope *you* are. Tell me about them, these dreams. Tell me your favourite one.'

After a pause, she said, 'D'you think they'd let a girl like me work there just for one day, Freddy? That's what I'd really love, you know. Just one day.'

'Suppose you got a craving for it, though!'

She chuckled. 'I already have! That's why it's my favourite fancy. But I should think a week of the real thing would be a pretty good cure.'

'Is that what your father's books all say?'

'No! The whorehouses in Hairyfordshire are full of the most desperate nymphomaniacs, with their Miss Laycocks eternally gaping and drooling for the touch of Cupid's piledriver. That's how I know it can't be true – because men wouldn't bother reading about it if they could go out and find such places in real life, would they!' She reached up her lips and kissed my ear. 'But I would like to try one single day – if it could be arranged sometime?'

'How d'you imagine it would go?'

She buried her face in my neck. 'Ask me some other time. I promise I'll tell you one day. But you can tell me about these two dozen who *do* work there. *Are* they nymphomaniacs? Just one or two of them, maybe?'

'I think there are several who don't mind taking the odd bit of pleasure as and when it occurs, but I shouldn't think they go out of their way to make it happen. This is just what I gather from talking to one or two. I could tell you a lot more in a month or so.'

'Why? What's going to happen then?'

'I hope to have rogered all of them by then, or most of them – one by one, of course.'

She clenched her fists and punched me in pantomime. 'Oh, you are so lucky, you men!'

'You said that before.'

'But I mean it. I wish I were a man.'

'Do you?' I asked in amazement.

She giggled again. 'No. But just for a day, perhaps – that's another of my just-for-a-day fancies. Sometimes I imagine I'm a man called Richard, rogering *me*, Rachel. It's very strange because I'm both male and female – not *exactly* at the same moment, but I sort of flit very quickly between, say, feeling my Captain Standish nosing his way into Miss Laycock's secret depths and then, a split-second later, feeling Miss Laycock swell and glow as Captain Standish forces his way in.'

She paused and gave a surprised little laugh. I asked her why. 'It's odd,' she said. 'Here I am, telling you all these lascivious things, and feeling as cool as a cucumber. If I were lying here alone, just thinking them to myself, my nipples would be quite swollen and ticklish by now, and Miss Laycock would be all feverish and wet. And my *bouton de plaisir* would be throbbing with lust. And Stinky Fingers would be all over the place, like baby eels.'

I heard the tremor in her voice and only just managed to get the lamb's bung on in time, before she crawled and wriggled all over me. And she left me with nothing to do, except to caress her nipples, and gently pinch them, and fold them tenderly as her elation progressed – and finally shoot her good and full between wind and water when the quake of copulation seized her.

And that was to be the pattern of our meetings for some considerable period. She revelled in quick, rather violent sex, but had little time for what Kitten called value-for-money encounters. She loved to lie in bed with me and talk about it for an hour or two, climaxing in a swift, urgent 'knee-trembler' – although, mind you, throughout our conversation our hands would stray tenderly all over each other's bodies and we would masturbate each other affectionately from time to time. She loved to feel my spermspouter firing off among her fingers and she got very good at squeezing Iron Jack at exactly the right moments, releasing the pressure just before each squirt.

It made her wonder whether she couldn't manage something of the sort with the walls of her vagina, and we spent many happy evenings thereafter, 'training' her quim (or, rather, the muscles she would use to nip off a pee in full flood) to squeeze like her hand – and in fact she became quite good at it.

But I am once again getting ahead of my story, not merely in terms of chronology but in terms of my sexual education as a whole; for, as I have already said, the progress of my discoveries with Rachel were intimately paralleled by those I made with Kitten at Lazy Daisy's.

I kept my promise to Kitten in all respects but one. Instead of waiting until the house closed down at two that Wednesday night (or Thursday morning), I went there just before midnight. I had the use of my newly acquired fortune by then – or, at least, of the interest from the investment trust Graustein had set up for me – and I hoped to spend a couple of quid on taking Virginie upstairs. I was quite interested in finding out what Maisie meant by 'very sexy,' but I was even more interested in hearing her account of last Sunday's jaunt with the Young Turks in Headingley – before Kitten gave me her version.

In a way I got my answer before I met either filly. At least I learned that they must have pleased the young officers mightily, for they had both been invited back there for the regular Wednesday evening 'bacchanalia,' as they called it. The pair of them had returned to Lazy Daisy's at ten that evening after having (as it turned out) been rather lightly used by the Young Turks. So, instead of being let off for the rest of the night, they were both in service in the salon. I found them half-naked, side by side on a large cretonne sofa in the anteroom, giggling at their reminiscences of that afternoon's escapades.

For some reason I felt acutely aware that Virginie was some years older than me. I felt I could not simply march up and take Kitten away from her, just like that; so I invited them both to join me in a spot of supper – which, of course, they were delighted to accept. I felt a little easier once their glorious figures were clad in kimonos, though the way the silk clung to them was as revealing as the flesh itself.

Virginie remarked that she had not seen me since last Friday. 'You are a wise young man,' she said, 'but really you would have been even wiser to stay away a whole week, you know.'

I asked her why and she replied that it was well known that a man was born with only so many shots in his locker and if I was going to fire six of them into a girl in a single hour, I should pass six days in abstinence to make up the balance; otherwise I should be spent out and ruined before I was forty.

I thanked her and said I'd consider her advice most carefully. I didn't believe it then – and, of course, I *certainly* don't believe it now, at the age of sixtyish, when (having fired some twenty thousand shots from that same locker) I can still roger a woman three or four times a night. (The *right* woman, of course.) If I was born with twenty-thousand shots down there, I should have weighed more than sixty pounds at birth. So *hah!* to you, Virginie, wherever you are!

For me, Virginie's advice was all of a piece with those tedious lectures at school on the supposed dangers of 'pulling wires,' which (as I discovered two years after the lecture in question) was that particular master's euphemism for tossing off! He was the Reverend Philomenus Stock, our headmaster, and I hope his descendants blush to read his name here, for his hand was never out of our pockets. At least once every term each boy in the school would be made to sit on his lap while he 'assured himself we were carrying nothing dangerous or sinful in our trouser pockets.' He emptied our pockets, all right, but his real purpose was to get our little pegos stiff and give them a few tender squeezes. Then he'd lock himself in the head-man's bog and toss himself off like a fury. I watched him at it many a time, for the sickroom bog was immediately above and some obliging fellow had at some time cut a little hole beside the gas pendant in the ceiling.

So that's how I knew those lectures on pulling wires was just so much sermonizing tosh – the sort of thing a reverend gentleman had to do to earn his crust. I was surprised to hear a pretty filly like Virginie spouting the same kind of claptrap, though. 'At least you've had the sense to give your balls a rest for five days, anyway,' she concluded.

My face must have given me away, for I saw Kitten smirk and I could almost hear the clicketty-click in her brains as she stored the questions away.

We were none of us very hungry; welsh rarebit and a bowl of strawberries were all we consumed. When we stood up to leave, Kitten said in the most casual manner, 'Would you like to take both of us upstairs, Freddy? We're very *sexy* together.' She glanced toward Virginie and they burst into laughter.

I don't know whether it was that slightly dismissive laughter or her use of the word 'sexy' – which was not nearly so common at that time as it is now – but I found myself saying, 'I was just about to suggest it myself.'

The laughter stopped at once. I could almost *touch* their surprise when, in Madame's boudoir, I took out my purse and shook out nine sovereigns without a qualm – one was for the meal, of course, and four for an hour with the two girls. But the other four? 'I'll keep Kitten for the whole night,' I said grandly.

Poor Kitten! Her eyes almost fell out of their sockets. I'm sure she had suggested a threesome to avoid having any serious conversation with me. Now I had all night – and for any kind of 'conversation' I liked!

'Try the Prince's Boudoir,' Madame suggested as we left her.

It was a room I had heard of but never actually seen. It was quite separate from all the others and could be reached only by a private staircase from a small antechamber on the far side of the ballroom; tradition held that the Prince of Wales, later Edward VII, had passed a night with two of the original Lazy Daisy's fillies up there. After that, if ever a customer chose two girls for a romp, he was offered the Prince's Boudoir if it were free.

Kitten was now thoroughly intrigued by my behaviour.

She had not expected me to invite both of them to a supper (well, fair dues to her, nor had *I* expected it, either!), and she had certainly not expected me to take her mildly taunting jest in earnest – much less to pay for it all so easily, and *then* to pay for an all-nighter with her into the bargain. It was greatly to her liking, though, for any girl who did an all-nighter was excused service in the salon until six the following evening. I felt a new sort of respect from both of them as we strolled through the ballroom, one on my either arm.

As we reached the door into the antechamber I deftly pulled the kimonos off their backs and laid them on a nearby chair. Kitten and Virginie twigged at once what I wanted and, linking their arms round each other's waists, walked ahead of me up the private staircase. 'Walked' is the wrong word. They *slinked* up those stairs, leisurely, languorous, and lustful. Keeping perfect time with each other, they swung their hips wide, they arched their backs, making their cute young bottoms pout for me . . . And when we reached the top – or, rather, when they reached the top and I tarried several steps behind them – they needed no second bidding to pause and spread their limbs wide apart, allowing me to peer up into their forks and feast my eyes on the promise of the feasting to come.

This is one of my favourite moments with any woman on our way to an enjoyable romp together. With an amateur partner – an *amateuse*, perhaps – I like to trick them into such stimulating revelations; with a professional, of course, one can't trick them into anything they haven't done a hundred times before, but there are compensations. First, their lips down there are so much meatier, being engorged with chronic sexual excitation; and secondly, if you can catch one within a minute or two of taking a sweet adieu from her previous partner, you can often see fresh drops of his seed drooling out of her receptacle and glistening along the rim of that well-rutted thoroughfare. To poke a woman who is full of the gluey warmth of another man's spending, to whip it into a creamy foam with one passionate poke after another, is a pleasure no man should die without tasting once.

On that evening, although I had no doubt their exquisite vaginas had swilled and gurgled with the spending of a dozen lusty Young Turks – and more – all trace of it had long since gone. My pleasure, perforce, was more of the imaginative kind as I stood there, gazing up in reverence at the miracles of their quims; I let my fancy roam over a vision of all the stiff military nimrods that had hunted up those agreeable fissures in Headingley that day. And now I was to cap the lot!

The Prince's Boudoir was, in fact, two rooms, separated – if one wished – by a heavy curtain. The outer room was about fifteen feet square, with looking glasses everywhere; it was furnished with two chaises longues, silk rugs, dozens of cushions, and a couple of curious little humpbacked footstools, which reminded me of upholstered turtles.

'What are they for?' I asked.

Virginie giggled and lowered herself over it, face down, so that it raised her derrière in a way I would have thought anatomically impossible. 'It's nice for poking in the bumhole,' she said. 'You wish to try?'

She wriggled her legs wider apart and I could see that her bumhole did, indeed, have the appearance of a much-poked orifice. I glanced at Kitten and saw her staring at me with distaste – not so much for me as for what my innocent question had provoked Virginie to do. She shook her head and raised her eyebrows as if to say, 'Please don't!'

'Not tonight, thank you,' I said. 'Let's see what's in the inner room.'

The outer room, where we stood, had one large sash window, shuttered at that hour, of course. The inner room, which Virginie now revealed to us by springing to her feet and drawing the curtain, had no window at all. In that same moment it became my favourite room in the house – indeed, to this day it remains one of the favourite poking rooms of my entire life. It was so like a womb! The walls were richly hung with dark crimson silk, padded and buttoned like a club armchair. There were no pictures, but six dimly burning wall lamps gave a soft, gentle, all-round illumination. I had expected to see a four-poster, or at least a half-tester, festooned with silks and satins; instead there was a broad daybed, softly padded in dark-gray velvet, but extremely simple in its design and construction.

I was still taking in these details when I realized the two girls had almost finished undressing me.

'Whoo!' Virginie exclaimed the moment Iron Jack leaped free of my shirt. Her wide-open eyes and slow, lascivious smile managed to convey that it was a long time since she'd seen such a leviathan. But I caught Kitten staring at her in amazement – and knew at once that it was, in fact, a very *short* time since they'd seen leviathans even greater – true belly ruffians, indeed. 'Are you *really* only twenty?' Virginie added, keeping up her flattering badinage.

And the curious things was, even though I knew very well it was all a pretence, I was nonetheless flattered and I wanted her to go on pouring it all over me. 'I'm afraid so,' I admitted ruefully.

'Oh, don't be afraid, Freddy darling,' she said, throwing her arms around me and wriggling her naked body tight against my right side – presumably leaving the left for Kitten. Kitten certainly presumed as much and performed the same enticing favour for my untenanted side a moment later.

My loins still melt at the treasured memory of that moment – the very first time in my life when two naked and adorable girls pressed their lithe young bodies tight against mine, leaving just sufficient room between them for Iron Jack to beat his dizzy knob against the flat of my belly. The feeling of their two forested mounds crushed firmly against the tops of my thighs, and the sumptuously fleshed curvature of their pert young derrières beneath my caressing hands, and the mere *thought* of the juicy heat of their vaginas, both only inches from the throbbing tool that was even now desperate to measure their welcome . . . it almost overwhelmed me. *Please don't let this ever stop*, I prayed to the oldest god in the pantheon.

'What d'you want us to do for you, Freddy?' Virginie whispered in my ear. 'Would you like to see a little exhibition, eh? Nuns at their Naughty Romps? Schoolgirls after Lights-Out?'

I gulped and managed to whisper a feeble, 'No.'

'What then?'

I tore myself from them, tottered to the bed, and threw myself flat on my back. Iron Jack whanged like a gendarme's baton against my belly. 'Do anything you like, but do it all to *me*,' I begged.

I think I was probably the first man who had ever declined her offer of Nuns after Lights-Out, or whatever it was. At all events, my refusal intrigued her enough to ask me a genuine question for a change. She knelt beside me and, leaning over, kissed me tenderly on the mouth; and as our lips parted she asked, 'Why not?'

'Because I want *you*,' I murmured drowsily. But I put enough emphasis on that one word for her to know that I didn't want a show, I didn't want a performance, I didn't want a fantasy. When she offered her body for me to enter and enjoy, I wanted it to be *her* body and *her* offer.

As the implications of my answer sank in, she lost her skittish remoteness and turned quite serious with me. 'Is that all. You don't want much, do you!' she exclaimed sarcastically.

'Oh?' I came slightly more awake in my surprise. 'Am I asking a lot, then?'

She laughed ruefully. 'I'm sure you don't think so!' And she pulled a rather enigmatic face at Kitten, who grinned fiendishly and said in a schoolgirl's singsong, 'Didn't I warn you!'

'All right then!' Virginie said with savage relish. 'Let's just see if he knows what he's asking!' And down she went between my thighs, easing them slightly apart with gentle but irresistible pressure from her forearms. I felt her hot breath swirl around Iron Jack, caressing my bush. I lay right back again and closed my eyes, relaxing as completely as I could. A moment later her deft fingertips were at play all over my jewels – column, knob, glans, scrotum, balls, the fork of my parted thighs, my mound . . . everywhere. They were soft as marshmallow, those fingers of hers, and restless as butterflies. And they were as cunning as only years of skilful play could make them – play with the nerve-rich flesh of those hair-trigger six-shooters we men dangle between our legs.

How many hundreds of them had she tickled and tempted in order to learn so precisely what she must do to keep me simmering close to eruption, yet never once boiling over? A moment later, when her lips and tongue joined in the music, I no longer cared when or how she had acquired that skill – just as long as she never stopped expending it on me! As the flames of brandy play around the Christmas pudding, so the thrills from her tickling fingers and dancing tongue flickered around my cracksman and set him on fire. Swollen as he was, I felt him stretch still further, until it seemed his very skin would burst with the feverish lust she managed to draw up into him.

And that was the moment when Kitten chose to sit on my face. Being Kitten, though, she managed it with the utmost finesse. When her thighs first clamped against my shoulders (my eyes were closed in drowsy yearning, remember) I imagined her to be kneeling the other way round. I thought she would lean forward and dangle her bubbies like soft melons upon my face. I parted my lips and half stuck out my tongue, ready for the first tease of hard nipple. Instead – and in swift sequence, so that it was a jumble of surprises – the bosky tendrils of her bush tickled my cheeks, the vixeny perfume of her sexual glands filled my nostrils, the warmth of her fork closed around my face, the cool tip of my nose knuckled upward into the wet heat of her vagina, and my tongue (quicker off the mark than me!) shot rigidly out like a miniature Iron Jack and grazed among her fleshy rilles and all around her rosebud of delight with dizzy hunger.

A moment later her fingernails rested on my nipples and, with the smallest of twitches, sent bolts of lightning through and through me. How I emerged from that sensual Niagara without shooting my bolt I cannot now imagine; it was a tribute to Virginie's skill, I'm sure. At the very moment when I felt my loins gather for the first barrage of the old twenty-gun salute, she gave my knob a hard squeeze from the tip down, driving most of the blood and all my desire from it – for only a second or two, though that was long enough. Then, leaping to her feet, she said, 'You really ought to explore the possibilities of those chaises longues next door, Freddy!'

Kitten was less enthusiastic about moving; she was enjoying the novel sensations of my tongue and nose – and so, indeed, was I. Rather than break off abruptly, she went forward and down, taking Iron Jack between her lips and swallowing him as deep as she could. This sucked most of the strength back into him; and my close-up view of her glistening wet quim spread wide before me, and the civet perfume that lingered all around my nostrils now, did the rest.

'Come on!' Virginie gave Kitten quite a slap on her invitingly stretched bottom.

As we both struggled to rise and follow her back into the outer room I was surprised to see patches of Kitten's skin blush bright pink, all down her back; I did not then know that such flushes were a token of high pleasure, but they surprised me nonetheless.

Virginie had meanwhile pulled the two chaises longues into a line, head to head, so that their sloping rests formed a kind of tent. I should explain that these were the simpler sort of chaises, with a sloping backrest about two feet long but without that low, padded rail down one side of the horizontal bed. Some people call them davenports but they were always called chaises longues at Lazy Daisy's. They permitted a filly to sit astride them, leaning against the sloping backrest with her feet on the floor, one on either side of the horizontal bed part – where, to be sure, a man could lie at his ease while he worshipped at her open quim. But that is not what Virginie had in mind for us now.

She carefully placed the two chaises so that about ten inches of open space separated the tops of the backrests. Then she knelt upon it, facing the slope and burying her knees about a foot apart in the angle it formed with the horizontal bed. Finally she leaned forward against the sloping rest, folding her arms on the top of the *other* chaise longue and resting her head upon them – thus leaving her gorgeous bubbies hanging free in that ten-inch space she had so carefully arranged.

'Now then, Freddy,' she said, smiling archly up at me and giving her derrière a provocative wriggle. 'Does that give you any ideas?'

I knelt behind and practically fell into her; that miracle moment when male meat makes merry magic among maiden's marvellous membranes . . . mmmm!

'What's it like, Freddy?' Virginie asked.

I'm sure she was expecting some generalized answer like, 'Wonderful!' or 'Splendid!' But I misunderstood; I took her quite literally.

'I've only been inside the quims of three girls so far,' I told her. 'All within the past two weeks. Yours is the fourth. But I'll tell you this – you're all quite different.'

'Eh?' she gasped, for I was rodding her rather enthusiastically while I spoke.

'Yes,' I explained, slowing down slightly. 'Maisie's was all soft and creamy. Kitten's is narrow and fine-grained – pure bliss. Rachel's felt like tight-folded velvet. But yours . . .'

'Yes?' she asked eagerly. 'Tell me the worst! Ruined with excessive use!'

'Oh no. Nothing like that. But it changes as I go in. Out here, near the opening' – I pulled my tool almost all the way out of her and jiggled him around her vestibule – 'you're all soft and and succulent and yielding. But as I go deeper in' – I matched action to words in a series of ever-deepening thrusts right up into the gullet of that divine receptacle – 'it changes, by barely perceptible degrees, into something delectably firm. And right at the top here' – she emitted a little gasp when I reached it – 'it's excitingly resilient.'

'Oh, Freddy!' she cried, but I couldn't tell whether she was laughing or weeping.

I leaned forward, too, then, covering her back completely and getting my hands round to her gorgeous dangling bubbies, pleased to find that her nipples were already distended and slightly moist. The heat of them was delicious. 'These must be wonderful on a cold winter night,' I said.

'I'm quite fond of them tonight, for some reason,' she replied.

For some reason, too, Kitten laughed – and then squatted down beneath the tent of the two backrests, beneath Virginie's bubbies, and started to lick and suckle her nipples between my fingers.

I was about to ask Kitten if she couldn't think of anything better to do – like increase the pleasure of the one who was paying for all this, for instance – when Virginie shouted out, 'No, Kitten! Please? No!' – but in such a way you could tell she only half-meant it, then only quarter-meant it, then didn't mean it at all, though she went on gasping 'No!' and 'Please?' for quite a while longer.

I didn't quite twig what sort of game they were playing but I could feel powerful emotions at work between them and so decided to stay on the touchline. I levered myself more upright and began to scratch Virginie's back with long, gentle strokes that hardly touched her. What a superb body she had! Neat, compact, exquisitely curvaceous, and – good heavens! – covered in strawberry-coloured blushes, just like Kitten's earlier!

Until that moment I had been rodding away inside her like a ferret, wanting to get my first fusillade away as quickly as possible before getting down to some serious copulation with the two of them. But the moment I saw that Virginie was nearing her own crisis, instinct took over. I slowed down from about three thrusts a second to something around ten a minute – long, careful, deliberate pokes, savouring every millimetre of her vagina on the way in and again on the way out. I began to shiver at the new, sensuous discoveries I was making. At the same time I got one hand around her, just below her belly button, and explored southward until I felt the first invagination of her cleft. There, instead of delving in and trampling all over her little *coquille de plaisir*, I started a gentle fluttering movement, which released her pleasure almost at once.

She gave out a long, deep moan, which sounded almost like a cry of despair, and began twitching beneath me and gasping away like some being at the end of its tether. The blotches in her skin bured an almost supernatural scarlet and the sweat just poured from her.

Then, after a few moments during which she lay like one dead, she gave a shiver and pulled herself away from me, slipping out sideways and staggering a little.

Kitten scuttled out from where she had been crouching and, staring up at her, said, 'Well?'

Virginie did an exaggerated collapse upon herself. 'Fluke,' she panted. 'He hit me when I wasn't looking.'

Kitten gave a sarcastic laugh and, leaping to her feet, went over to one of the cupboards. She returned, pulling on a pair of trousers – that is, they had the shape of trousers but, being made of the filmiest gauze, they did nothing to hide the graceful limbs inside them; they merely softened their outline and colour. As she came close to me, back in the well-lit part of the room, I saw that the garment was, in fact, open right through her fork, from waistband to waistband. However, as the waistband in question was delightfully low – two inches below her belly button and only just above her bush – it was a very *practical* opening. They are known, rightly or wrongly, as hareem pants.

'Here's another thing boys and girls can do on a chaise longue,' she told me, taking me by the hand and pulling me toward the foot of it. 'Or this particular one, anyway.'

Her words prompted me to examine that end of the chaise more carefully, and I noticed it had an unusual form – tapering to a flattish end like a coffin. Kitten sat me on it, *well* on, so that the end of it touched the backs of my knees. Then giggling with half-suppressed merriment she faced away from me with the backs of her knees touching my kneecaps.

Every action of Kitten's was done with such style and grace; she glided like a queen, like a swan at dewfall. So when I say she now began to move her hips and her glorious young bottom before me in the most enticing manner, you must not imagine some vulgar rear-view of a Port Said belly dancer. What she gave me was an artistic performance to take my breath away. You will never have seen a girl who could move like Kitten. I never yet saw her equal – in forty and more years of close observation of naked young girls moving in every possible way, none came close to even suggesting her. Thus the girl of my most treasured memory can only be the girl of your most treasured dreams.

My hands reached out to touch and caress what my eyes could scarce believe. She had muscles and curves and dimples – and bony bits and fleshy bits – that, had the dying Michelangelo achieved their form in marble, he would have ordered all his other works to be destroyed, in shame at their ordinariness. To see her nakedness from across the room was to break into a sweat; to hold it in my hands, my trembling hands, to let my trembling hands roam free over those perfect curves, was to burn with the fires of Olympus. I truly think the gods themselves forsook their games that night, and looked on at us in wonder.

The peculiar shape of those chaise longues had a delightful effect on Kitten's anatomy as she backed herself nearer and nearer toward me. The taper of those ever-widening sides forced her knees ever-wider apart. Inevitably, the opening through the fork of her hareem pants grew wider, too – and that, in its turn, brought the fleshy oyster between her thighs closer and closer to that part of my anatomy which beat the air in a frenzy and swelled hot and red in his lust to plumb and rake the depths of that same flesh.

The joiner who carved that chaise longue was, I'm sure, an equal anatomist with Professor Gray; he was also a geometrician to beat Euclid into a cocked hat. He knew that the knob on my hypotenuse was equal to the tangent on Kitten's derrière at the precise moment when the conic section of the taper pushed her knees so wide apart that she collapsed upon me by force of gravity. So he was the equal of Newton, too. But at that sublime moment I felt greatest of all. I was Zeus and Hercules and Eros, Casanova, Don Juan, and that randiest of princes for whom the room itself was named – all rolled into one.

But Kitten herself was in a more skittish mood than I – or perhaps, knowing we had the whole night ahead of us, she wanted a less frenzied, more playful pace. For no sooner had she sat firmly on me, arching her back and taking Iron Jack's knob deeper into her than he had yet been inside any female belly, than she wriggled herself round sideways-on to me – still impaled on Iron Jack – and leaned back on her slender, double-jointed arms, smiling at me her most gamine smile.

This wanton display of bubbies and belly left my hands frantic as to what to touch and fondle and caress first – and then she increased my choice by throwing wide her thighs. Soon my eager fingers were roaming through the mossy hills and moist valleys of paradise itself.

Virginie meanwhile was rearranging the two chaises longues yet again. Now she shunted them side by side to form one broad bed with a single continuous backrest. Kitten, who could look over my shoulder and see what she was doing, broke into a broad grin and cried, 'Oh, yes!' – and, leaping off me as suddenly as she had collapsed onto me only moments earlier, raced to join Virginie at the other end. When I rose and turned to follow, the pair of them were already standing beyond the chaises longues, leaning toward me over the tops of the sloping backrests. I thus saw two bewitching smiles, two pairs of sparkling eyes, four slender shoulders, catching the light, and, swinging delightfully in the shadows beneath, four glorious bubbies – any one of which would make the palms of a saint itch.

But, as a saint may forgo the pleasure of caressing such delightful organs – because he knows a richer reward awaits him on the other side – so, too, I now found the strength to forgo the same pleasure because I, too, knew a richer reward awaited me on the other side of those girls. From somewhere I found the strength to walk those extra three paces, and to turn and worship the two most delightful derrières a man could ever hope to see – or a saint to forgo.

In fact, they were crouched so far over the backrests that they offered more than their derrières for my worship; four succulent, hairy lips grinned saucily up at me. Never was the expression 'vertical smile' more lasciviously illustrated. Never did Iron Jack beat more furiously in his indecision as to which heavenly manhole to sample first. It was Virginie who decided for him, by arching her back even further and pouting those lovely, ferny parentheses in a plea no red-blooded man could deny.

'Just waggle the tip of your fellow up and down our crevices, Freddy,' she said when I was near enough to take her temperature.

I followed her suggestion – and cried out in astonishment at the thrill it gave me.

Virginie, who had been pleasuring half a dozen men a day for the past several years, had the soft, brownish, meaty lips of the true professional; thick and protective, they could swallow the whole of my knob without his going a fraction of an inch into her hole proper. Kitten's were still red as fire from over-excitation – though not half so bad as when I had seen them last Saturday; they were not yet thick enough to embrace the whole of my knob but their heat and the glorious redhead aroma that rose up to my nostrils were more than compensation.

I spent a full ten minutes, I'm sure, at that delightful game – wiping Iron Jack up and down, up and down those warm, wet, self-lubricating crevices – but at last I plunged his desperate head inside, the full depth of him. I gave each in turn a single poke, in-and-out, making it as lusty and swift and deep as I could: Virginie, Kitten, Virginie, Kitten . . . thrust, thrust, wham, bang – it was a most delightful game! But the moment I chose to stay inside Kitten and give her novice quim my most amorous attention, Virginie cried, 'No! Do her the same way you did me earlier.'

Nothing loth, I went round to kneel on the bed of the chaise longue while the two of them manhandled an armchair for her to rest her head and shoulders on – again leaving a space where her bubbies could swing free and invitingly caressable.

When Kitten came round to join me – to take up the position Virginie had adopted earlier – I was treated to a display of such grace and elegance that I knew at once the difference between these two lovely fillies. Virginie was merely superb; but Kitten was far beyond the scope of even the finest words of praise. To see her slender, willowy body slide into position before me on the chaise longue was to watch one of the truly great moments in the history of ballet. The music fell from the crystal spheres of heaven itself; the libretto was older than civilization; but the way Kitten inserted herself beneath me, the sinuous charm with which she parted her thighs, planted her knees, arched her back, and wriggled her bottom – and all for my delight – was hers and hers alone.

I lingered five long, loving minutes working myself slow-slow-slowly into her, stroking the sinews of her back and leaving Virginie and her tongue to work the magic of revenge on her bubbies and nipples. Then I got my knees outside hers and pulled her thighs hard together, flexing her firm young vagina even tighter round Iron Jack. I covered her back as fully as I could and added my teasing, tantalizing caresses to those of Virginie around her nipples and aureoles. In that position, holding her pinned as tight as possible in every joint, I poked her as slowly as I knew how. I doubt that Iron Jack felt the top of her dumb glutton more than four or five times a minute. After fifteen minutes or so of this, I was no nearer my climax than when we had started – though I experienced new and profound thrills at every turn; but she was almost going berserk on the very edge of her ecstasy. I could feel the thump of her heartbeat and the shock of each sudden gasp for breath.

Then, just when I decided to relent and poke her fast enough at last to brim her over, Virginie hastened out from under her breasts and – her eyes sparkling with merriment – manhandled me onto my back with Kitten lying on top of me, both of us facing the ceiling. In fact, she rolled us into this position on the other chaise longue. Then, pushing the one we had just vacated away, she made room for me to spread my thighs wide and place both my feet on the ground, one on each side. Grasping Kitten's knees, she forced them wide, wide apart until her heels, too, were on the ground. Then, while I tickled and pressed Kitten's hugely engorged nipples, and Iron Jack stretched his full length inside her belly, Virginie put her tongue to Kitten's *coquille* and plied it with such skill she brought her as close to erotic insanity as any girl is likely to get – and survive to tell of it after.

I was so impressed by the lascivious fevers and agues that shook her entire frame upon me that I barely noticed the onset of my own eruption; I chanced upon it, so to speak, halfway through and realized it was of prodigious size and ferocity.

After Virginie had gone, Kitten and I went up to one of the old servants' rooms on the top floor and bedded down for the night. For a long while we hardly exchanged a word. Naked as babes, we lay side by side between the sheets and I held her in my arms. And after a while she began to cry softly. I said nothing. And then I began to cry, too. I don't know why, and I don't suppose Kitten did, either. We were certainly not miserable. It was an odd – and, at that moment, oddly appropriate – way of relaxing.

'D'you want to screw me again?' she whispered when the last of her hiccups had come and gone.

'I don't think I'll ever *screw* you, Kitten, as long as you live,' I told her.

She kissed me at the base of my neck and licked the salt of my tears. 'Sorry! I don't know what to call things any more. It's all been so confusing – this week. Everything's so new. That's what made me cry, I think.'

'D'you want to sleep now?'

She gave a little shiver and raised herself on one elbow. 'Is that what you want? Could you bear to stay awake and talk for a while? Not long, but I'm just so . . .' She gave another shiver.

'You went back to the Young Turks again today?' I asked.

'Who is Rachel?' she fired right back.

So I told her – everything I could. Who Rachel was. How she started it all. What we had done since last Saturday evening. The things she said – even her desire to become one of Lazy Daisy's fillies for a day. It took about twenty minutes, during which Kitten listened in fascinated silence, asking only those questions necessary to stop the conversation from becoming a monologue. At last she said, 'Don't you think it odd, Freddy? Your Rachel thinks and behaves like a whore – not a real whore, of course, but what men imagine a whore is like. And yet here we all are, two dozen of us, and not one among us thinks and behaves like that at all.'

I admitted that the same thought had occurred to me. But, I added, I thought the differences were very slight anyway. Certainly I noticed very little difference between my frolics with Rachel and my frolics with her and Virginie earlier that night. I didn't believe there was such an enormous gulf between the filly in Lazy Daisy's and the woman outside.

Kitten laughed.

Feeling rather miffed, I asked her what was so funny.

She apologized and showered me with kisses – saying she was actually laughing at Virginie, not me. 'There's an exception to every rule, Freddy – and for some strange reason, you are it. For me, anyway – and now, it seems, for Virginie, too. And for Maisie. Three out of three! So it must mean something.'

It didn't mean a thing to me, and I told her so.

'You remember when you saw me last Saturday – after my first day on my back?'

'Actually,' I reminded her, 'I saw you after your first *lay* on your back with Lieutenant Wonderful.'

She laughed at my name for him but she was not to be deflected from her point. 'And I told you he had been an oasis in a desert? D'you remember that? I don't think men will ever understand this point. I don't think you can imagine putting your pego inside a woman – just any old crone who walked in the door – and feeling no pleasure whatever from it. Can you?'

'He wouldn't even get stiff without *some* feeling of pleasure.' (I wondered about waking up piss-proud, where the erection doesn't *start* from pleasure; but even there, the minute you put a hand to your old man, the old electric juices start to flow.)

'No, well, there you are!' she said. 'So you can't imagine one of us girls having a man's stiff pego poking away furiously inside us without giving us at least some pleasure, too – can you?'

'It is difficult,' I agreed. 'What if he caresses you down here, though?' I demonstrated. 'And does this with your nipples? And so on.'

She shivered and took my hands off her body, kissing the fingers to show she was not actually rejecting me. Then she reached round me and scratched my shoulder-blade gently. 'Is that nice?' she asked. When I said of course it was, she said, 'Well, it's as nice as that. Friendly-nice. I can enjoy lots of friendly-nice pleasures like that with the gentlemen who take me upstairs here – but that doesn't get me within a million miles of the Big One.'

'Like tonight?' I chuckled, thinking how inadequate the words Big One were for *that* eruption!

'Oh God, Freddy – I almost died. I'll swear my heart stopped.'

'That was more because of what Virginie did to you. Not what I did.'

'I know! She was taking her revenge. Because you gave *her* the Big One, too – and I warned her you would and she said never while she lived.'

I asked what I did that was different from other men; I couldn't imagine a different way of enjoying a woman, other than the one that came to me so naturally.

'It's not what you do, Freddy,' she told me. 'It's your attitude. It shines out of you . . .'

'Attitude?' I interrupted with a bewildered laugh.

'Yes. Tell me – what's your attitude to me? And to Virginie?'

I thought it over briefly and said, 'Gentle admiration, I suppose.'

'There you are!' she said happily; I did not realize she had been holding her breath for my reply until then.

'Am I?' I asked, still none the wiser. 'What else could I possibly feel? To me this house is like a shrine to *all* women. I can hardly believe my luck that such wonderful creatures as women are abroad in the world. The body of a beautiful woman is not simply an argument for God's love to man – to me it is proof positive. This' – I ran a caressing hand down her gorgeous body – 'is also a shrine

– the shrine where I worship. Sometimes when I think of you, Kitten, I draw a deep breath as deep as I can, and yet I still feel I'm suffocating. I cannot contain the worship I feel for you, and your body, and the pleasures you afford me. I want to . . .'

She stopped my lips with a kiss. I felt tears on her cheek again. 'It's all right, Freddy, darling. I *know*, you see. You've no need to tell me. It just pours out of you, every moment we're together. Maisie said the same. Virginie wouldn't believe it – but now she does.'

'But surely,' I protested, 'every man who comes here worships at the same shrine as me?'

'Ha!' She almost collapsed in ironic laughter. 'Most men think of us as sewers! We help keep *decent* women pure! We are receptacles for their night soil. Oh, not all of them. Some of them are very friendly, very amusing . . . they're good company. I'm not complaining. Life here, hard though it can be on occasion, is ten thousand times more interesting than life at Hetherington Hall – so I'm eternally grateful to my father for his suggestion! What was I saying? Oh yes – there isn't another man like you, Freddy. You radiate your adoration like the sun. And we're all so starved of genuine adoration that we cannot help responding.' Her arms stole round my neck and she rested her beautiful head on my chest. 'In fact, it brings me to what I really want to ask you tonight – before some other girl does. Will you be my macquerau?'

I made some vague, questioning sounds; I remembered hearing the word before, from Maisie, I think, but it had no immediate meaning for me.

'You don't have to say yes. I'll quite understand. But what it means is that every Sunday night at midnight you can come here and sleep with me until nine next morning – free. And when my friend the cardinal calls on his regular monthly visit – *I hope!* – I don't have to stay here and mope around. I can go to your apartment in Leeds and mope around there, instead. And if you're wondering how you can afford an apartment, that's the third thing a macquerau does – he takes all the money a girl earns here and looks after it for her. I've got nearly a hundred pounds for you, and I've only been here – or working, rather – for five days.'

'Six,' I said. 'You started with me last Friday.'

She kissed me tenderly. 'Five,' she murmured. 'I started *work* last Saturday. What's your answer? You don't have to give it now, of course. You can think it over.'

'It doesn't involve . . . love or anything like that, does it?'

'Oh!' She roared with laughter and, leaping up so as to straddle me, lashed out at my face with her bubbies. 'Diddums!' she exclaimed as she settled down again. 'Issums afraid of a little love, then?'

'No,' I replied awkwardly. 'I just don't want it to get in the way. That's all.'

'Get in the way of what? Your chance to screw the tail off every filly in this house?'

'For example,' I said. 'Also, I think you should know that I've got quite a bit of spare cash knocking around. I had a big win on the geegees. I can feel another one coming up next week at Doncaster. So I . . .'

'Are you a *gambler*, Freddy?' There was horror in her voice.

I laughed. 'Are you a *prostitute*, Kitten?'

She had to laugh but she didn't like the comparison. Then I explained my system – how I wasn't really gambling on horses or betting against the bookmakers, but really against the poor judgement of all the other punters. 'I never place a bet on *any* horse unless I think the odds should be down to a third of what they actually are – and even then I can be wrong four times out of five and still make up all my losses on the fifth. I'm betting against the other punters, really.'

'What's a punter?' she asked. With her background, of course, she'd never heard the word.

'A man with dreams of getting rich but who, in fact, gives a bookmaker a lot of money in return for a few moments of excitement, loses it all, and goes home sadder but (luckily for me) never the wiser.'

She laughed and clapped her hands with delight. 'It's perfect, Freddy! Substitute Madame for bookmaker and you have the perfect description for the gentlemen who take us upstairs. Punters! That's what I'm going to call them.'

'They don't have dreams of getting rich,' I objected.

'They dreams of getting a richly rewarding *experience* between our thighs,' she replied – which I could hardly deny.

'Madame tries to make us call them *lovers*,' she said scornfully. 'But we absolutely draw the line at that – among ourselves, anyway. Our *gentlemen* is what most of us say.' She sighed and recalled her original question. 'So you don't want to be my macquerau, then?'

I kissed her and caressed her, long and sweet, until I felt her responding. Then I told her. 'I don't want to be kept by you, Kitten, and I don't want to keep you. I don't really know *what* I want to do or be in life, if you must know. But if it's going to be you-and-me together, somehow, then we're going to be equals as far as is humanly possible.' I chuckled. 'Gambler and prostitute! D'you realize something? When we've both become absolutely proficient at our respective professions, we can go anywhere in the world? They're the two most portable professions you could possibly imagine!'

She lay back and stretched herself luxuriously. 'Absolutely proficient!' she sighed. 'Doesn't it sound marvellous! D'you think I'll ever be as good as Virginie? Or Maisie?'

'Oh, Kitten!' I protested. 'In so many ways you're

streets ahead of them, even now! I'm almost afraid to tell you this in case you get self-conscious about it, but the way you move your body is like a dream. When I was kneeling on that chaise longue down there and you slipped yourself in front of me and took up the position Virginie had been in earlier . . .'

'Oh, but she was so *sexy!* The way she wiggled her bottom at you and smiled up over her shoulder! I just felt so envious!'

'All the tricks! You don't need any of them. When you move your body so as to offer it to a man, you aren't just sexy. Any young girl can be sexy. You are every man's most ardent dreams of sex made incarnate.' I chuckled, being a little embarrassed at getting so carried away. 'Of course, I speak from vast experience in this particular matter!'

'Four girls,' she said, and I thought she was agreeing with my point. But then she went on. 'Only four girls, and yet you could describe our quims like . . . I don't know what. The way a connoisseur describes fine wines. Actually, that brings me very nicely to the other thing I wanted to ask you, Freddy, dear – once you agreed to be my macquerau. Can I take it you have?'

'I'll be your partner in our joint adventure with the whole wide world, Kitten. Proudly. When you're mistress of your trade and I'm master of mine, no one will stop us. Hand me your money, if you like. I'll invest nine pounds out of every ten in your name, and in the most copper-bottomed government funds. And I'll bet for you with the tenth – if you agree. And if you want to call that "being your macquerau," if you want to tell the other girls that's what I am, I shan't contradict you.'

'And you will come and spend every Sunday night with me? And you will rent an apartment in Leeds where I can stay when the flag's flying?'

'What's so important about Sunday night? I can come

and spend any night you like with you.'

'No, but Sunday.'

I waited for her to explain why.

'Oh, very well!' she grumbled. 'The thing is, you see, that those girls who don't have macqueraux of their own sort of get together in each others' beds down in the dorms and . . . make up for it.'

'Did it happen to you last Sunday?'

I felt her nod.

'And you don't like that, I suppose?' I slipped an arm around her again to comfort her.

She didn't reply.

'Of course, you spent all afternoon at the Young Turks!' I exclaimed as if I had forgotten.

'Perhaps that was it,' she said softly. 'It was such a . . . such a . . . I was so stirred up all that day.'

'I saw you leave the place to go there,' I could not help blurting out. 'I watched you and Virginie getting into the coach.'

Again I felt her nod. 'Maisie said she thought she saw you in the bushes.'

'How many of them were there?' I asked. 'It sounded like several dozen.'

She stiffened. '*Sounded* like? Did you come to Headingley and eavesdrop?'

'No. I just dashed after you on my bike and watched the two of you go in.'

'Well, it was only a dozen,' she assured me. Then she laughed. '*Only* a dozen!'

'Was it hell?' I asked hopefully.

She clenched a fist and beat me lightly on the chest. 'I'm going to tell you the truth, Freddy. I'm always going to tell you the truth, because the moment I start lying to you is the moment it becomes pointless for us to go on being together. Agreed?'

'Agreed,' I said miserably.

'And the same goes for you? Your honesty about Rachel tonight – you'll go on being equally honest about any others?'

'Yes.'

'Then I'll tell you. Last Sunday was the sort of day I know I'll never experience again – because those exact circumstances will never occur again, either. I was feeling quite excited even before we set out – sexually excited – you know what I mean. I'm not talking about schoolgirls getting excited over a new pony. I was all wet between my legs and my heart was going pitapat and I had butterflies in my tummy and my nipples were all – well, I could hardly bear for them to touch my blouse. And all because I knew the first man who was going to screw me was Tooley – the one you call Lieutenant Wonderful. You may think you're only being sarcastic, but he is wonderful. I'll tell you how wonderful he is – he's *almost* equal to you! There now!' She tickled my belly gently. 'Greater praise I know not! Anyway, after nine screws the previous day, all pretty dead – sexually, I mean – in other ways they were quite interesting, as I told you. Anyway, after nine screws during which my quim might just as well have been made of old boot leather – in fact, I was beginning to wish it was! – *he* took me upstairs and gave me the thrill of thrills. Again and again and again and again – an hour of wanton abandonment and bliss. And he was the man who was going to take my dress off at the Young Turks and do it all over again. And he did! But he got me going so much, I just couldn't seem to stop. I won't say I reached the Big One with all twelve of them, but certainly with eight – and more than eight times! God, I just lost count! And even those who never took me to the mountaintop, kept me climbing happily and soaring somewhere near it. But I was *dead* when we came back.'

'And after all that one of the fillies here expected you to cavort half the night with her! How heartless!'

She laughed, but with little mirth behind it. 'No, Freddy. That wasn't the way of it at all. Of course, when she first suggested it . . .'

'Who? Which girl was it?'

'I'm not going to tell you – you'll understand why in a moment. Anyway, when she first suggested it, I was horrified. And when she started kissing me I wondered if I could survive it without retching. But when she put her head between my legs and started on Little Darling down there . . . oh, Freddy! I'll tell you how good she was – at that particular pleasure she was even *better* than you! And I was in such an excitable, sexy state that day, it all came flooding back. I just got thrill after thrill from it. And I even caught myself thinking, this is better than any man is ever going to be! And that's what frightens me, Freddy – you see? There are women here who will never again get a thrill out of any man. And I don't want to get like that – because I enjoy screwing with men, even if most of them don't give me any thrill at all.'

'Most of them don't?' I echoed. 'How many do?'

I could feel her reluctance to answer. 'Absolute honesty!' I reminded her.

'One or two a day, I suppose. Why shouldn't I? They try hard enough.' After a pause she added, 'It was four today.'

'Including me?'

She punched my chest again. 'I'm never going to include you in that tally, Freddy. The sort of thrill I have with you is just so far beyond anything I get with other men . . .' She laughed and corrected it to: ' . . . with *punters* that it would add a hundred to the score. No . . .' Her voice became dreamy again. 'The four today were all at the Young Turks.'

'Out of how many? How many officers in all screwed you today?'

'Four,' she said. 'They all screwed Virginie, too – twice.

They screwed each of us twice. It was so funny! They got Virginie and me playing billiards, while they sat around the table and watched – very close!'

'Naked.'

'Of course!'

I could picture it. Lots of bending over – bubbies dangling on the green, gorgeous derrières thrust provocatively out . . . one leg lasciviously raised to the cushion for an awkward cue shot . . . and the Dumb Glutton spread wide in mute supplication! Thank heaven my jealousy had not thought of such a picture to torment me earlier or I should have been a nervous wreck.

'D'you know anything about that place?' she asked.

'I know what the building looks like from the outside. That's all.'

'It's really a private brothel for the young regimental officers of the district.'

'On Wednesdays and Sundays,' I said.

'No. All the time. They've got four girls living in all the time. We girls from Lazy Daisy's allow two of them a day off on Wednesday and the other two on Sunday. Actually, there are six of them but only four in service at any time – for the same reason as here. Those four serve as what they call 'pretty female waiters' in the restaurant and bar and smoking room and so on. And a Young Turk can take any of them upstairs and screw her at any time – except that there must always be two to do the waiting downstairs. In other words, only two of them can be upstairs, being screwed, at any moment. At ten o'clock the bar and restaurant close, then they can screw all four of them until midnight – and they do! They're mostly quick ones – twenty minutes – so each girl gets screwed by half a dozen young fellows in those two hours. They lead a full life, believe me! Of course, we Lazy Daisy girls don't work in the bar or restaurant. It's six hours of non-stop screwing for us.'

'How d'you know all this?'

'I was talking with one of the girls. She want to come and work here. I almost thought of swapping with her! Actually . . .' She tapped my chest with one fingernail. 'Your Rachel might enjoy the Young Turks a good deal more than working one day here.'

'I don't think so,' I said, though I had given it no real thought.

'Why not?' She was surprised at my assurance.

'I believe what fascinated Rachel about it, about the *idea* of working here, is the *compulsion* that's involved. The absolute lack of choice on your part – or her part, as it would be. If a man chooses her, she's *got to* go upstairs with him. And whatever he says he wants to do with her, she's *got to* permit it.'

'*And* make him think she loves it, too! And be ready with something even more exciting when his invention runs out!'

'Yes, but it's that element of compulsion which truly excites her, I think.'

'Has she actually told you that or are you just guessing?'

'I'm just guessing. I just feel it about her, from the way she spoke.'

After a pause Kitten said, 'I'm sure you're right. I'd never thought about it before but that element of compulsion *does* remove a lot of the possible guilt. Sometimes it's frightening, Freddy – the way you understand us better than ourselves.'

'Come!' I gave an embarrassed laugh. 'I may be quite wrong. I must ask her. She'd love to talk to *you*, Kitten.'

'I think I'd quite like to talk to her, too.' She hugged my arm. 'When we've got our apartment, you can bring her there. And we needn't just *talk*, either!'

When our laughter died I asked her if she'd kept her promise about the diary.

She yawned. 'I'll show you tomorrow, love. I *must* get

some sleep now. Just one other thing – the other favour I wanted to ask you.'

'Yes?'

'It occurred to me tonight, when you were telling Virginie what different quims the four of us have. How acutely observant you are, and how useful that could be to me. If I really am going to take this new profession of mine seriously, I've got to try to see the work from the gentleman's . . . I mean the punter's point of view. When he comes up the drive, what's he hoping for? When he gets into the salon and sees eight girls to choose among, what does he look at? What arguments go through his mind for and against this girl and that? I've tried watching their eyes but I can't really see anything. How does a man watch a girl going upstairs ahead of him? Where do his eyes stray?'

'I can only answer those questions in my own particular case,' I objected.

'But there is one thing more you *could* do, if you were feeling terribly, terribly kind towards me. Please?'

'What?'

'You could screw all two dozen of the fillies who work here – one by one – and tell me all about it. Write a report on every single one – her good points, her bad points. Things I could profit by. And you could actually take me to bed and teach me some of them!'

I was fighting for breath – and trying not to show it.

'Well?' she asked.

I groaned. 'The things we do for our friends!'

Two dozen fillies! Oh me, oh my! Two dozen pairs of come-to-bed eyes, and soft, wet lips promising heaven, and rounded feminine shoulders and soft, pretty bubbies of every size and shape for me to cuddle in my ever-eager hands, whose size and shape is universal; two dozen soft bellies, and supple waists to lead a man round to enticing, pneumatic derrières; four dozen arms, cunning in the art of the amorous embrace; two hundred and forty nimble young fingers, skilled at the caresses that drive a man's spermspouter to the verge of mania – and twenty-four mouths and throats to aid them; and four-and-twenty vertical smiles to twinkle at me, to open up for me, and all heaven beyond them! Oh, that soft, moist, warm, living, responsive, exquisite vagina – that sacred void, that consecrated grotto, whose possession is woman's choicest pearl and man's most desperate endeavour! Oh, those supple, juicy, tender holes, each unique yet each divinely fashioned to receive Iron Jack, to suck him in, to enfold him, to cleave to him, to caress his knob and squeeze the shaft of him, and to accept at the last the sticky broadside of his sporting joy! Twenty-four of them, and all for me! I could not believe my good fortune and Iron Jack could hardly wait to feel himself nosing proudly up those hair-girt holes. I sang while he danced, the whole way home.

I broke the good news to Rachel with some trepidation, however. Her attitude to my dalliance with Kitten had been liberal enough but I would not have blamed her for feeling that to disport myself with all two dozen of Lazy Daisy's fillies, one after the other, was carrying indulgence, hers and mine, too far. But I was wrong. She was, if anything, more excited about it than me; also, not being knocked sideways at the prospect of so much dizzy pleasure, she was more methodical, too.

'You'll have to do more or less the same thing with each of them,' she told me. 'Otherwise comparisons will be meaningless. What we've got to do is work out a drill . . . no! Not the best word in the circs! A procedure. Yes – we've got to work out a procedure for you to follow with each one of them, so you'll be comparing like with like, you see?'

I did, indeed, but I was in no great hurry to perfect this

procedure since the process of refining it involved many happy trials and numerous delightful adjustments – all of which required Rachel's devoted help. In fact, it took us about twelve hours, spread over the following three nights and Sunday afternoon (when Kitten was once again spreading the relish for the Young Turks in Headingley, this time partnered by a filly called Geraldine). When I arrived at Lazy Daisy's at eleven o'clock that night, guessing rightly that Madame would not send her back into the salon, I claimed my quim-privilege as her new macquerau and squired her up to the Prince's Boudoir, which, by good fortune, was unoccupied. I had taken a liking to that place. I relished the chance it offered to shepherd a girl from one room to the other and enjoy her in many different attitudes and positions.

But Kitten, I could feel, resented it – for which I cannot blame her. She wanted us to get between the sheets in a cosier, more intimate room and lie in each other's arms, and talk for an hour or more – simply recovering from another day of gluttonous copulation with her officers – before we cherished each other with our own kind of gluttony. This instant sport in the Prince's Boudoir was too reminiscent of the games she'd been required to play all week. So I was obliged to explain my intentions. I had hoped to try out Rachel's *Procedure* on her without her knowledge, to see if she thought it too mechanical and too obvious a test of a girl; but her resentment made me realize such a stratagem never would have been possible between her and me at any time – much less after a hard week's grind.

Talk about professionalism! The moment I explained my real purpose, her whole attitude changed from pique to cheerfulness, from lethargy to bubbling enthusiasm, and she couldn't wait to begin the 'programme,' as she called it, as if it were an etiquette for a dance. It ran as follows (the rather clinical language being Rachel's contribution, borrowed from the more scientific part of her father's clandestine library):

FAMILIARIZATION (20 minutes)

1. Cunnilingus. Place the girl on her back on a bed or against the slope of a chaise longue. Ask her to draw up her knees and open her thighs as wide as is comfortable. If her quim is not easily accessible, support her derrière with cushions or a pillow. Feast upon her quim until sated. Work your tongue up and down her labia and linger in the furrows between them. Thrust it deep inside her vagina and tickle all round while up there. Play near her clitoris and press your tongue moderately hard against it, but do not overdo direct stimulus. How convincing are her responses?

2. Fellatio. Lie back and spread your thighs and give your penis a good airing. Get her to tease and tickle it with her fingers and tongue. Does she favour the sensitive midline and the underside of your glans or does she seem to think the whole surface is equally randy? Does she blow on your knob to cool it and then quickly plunge it into the heat of her mouth? In short, does she know what stimuli will excite you most? (Reminder: Don't suppress your responses or you may mislead her.) Get her to swallow your penis as far as she is able. Can she get it deep into her throat? Does she swallow hard and does she apply the pressure of it to your glans rather than to the extreme tip of your penis?

3. Soixante-neuf. Engage with her in 'soixante-neuf' – first side by side, then with you on top, and finally with her on top. Does she encourage you to certain actions and discourage you from others in these positions? Does she appear to know that the upper surface of your knob is less sensitive than the underneath? Does she make allowance for the fact or does she suck away as she did in the fellatio position?

COITUS (20 minutes)

Your purpose is to copulate with the girl, without ejaculation, in up to thirty different positions, divided into four groups: standing, sitting, kneeling, and lying down. In each group you can mount her from behind, from her left side, from her right, and face-to-face. There are further variations in the positions of her legs; and in most of the lying-down positions there are three variations – her on top, side by side, and you on top.

1. Standing

(a) Bend her forward over the back of a chair or chaise longue and prepare your penis for entering her from behind. Grasp your penis firmly in one hand and rub it up and down her furrow first, both to pick up lubrication and to see if she responds. Penetrate her slowly, taking several dozen strokes before you get into her as deep as you can. Vary the stroke depth and rhythm; keep her alert, don't let her settle to an automatic pace. Note the length and texture of her vagina; it may change later as she warms to the sport.

(b) Slowly bring her upright. Fondle her labia near her clitoris but avoid direct pressure on it. Try quick, gentle vibrations of her mound. Fondle her breasts and nipples. Rub your fingertips upwards from the bottom edge of her aureoles. Rake your fingernails gently from the outer edges to the middle. Pinch her nipples *gently*. Fold them very gently. Note her responses.

(c) Stay deep in her and turn her sideways-on to you. For this she will have to raise the nearer leg; support it for her and curl your back to get in under her. Poke her as deep as you can – the way a wasp curls its abdomen right round to sting its victim. Feel the different texture of the side of her vagina.

(d) Repeat (c) from her opposite side.

(e) If she's athletic enough, lean back and get her to do a high chorus-girl kick to being her face to face with you. Again, poke her with varying pace and depth in this new position. Caress her derrière, waist, and breasts. Stir her nipples and press them gently. Tickle them with your little fingernails. Gently scratch the full length of her back. Get a finger moist in her juices, insert its tip in her bumhole, and wiggle it about. Note her responses to all these movements. Note the texture of her vagina in this position. Note what caresses she gives you in return. Does she follow you or invent caresses of her own?

(f) Ask her to raise one of her legs and place it around your waist. Note what effect this has on the texture and grip of her vagina.

(g) Ask her to raise both legs and clamp them round your waist. If your spine won't support her weight, keep her derrière on the back of a chair, chaise longue, etc. You are now as deep into her vagina as it is possible to get. Can you feel the top of it? Does she show discomfort? Note the feel of her vagina at this degree of penetration. Is it now softer and wetter than when you first penetrated her? Wriggle your hips from side to side and note how much lateral movement of your penis her vagina permits.

2. Sitting

(a) Sit well into a chair (not an armchair) or on the end of a chaise longue, with your knees together. Ask her to stand with her back to you and with her legs parted over your thighs. Caress her thighs, hips, back, and derrière, tickle her labia, and finger her vagina as you slowly draw her back toward you. When she's near enough, grasp your penis and waggle it up and down her furrow. When she's very close, spread your thighs, forcing her to collapse down onto you. Little actual poking is possible in this position but you can finger her labia and all around her clitoris and caress her breasts and nipples. Note how vigorous and active her vagina is in a position where you can do little to poke it to life.

(b) Move her sideways-on to you (she should be able to do it while still impaled on your erection). Wriggle your hips as much as possible in all directions and see how elastic her vagina is.

(c) Again if she is athletic enough, she should be able to swing a leg through a full arc so that she is now sitting astride you, face-to-face; otherwise penis and vagina must part company for two seconds. As in the other sitting positions, little movement is possible but there is plenty of opportunity for caresses, kisses, and fondling of all kinds.

3. Kneeling

(a) Invite the girl to kneel at the bedside as if in prayer. Kneel behind her and take her derrière between your hands. Assess its voluptuous and lecherous qualities and note how lustfully she moves it, how knowingly she appreciates its lascivious character.

(b) Move in tight behind her until your penis is pressing hard up into her fork and buried in the full length of her furrow. Give a few languorous thrusts in this position and see how robustly she responds.

(c) When, after several thrusts, your glans is hovering around her vestibule, let it linger there and see how swiftly she moves to get you into her vagina proper. Copulate awhile with her in this position, noting her responses to any changes you may make in pace or degree of penetration.

(d) Lay her on her back across the bed with her fork at its very edge. Observe what lewd invitations she makes – by spreading wide her fork, parting her labia with her fingers, diddling her clitoris, and otherwise caressing her body. Encourage her with beaver kisses and further cunnilingus.

(e) Move into her fork until your penis is engulfed in the full length of her furrow. See if she encourages you by pulling your organ tighter to her, making your glans rub her clitoris.

(f) Push your penis in to the full depth of her vagina and copulate with her, using many variations of pace and depth. Note how aptly she responds to each.

(g) Raise her legs until her heels rest on your shoulders. Hug her thighs tight to your torso and copulate vigorously into a vagina which, in this position, will be at its loosest.

4. Lying down

(a) *Doggy position*. Invite her to kneel on all fours on the bed and mount her from behind like a dog on a bitch.

(b) *Pasha's Favourite*. Get her to lie face-down on the bed and mount her from on top. Variations include: (i) clamping her thighs tight together between yours (tightens the grip of her vagina and increases the friction of each thrust); (ii) pushing her thighs apart by inserting your knees between hers (softens the grip of her vagina – useful to avoid premature excitement – and lets you go in deeper); (iii) lying precisely upon her with the points of your knees in the backs of hers – deep penetration into a firmly clenched vagina is possible in this position, but does she realize that?

(c) *Two Spoons*. Holding her tight-notched on your erection, roll onto one side from this position and continue copulating. Variations include different degrees of rounding of her back to complete raising of her knees to her breasts. Each position affects the shape and length of her vagina; how well does she exploit that fact?

(d) *Stargazers*. Continue the roll until she is lying on top of you, still impaled on your erection, both of you looking up at the ceiling. Here you will have total freedom to caress her body – thighs, clitoris, mound, stomach, and breasts. Use it and note how wantonly she responds to each.

(e) *Two Spoons*. Continue the roll again and test as in (c) above.

(f) *Front-to-side*. Ease her onto her back, still keeping your penis inside her. This is the horizontal equivalent of the position you tried in 1(c) above, except that now you do not need to support her raised leg. You can therefore slip your lower arm over her shoulder to fondle her breasts while your upper arm caresses her stomach, bush, and clitoris, or scratches lightly the underside of her thigh. You can also slip the upper hand under her thigh and finger her bumhole in this position. Note her responses to each of these caresses.

(g) *Canoeist*. Still with your erection inside her vagina, roll on your back and pull her on top of you into a sitting position – at the same time turning her to face you, so that, when the manoeuvre is complete, her heels are beside your ears. In this position everything is up to her. How well does she cope. For variation, grab each other's arms in the 'Roman handshake' and let her lean back while you half sit up. When you draw her upright again, lie fully back and let her straddle you, knees bent double. You are now in the position called:

(h) *Girl Jockey*. While she rides you like a New-market pro, you have the freedom of her stomach and breasts.

(i) *Domina*. Let her straighten her legs and lie full out upon you. With slight variations of her leg position all parts of her body are accessible to your caresses, especially her breasts, derrière, and bumhole. And by varying the angle of your hips you can change the degree to which you penetrate her vagina.

(j) *Right Fish*. Roll onto your right side and continue to caress and copulate with her. In this position it is easy to become dislodged; how skilfully does she help you avoid that fate?

(k) *Left Fish*. Roll all the way round onto the other side and repeat (j).

(l) *Orthodox*. Roll her onto her back and copulate all the way to orgasm inside her. This is the Finale phase of the procedure.

FINALE (10 minutes)

The variations of leg position here are numerous. At one extreme she holds her thighs tight-clamped together while you grip them between your knees, like a huntsman going at a fence. At the other, she gets as near to doing the splits as she can while you keep your heels together and your legs straight. There is also a position where you have one thigh outside hers and one between them; this causes intense friction between your penis and one side of her vagina. Then there are all the positions where her knees are bent, either with her heels on the bed or with them raised in the air – perhaps in the 'dead-donkey' position or perhaps clamped around your waist with her heels digging into your buttocks and giving you hints as to what rhythm to use. And finally there is the 'capsized canoeist' position (the opposite of (g) above) in which she lies almost doubled-up underneath you with her heels by your shoulders. In this position you can make further variations of your torso, from horizontal to almost upright, each of which imparts a different degree of curvature to her vagina and permits a different depth of penetration to your penis.

Try all these positions and variations; choose the one in which she excites you the most; copulate with her all the way to your climax.

AFTERMATH

Does she let you soak it as long as you want?

If you stay hard, does she jiggle around to encourage you to another go?

If you go soft, does she jiggle even more wantonly to encourage you even harder? (Kitten's only comment during her reading of the entire programme came at this point. 'If *you* go soft, Freddy, call the doctor!' she said.)

Does she give you the impression that what you have just done with her was one of the more enjoyable acts of sexual intercourse she can remember?

Does she continue to treat you tenderly, affectionately, all the way until you part?

Does she make you want to 'come again' with her?

When Kitten reached the last sheet of paper she scanned the whole thing through again, glancing briefly at each of the headings, and then clasped it to her bosom with a sigh. 'How could she know enough to write all that?' she asked in amazement. 'It makes me despair.'

'You wouldn't despair at all if you knew her,' I said. 'Funnily enough, Rachel is fascinated out of her wits by sexual intercourse, yet she is not actually very interested in Doing It.'

'How can you say such a thing!' Kitten brandished the papers at me.

'I mean she loves reading about it, and talking – and dreaming and thinking about it, too, for all I know. She adores preparing for it and all those little anticipatory things one does. But actually *doing* it . . . san fairy ann!'

Kitten shook her head in bewilderment.

'It's true,' I assured her. 'The first time I poked her, I did something she rather liked. In fact, it gave her what she calls an *orgasm.*'

'That's the proper word, you know.'

'I know it is. But does anybody use it? Do you? Do the punters?'

She grinned and shook her head. 'They say spending, or

169

coming. I call it doing a sticky.'

'Anyway, I repeated the action that gave her the thrill – thinking she'd surely want to experience it again – which was reasonable, yes?'

Kitten nodded.

'Not a bit of it. She told me to go on and try something new. I asked her if she didn't really enjoy it . . . didn't she even *want* me to do it again. "You can do it again next time," she said. So there! Twenty minutes is her ideal copulation time. Anything longer and she gets very tetchy.'

Kitten shook her head in amazement, and then returned to her earlier point about the word *orgasm*. 'She's so lucky to know all the proper words for everything,' she said. 'I'd love to know them, wouldn't you? I mean, *vagina* . . . *penis* . . . *clitoris* . . . *labia* . . . *orgasm* . . . Aren't they exciting? And *fellatio* and *cunnilingus!* Don't you just adore *cun-ni-lin-gus?*'

'I was wondering if you'd ever ask,' I said as I dived into her beaver.

'No!' she shrieked, kicking her legs as if I were tickling her.

I didn't stop, however. Then I heard her rustle Rachel's programme again. Then she said, 'Oh yes – that's where it begins. Go on!'

While I did so, she wriggled out of every stitch, except her silk stockings, and then we went through the entire canon.

It took us ninety minutes, in fact, because there were several bits we enjoyed so much we did them twice, and sometimes thrice.

When we had recovered from our last gasp she stretched out fully in the bed; Kitten had a way of stretching – luxurious, lascivious, and lecherous – that somehow made me thoroughly aware of Little Darling, the vagina that was undergoing the complementary degree of stretching – also luxurious, lascivious, and lecherous – hidden in her belly. I shivered with an instant revival of my lust.

'How many marks did I earn, then?' she asked.

'You've set the standard,' I told her. 'Ninety-nine out of a hundred.'

She pouted and pulled a punch on my arm. 'What was my one failing? Why not a hundred?'

'If Rachel ever heard I'd given you a hundred on her test procedure,' I replied, 'she'd never forgive me!'

It was mid-August before I found the apartment to suit all my requirements. It was in an alley off the north side of Head Row, one of the principal shopping streets in the city – in other words, a female caller might easily tell her mother or friends that she was 'going shopping' and keep an assignation with me without actually lying.

By then I had begun my labour of love in aid of Kitten's career. These are the exact words I wrote in my reports to Kitten of the first seven (I had, of course, already covered Maisie!). The others will follow at their appropriate places in the narrative:

1. Miriam Dela——t ('Maisie'): a well-educated, accomplished woman of twenty-three, good-looking and slender with long, straight ash-blonde hair. Her parents are in retail trade. Her eyes are an attractive pale turquoise; her nose retroussé; her upper lip is thin and elegant, her lower lip full and more wanton; her chin firm. Her breasts are of medium size, firm, and rather high on her chest, which itself is large and strong, her nipples are big and soft. Her waist is slender and her belly slim but her figure swells to a most generous pair of hips. She has slender thighs which do not quite meet at her fork. She boasts a prominent mound of Venus. Her quim at rest shows only her outer labia – two thick, meaty lips, which, on parting, reveal a

delicate, uncomplicated quim. Her vagina is firm and resilient and she can make it juicy and well-lubricated at a moment's notice.

Her strongest point is the confident professionalism she always radiates. She somehow manages to imply that no matter what your desire might be, she is fully capable of meeting it.

2. Monday, August 2, 4p.m. – Geraldine Daun——y ('Gertie'): an attractive, well-fleshed woman of twenty-three with longish, wavy chestnut hair. She is the accomplished elder daughter of a hospital almoner. Her eyes are green and haunting, her appearance calm and solemn. Her breasts are smallish with large, prominent nipples. Her body is firm and vigorous in action. Her quim at rest shows all four lips in sinuous parallel lines but no other features. Her vagina has a soft, yielding texture.

She, too, is a calm, competent partner in the arts of venery; but she is slightly different from Maisie in that she radiates a sense of completely uncritical patience. Every inch of her body, she implies, is *totally* yours – which must serve her well with her shyer, less ebullient punters.

3. Wednesday, August 4, 7p.m. – Sarah R——son ('Sal'): an enjoyable, willowy girl of nineteen with short, curly, light brown hair; the clever but uneducated daughter of a hearse furnisher in Barnsley. Her pale-brown eyes gleam merrily and more than compensate for the prim effect of her nose and mouth, which are rather thin. Her breasts are large and superbly rounded on a rather slender body; her nipples are small. Her belly is almost concave, which shows off her prominent mound to perfection. Her bush is pale and her cleft is always visible. When she parts her thighs her labia unfold like the petals of a flower; the flesh of her inner labia and hole is attractively anaemic. Her vagina is slender and firm.

A strong point with her is her readiness to take the initiative the moment her partner shows the slightest uncertainty. She proved most resourceful and seemed always ready to offer an interesting new pleasure at any moment.

4. Friday, August 6, 11p.m. – Virginie M——chier ('Froufrou'): a tall, graceful young woman of twenty-three, with wavy ash-blonde hair worn in a pigtail down to between her shoulderblades and cut long over her brow and eyes. She is the bright, intelligent daughter of a Normandy farmer; she has come to England in order to earn a good dowry, by which means she hopes also to retain her reputation at home. She usually wears a black velvet band horizontally around her forehead. Her pale-blue eyes are haunting – especially when only half-glimpsed through her fringe. Her nose is aquiline of a characteristic French type and her lips are full and luscious. Her skin is pale, smooth, slightly waxen, and fragrant. Her breasts are delightfully full and heavy, with large, dark aureoles and prominent nipples. Her belly is concave and her waist slender but her hips swell generously to an ample derrière. Her mound is prominent and sparsely mossy, deeply divided by her cleft – which runs straight through her fork and is continuous with the division between her buttocks. Her inner labia are simple and sharply delineated at the front but turn into a confusion of folded flesh around the opening of her vagina, which has a tight grip and seems curved toward her back.

Her strong point is undoubtedly her skill at anal intercourse. This, apparently, is the favourite French method for avoiding babies and is common both inside marriage and out. She can do things with that part of her anatomy that I would have sworn were impossible to anything but an extremely skilled hand. If you wish to develop this skill yourself, Kitten, dear, we shall have to work on it *together!*

5. Monday, August 9, 3p.m. – Annie O——vy ('Fizz'): a short, vivacious seventeen-year-old with tight-curled blonde hair that hugs her head. She is the accomplished and well-educated daughter (orphan) of a non-conformist preacher. Her alert pale-blue eyes dominate a face that bubbles with a sense of fun. Her lips are like a porcelain doll's. Her breasts are small, perfect hemispheres on her spare, rounded torso. She has a little mound, like a child's, and – also like a child's – it is deeply divided by her cleft; her bush is sparse and scarcely visible. The opening of her vagina is much closer to her bumhole than in most other women. She is best enjoyed from behind, where her ample derrière is all the padding a man could desire. Annie has only been gay for six weeks and has still not developed her professional personality to the full. She is, however, going along the right lines. Her great asset is this strange combination of juvenile and mature female attributes. Her manner is winsome and little-girlish and, although she must have been poked about at least 150 times before I took her upstairs, she managed to suggest that everything we did still seemed terribly novel – and naughty, in a giggly sort of way. The suggestion that she is just bubbling over with fun and naughtiness must be highly stimulating to her partners. It certainly was to me!

6. Wednesday, August 11, 8p.m. – Alice C——rell ('Lysia'): a solemn, serious beauty of twenty, with glossy black hair cut to shoulder length. She is the well-educated daughter of a gentleman who has twice been an un-successful parliamentary candidate for the Bradford constituency. Her dark, deep-set eyes and earnest, oval face suggest pleasures profound rather than frivolous. Her slender, sloping shoulders support breasts of classical loveliness – taut and smooth above, soft and rounded beneath, with large, smooth nipples. Her slender waist

fattens superbly to generous hips and a smooth, well-fleshed derrière. Her mound is small and her dense black bush hides her quim entirely, making its flesh, when parted, glow like a pink flame. Her outer labia run right up into her mound but her inner labia unite at the front of her fork and continue in a single swelling or ridge, giving her innermost charms the appearance of a pink lily, newly burst from its bud. Her vagina is tight and juicy.

Her strongest point is her seriousness; it lends great dignity to an act that can otherwise seem trivial and worthless. You might try it as a variation with your most regular punters – as if it were a mood that sometimes overcame you.

7. Friday August 13, midnight Yvette St F——eau ('Nana'): a stocky French peasant girl of nineteen with long, straight shiny hair, deep brunette in colour. Her hazel eyes are gentle and kindly, but rather reserved; her face is plain but pleasing with a firm, strong jaw and stout neck. Her body is built like a fortress, rounded and sturdy. Her breasts are small and rather high on her chest; they point outwards, which is very attractive, especially when her nipples swell, as they often do. Her belly is firm and well filled but not fat. Her mound is small and hidden inside her lustrous dark-red bush. The perfume of her quim is prodigious. Her labia are of average size; the inner ones form a perfect Gothic arch to the shrine of her vagina, which is soft and yielding.

I believe Nana has little to offer from which you might benefit, Kitten. You and she are chalk and cheese. But the languorous way she caresses and plays with her own quim while she spreads it for one's inspection is delightful.

I had shown each report to Rachel as I completed it. Not

only did it whet her appetite to work at Lazy Daisy's for a day, it also made her keen to meet Kitten and talk about her favourite obsession. Kitten, however, was reluctant, for reasons she could not explain; she just spoke vaguely about not feeling ready yet.

My suggestion about anal intercourse was timely, however. Several punters had expressed a preference for it but she had told them it was not something she cared to offer. Madame had given her two weeks to change her mind, otherwise she would be sent to a more modest, 'bourgeois' house in Bradford, where the girls merely offered straightforward vaginal intercourse in a few 'orthodox' positions in encounters that lasted a mere twenty minutes and were obviously pretty mechanical. A girl earned no more than five shillings a time and was expected to pleasure between two and three dozen men a day.

Poor Kitten was very depressed at this prospect and was thinking of getting Tooley to take her on as a pretty female waiter at the Young Turks. In fact, she would have done so if one of the girls hadn't let slip that several of the officers there also favoured the back door. So my suggestion that we should work on it together could not have come at a more opportune moment.

Funnily enough, though, even if Frou-frou had not initiated me into the art, I should still have been ready – thanks to another of those extraordinary accidents that shaped my early sexual education.

It happened one night that the Cohens were giving a dinner party. On such occasions Rachel's parents sometimes seated her at the table, sometimes not. I went over the roof to her room in the hope that she was not dining in style on that particular night. However, I was proved wrong. On my way to Rachel's balcony I had to pass Nannette's window; I had ducked going past for I saw she had a lamp burning there. On my way back, however, the room was in darkness, so I took no care to conceal my exodus – which was how I came face to face with her, leaning on the sill and staring out at me with a certain smile on her lips. I did not notice the smile at first because her nakedness distracted me – especially those two superb bubbies with nipples like alpine strawberries, resting on her window sill.

'I thought so!' she said accusingly. 'I've had my suspicions about you two for some time. Come on!' And the dark of the room swallowed her.

By the time I reached her bedside she was between the sheets. She stretched out a delicate hand to turn up the wick and the back of her forearm brushed against Iron Jack, who was almost tearing the cloth of my trousers in his eagerness to get out.

'Oooh!' Her eyes went wide and her nostrils flared. 'Can I see . . . please?' She rubbed her arm up and down against the bulge.

I took my time, as if I were unwrapping a present for her – which, in a way, I was. I had the curious sensation that I was experiencing the sort of feelings the girls at Lazy Daisy's must have when they undress their bodies in that deliberately provocative way for a punter – that same mixture of pride in their charms and resentment at having no choice. Admittedly the element of compulsion in the two cases was quite different. With the girls it was imposed on them by their way of life; mine was all from the inside – that irresistible urge to possess every available cunny in the world, the moment I get the first sniff at it. But, as Burns might have said, 'A compulsion's a compulsion for a' that!'

The moment Iron Jack burst free of his confines she gave a gasp and both her hands came snaking out to grip him with a loving firmness. She certainly knew her way around his nerve endings; I didn't need to tell her a thing. Before long she had me reduced to a quivering mass of frustrated desire.

It proved infectious, for she was soon trembling, too. That was when I first appreciated the greatest difference between a partner who does it for love and one who does it for money. The moralists of my young day would never admit that *any* female did it for love. According to them, good-hearted women recognized a sort of dreary duty to their menfolk and so put up with Doing It for the sake of filling the nursery and serving the Empire. During my lifetime I've been able to watch these sophistical moralists undergo a complete shift of position – without getting a fraction of an inch nearer the truth. Now, *all* decent women enjoy Doing It – *but only with their husbands!* Sexual pleasure, once considered to be no more than an awkward necessity, is now absolutely the greatest, most wonderful, utterly super thing ever – but, naturally, only as long as it is tasted inside the marriage bed. Stolen pleasures, adulterous pleasures – and worst of all, paid-for pleasures – are as different from 'the real thing' as the moon is from the sun. One day soon, perhaps, we shall have the simple honesty to admit they are about as different as chocolate fudge is from chocolate cream.

In my experience, the pleasure I had with the fillies of Lazy Daisy's at two quid a time, were every bit as intense and as enjoyable as those I had with Rachel, Nannette, and hundreds of others who parted their thighs for love – but equally enjoyable is not identically enjoyable. Indeed, there were big differences. Where the fillies were bold, unabashed, hedonistic, playful, attentive, accommodating, patient, resourceful, skilled, and tireless, the *amateuses*, if I may so call them, were more challenging. Many of them required to be seduced before they would yield up their treasure – even on the twentieth occasion. And when they did, many of them proved woefully ignorant of what gives a man most joy. Quite a few of them believed a man could find his pleasure at almost any part of the game – whose real purpose was, therefore, to satisfy the female's almost boundless capacity for orgasm.

However, in the matter of sheer relish for the game, the *amateuse* puts the *pro* in the shade. That, as I say, was what I first noticed with Nannette that evening. She lay at my side, fondling Iron Jack with as much skill as any pro but – unlike any pro I ever knew – she was also *trembling* with the urgency of her desire. Her entire body quivered with passion and when I lifted my hands to her bubbies I found her nipples were swollen almost to bursting and covered with a fine exudation of moisture. When I began to caress them she broke into a sweat all over and the whole bed soon reeked of naked female lust. Pros are skilled at many kinds of simulation but *that* is an emotion they cannot mimic.

When I put my hand down to her cleft I found a hot cauldron of sticky juices, seething away in preparation for the triumphal entry of the cause of all the excitement. However, the moment I slipped my knee between hers, to winkle apart the pillars of her temple, she stiffened and clamped them even tighter together. 'Please?' she begged in that appealing French accent of hers, 'Only use Miss Brown, Freddy, hein? Do not penetrate Miss Laycock at all. I keep 'er special for my 'usband, Jacques.'

These charming Victorian archaisms for the anus and the vagina would have puzzled me if I had not already heard them from the lips of the girl who was both her mistress and mine. They came, of course, from old Cohen's secret library. Nannette must have had them directly from the old boy himself. It amused me that he and his daughter both used the same coy names for those organs though neither of them probably realized it of the other.

Intrigued, for this was before my encounter with Frou-frou, I slipped behind her and clasped her tight – 'lining up the artillery and getting the range of her,' as we were to say in later, less happy times. I had, of course, come furnished with my usual ration of lambs' bungs – half a dozen. And, as I had no idea what Iron Jack might encounter in his tryst with Miss Brown, I slipped one round him now. I had by then perfected a technique for unrolling a bung down his length in a single stroke – something a girl might easily miss in all the excitement – and, as I've said, once it gets wet a bung feels indistinguishable from natural skin. So after I had rubbed Iron Jack up and down her furrow a couple of times I had lost all sensation of wearing the thing at all.

The action was also delicious to her, for I chose an angle that caused the flat top of my glans to massage the hot little bud of her clitoris with the gentlest of pressure. Then, when I changed the angle so that it just failed to make contact with that delightful *coquille*, she lowered her hand into her fork and pressed my lad up into her cleft with a pressure I would not have dared exert. In effect, her fingers beneath Iron Jack and the deep furrow between her labia above him formed a temporary vagina of a most exciting kind – an excitement she soon augmented when she began to tickle him as he moved languorously up and down. Of course, she had no idea I was sheathed in the safety of a bung. So when my fine young spermspouter began to do his stuff, she gave a little cry of alarm and struggled to be free of his dangerous broadside. But I was ready for her and clamped her tight to me, covering her back and neck and ears with little love bites, nipping her ear lobes between my teeth and poking the tip of my tongue rapidly in and out of her earhole in time with my leaping lad below.

She immediately brimmed over into a most satisfyingly massive orgasm. How we failed to bring the entire dinner table up to discover who was murdering whom, I cannot imagine. But she was magnificent in her ecstasy – and fatalistic when it was over. 'I think I go home to France very soon, Freddy dear – after that.'

'After what?' I asked.

'That!' She held her hand up to the lamplight, clearly expecting to see half a gallon of my sticky drooling off her fingers. 'Hein?' she exclaimed.

Laughing, I pulled Iron Jack, shroud and all, out of her fork and, kneeling near her head, poked him into her field of vision.

And *vision* was the word! She gaped at the sight, exclaiming, 'I never seen! I never seen! 'Ow you do it?' Gingerly she poked at the dangling globule of sticky and gave a little cry of alarm when it shivered at her touch.

I rolled the bung up again until the last couple of inches simply slipped off the end of my knob – revealing him in all his pristine glory as when she had first clapped eyes on him.

'Oh!' She took the limp, wet bundle with the white goitre dangling beneath it and I watched the understanding dawn in her eyes. But what she did next was something I could not have predicted in a million years – ignorant as I then was of so many of the ways of Woman.

She sat up, half turned toward the lamp, lay the pathetic bundle in her open hand, which she then curled to form a tube, and poked at it with the tip of one delicate finger, not once, but many times. And after each poke she opened her hand and inspected the result. When at last one of the pokes succeeded in expelling the sticky, making it flood out and cover most of her hand, she laughed with delight.

I simply took refuge in the thought that women are odd creatures at the best of times.

'What is?' she asked, holding up the bung.

I explained.

'You 'ave more?'

'I always carry six, just in case.'

'In what case. You 'ave the case 'ere?'

'No, I mean in case I get an invitation to stay all night.'

Her eyes went wide once more. 'Six times! In ze night? You?'

I nodded.

'Oh, Freddy!' She made an expressive Gallic gesture of angry frustration. 'It's not possible for us tonight, *hélas!* Six times? Really?'

'More if you like. I find once I get beyond three there's none of that sticky stuff left to shoot – and so there's no real reason not to go on as many times as I like.'

'Ten times?'

I shrugged. 'Probably.'

'Oh! You come back tomorrow night after eleven yes? Not before – very important not before.' She grinned – a very French, very saucy grin – and added, 'Bring twelve of these, hein?'

'Oh! You mean that's all we're going to do tonight?' I asked in a disappointed tone.

'No-o-o!' She snuggled up against me, wriggling her glorious derrière into my groin. 'Now we both enjoy Mlle Brown, as I promise.'

And we did, too. I cannot say it was a greater pleasure than the more natural form of copulation, but it was certainly very different. I was too excited at its novelty to analyze it much but I had the strongest intuition that I had just made another great leap in the arts of venery, acquiring a skill that would stand me in good stead in years to come – not to say losing a prejudice that could well have blighted those same years had I continued to hold it.

And practice had made Nannette perfect at giving pleasure by using the powerful muscles of Mlle Brown's passage – and at receiving it through those same vibrant membranes. Of course, my delicacy of touch at the farther end of her divine cleft added spice to her feast.

And the following night, precisely at eleven, I and my dozen bungs were there, ready for a night of worship at the divine fork. The first thing Nannette did, however, was to take one of my bungs and vanish behind a screen. When she emerged a minute or so later she was naked as a babe – and carrying a large, soft bath towel, which she spread across the centre portion of the bed.

'Now,' she said, lying on her back and spreading her thighs in a most businesslike fashion, 'you may 'ave my virginity.'

'What?' I was aghast.

'Yes. Put on one of those bungs and enter Mlle Laycock.' She gave a wicked smile.

'But what of your husband to be?' I asked. 'Jacques. Are you not . . .'

'Please, Freddy. *Je t'en prie!* Just do like I ask. You'll see.'

The dumb mouth of her virgin hole gaped in silent supplication before my eyes, making a plea a thousand times more eloquent than the one her other lips had framed. I lowered myself upon her and began the slow, heavenly rite of female initiation.

After five minutes of 'outdoor frolicking' she was as juicy as ever she had been the night before, and trembling again, too, with the violence of her lust, and just beginning to sweat all over. So I eased Iron Jack into that most privileged vessel and let him relish every trembling millimetre of his stately progress into a paradise no man had tasted before him. I experienced only the slightest resistance from her maiden veils. I fancied I felt them tear before me. I would have stopped and withdrawn in tenderness for her distress if she had not at that moment given a great sigh of joy and, throwing her legs up round my back, pulled me into her, deep and tight.

She came at once, and went on like that, boiling and simmering, boiling and simmering, throughout the delightful twenty minutes it took me to explore and savour every novel feature of her virgin cunny. When it was over and she had marvelled yet again at the sticky white gobbet of my milt hanging securely in its membranous sac from the tip of Iron Jack, she asked me if I had ever taken a girl's maidenhead before. I mentioned my experience with Kitten, saying nothing of her profession. She asked about Rachel and I described that experience, too.

'So you never break a girl's veil before?' she asked.

'Not before tonight,' I assured her. 'Yours was the first. But I still don't understand why you permitted it.'

She giggled and shook her head. 'You 'ave not break mine, neither,' she said. 'See?' And, spreading her legs wide, she inserted two fingers into her vagina and fished around in there.

I, meanwhile, was horrified at the sight now revealed – not of her cunny, that was delightful and was already encouraging Iron Jack to his next safari – but of the blood that stained the towel she had placed beneath her. I glanced at my discarded bung, which was on a sheet of newspaper on the floor, and saw that it, too, was crimsoned with the blood of victory.

But then she found what she had been seeking and pulled it out with a triumphant, '*Voilà!*'

It was another bung, the one she had taken from me at the beginning, and it, too was dark with blood. She, meanwhile, was looking down at the huge stain between her parted thighs. 'I put too much in,' she said. 'Jacques, 'e never will believe so much.'

She smiled bewitchingly at me. 'Encore?'

'Encore!' I agreed.

It was shortly after I had enjoyed Frou-frou on August the sixth that Kitten came to me with Madame's ultimatum. She had just been favoured with the first visit of her little friend, the cardinal – much to her relief, of course! – so it was the start of her week away from Lazy Daisy's. Naturally, she spent it at my apartment in the city. I visited her there every evening and, with the help of cocoa butter and some superb muscle control, we were able between us to work her darling Miss Brown up into a beautiful condition – fully hardened and ready for any amount of traffic. It was one of the most enjoyable weeks of that idyllic summer as we practised all the skills I had observed in Frou-frou and Nannette.

Somehow during that week Rachel got to hear that Kitten was staying in my apartment. Tired of waiting for me to tell her Kitten was ready to meet her at last (indeed, I think she believed it was *I* who was keeping them apart), Rachel went to beard the lioness in her den. What happened at that interview I do not know. They refused to tell me, saying it was just 'girls' talk.' But they must at some point have discussed what are nowadays called 'sexual fantasies' – something for which there was no proper word at that time. Indeed, most people – including, I'm sure, all women – would have strenuously denied that females enjoyed fancies or daydreams of an erotic nature at all. Even men would have thought twice before admitting to same; such fancies would have carried the same stigma as, say, masturbation does today. So it was a bold thing for Rachel and Kitten to discuss the matter at all, much less admit to indulging such fancies.

It was, as one might expect, Rachel who first broached the subject. I know it for a fact because, two weeks later, she handed me a sealed envelope and asked me if I would be so good as to pass it on to Kitten, who was by then back at Lazy Daisy's, offering Little Darling or Miss Brown with equal abandon to all-comers. I obliged, of course, but unfortunately it stood too near a steaming kettle and fell open. However, no accident is so unfortunate that it cannot be put to good use. Accordingly, I made a fair copy of the contents before I glued the envelope together again and delivered it to Kitten – who again refused to let me see the contents on the grounds that it was yet more girls' talk. Before I reproduce it, however, let me catch up on the fillies I had tested on Kitten's behalf; I thought it particularly mean of her to keep Rachel's letter secret, especially in view of my own utterly selfless labours in aid of her professional improvement.

8. Monday, August 6, 2.30p.m. – Florence El——n ('Swan'): a pleasant-natured, responsive young lady of twenty-one with luxuriant and wavy chestnut hair. She is the uneducated but talented daughter of a Whitby fisherman. Her dark, greeny-brown eyes and gentle smile make one's time with her a pleasure from the first moment. Though of average height and build her body is slight and graceful. Her breasts are long pendulous cylinders with enormous nipples to round off their ends; when she raises her arms, they project at a most enchanting angle. Her slender waist and hips accentuate a generous and beautifully curvaceous derrière, beneath which one sees daylight between her thighs – half-filled with the fuzz of her sparse bush. Her crevice is small and does not divide her mound, which swells bountifully. Her short outer labia conceal everything until her thighs are fairly well spread, whereupon they reveal a quim of delightful complexity – indeed, very like the proverbial oyster after which that divine flesh is often named. Her vagina at rest is closed tight together and not immediately visible; it is sublimely tight in action.

You and she are so alike, Kitten, you might easily have attended the same rogering classes! You are both so natural and unflustered, and you both manage to suggest you are discovering some deep internal pleasure in what your lover of the moment is doing to you. She has a splendid little wriggle of her derrière, which I will show you next time.

9. Wednesday, August 18, 7p.m. – Emily J——s ('Pudding'): a (not to mince words) fat, short, jolly woman of

twenty-seven with straight, severely cut strawberry blonde hair. She is the uneducated but bright daughter of a Sheffield knife-grinder. Emily's face is wider than it is high, yet her features are finely drawn and elegant, nonetheless. Her merry eyes twinkle beneath beetling brows and fat cheeks, between which is an aquiline nose of some distinction and a mouth that seems to be always smiling. Though fat she is not at all flabby. My arms would not meet about her body, yet all they touched felt firm and lively. I was not particularly looking forward to my experience with Emily but she turned it into a rare pleasure and cured me of my unthinking distaste for chubby girls forever. Her enormous bubbies, like two huge feather bolsters, are especially exciting, both to caress and to lie on – and to lie *under*, indeed! Her quim is surprisingly small and delicate, like a pink bourbon rose that unfolds when she parts her massive thighs. Her vagina, contrary to what I expected, is amazingly narrow and tight.

I cannot think of the slightest parallel between you and her, Kitten – but you can safely recommend her to any punter who may pass a disparaging remark about her size.

10. Friday, August 20, 8p.m. – Dolly Mac——y ('Chuckles'): a tall, loose-limbed woman of twenty-six with long, glossy, wavy honey-blonde hair. Dolly is the comedienne of the fillies at Lazy Daisy's – a warm-hearted, vulgar, cockney 'gel.' A clinical description cannot possibly convey her real attractiveness for her face is horselike, with large, watery eyes and a mulish lower lip that beetles over a receding chin. Her breasts are flat and pendulous, with nipples that resemble large warts. Her belly bulges; she has no derrière to speak of; her legs are skinny shanks. Her quim is her most delightful feature, being the closest thing to an anatomy textbook I ever saw; her vagina, too, is welcomingly fleshy and firm. Yet an hour with her is

one of sheer delight. She is the perfect example of the triumph of mind over matter – that is, her vulgar humour and good-natured willingness to indulge her lover of the moment in every little whim certainly helps take one's mind off what matters!

11. Monday, August 23, 4p.m. – Susan Pel——n ('Kiddy'): a small, slight eighteen-year-old with short, straight auburn hair of a fine texture. Her father is a bank officer and her mother teaches at infant school. Sue's amazingly baby-like face makes her the natural 'infant' of the house. At first glance her body is that of an immature girl's on the verge of nubility – with awkward elbows and knees that seem almost double-jointed. Then you notice her breasts which, size apart, are gratifyingly those of a grown woman; her derrière, too, is as plump as Eros ever intended a woman to be in that region. Her outer labia are soft and puffy, like two pink sausages laid side by side; her inner pair are merely vestigial and her vagina is agreeably juicy and accommodating.

Of course, she makes the most of her childlike features. She throws herself into a man's lap and makes *ooh-naughty!* faces when his fingers stray into her cleft; and she gives perfect little cries of childish delight when he follows his finger with the organ nature intended for the purpose. You might try the same with really elderly punters, Kitten – the sort to whom any filly under the age of thirty is an infant.

12. Wednesday, August 26, 3p.m. – Louise Val——z ('Ebony'): a stately Mauresque girl of nineteen with tight knots of fine, frizzy hair that cling firmly to her head. Her parents belong to a North African people whose daughters regularly earn their dowries in the brothels of Algeria and southern France. Her talents were discovered there last year by a Leeds coffee importer, who 'imported' her

at once to Lazy Daisy's, where she thrives. Her fine-textured blue-black skin has an alluringly musky fragrance. It stretches taut over the elegant bone structure of her face, with her prominent cheekbones, deep-set eyes, and thin lips. Her neck is immensely long and elegant and its curvilinear lines flow beautifully into those of her breasts, which, though large, are splendidly uplifted and firm; her dark-brown aureoles are ample and seem blessed with several minuscule nipples as well as her real ones, which are glossy and smooth. Her belly is flat and her hips broad. Her backside, like that of many black-skinned fillies sticks out prominently – and most invitingly, too! It is both soft and firm and well furnished with muscles, which are not idle during action. Her mound is small and plucked clean of all hair. When it comes to the gap between the tops of her thighs, hers is the largest of any filly at Lazy Daisy's. Her labia (which she also plucks clean) are dark at their extremities but turn to a glorious salmon pink in their secret recesses. Her hole is large and florid, like a cabbage rose. Her vagina is loose and yielding with many interesting changes of texture and firmness – soft as jelly in one place, fricative as a cat's tongue in another, and with stimulating little rib-like folds in between.

She has a way of lifting up her breasts and offering them to a man that almost undid me on the spot – something we shall have to practise. Also she can squeeze the top of her vagina independently from the bottom – another little trick worth cultivating, I think.

13. Friday, August 28, 10p.m. – Gisela K—ch ('Heidi'): a short, slightly built German girl of twenty-one with longish, wavy black hair with a lustrous sheen. Her father has a farm and vineyard in Bavaria, where she hopes to return next year to get married. Her dark, luminous eyes (assisted, possibly, by belladonna) are infinitely appeal-

ing, as is her pretty, rounded face with its chubby cheeks
and cherubic smile. Her body is plump but solid and firm,
all except her breasts and derrière, which are generous
and soft. Her skin is velvety and dark and she is liberally
furnished with dark, glossy hair in all the right places –
beneath her arms, on her lower belly, up her thighs, and
into her fork. Her mound is large and prominent and,
being covered in dark tresses, makes an utter secret of her
quim. Her labia are small and delicate and the entrance to
her vagina seems impossibly narrow. But, she says, her
vagina will expand to accommodate all-comers. Her
thighs are short and powerful; they grip with a satisfying
embrace.

She showed me a delightful little game in which I knelt
over her supine body and laid Iron Jack between her
bubbies, which she then folded over him, making a soft,
downy cavity for me to poke. It is such an obvious
pleasure I'm amazed I had not thought of it myself, long
ago. I mention it on the off-chance no one has shown it to
you, either.

14. Monday, August 30, 5p.m. – Clara R——son ('Rosebud'): truly an English rose of a girl, aged twenty, with
short, curly brown hair, tinged with ginger. Her father is
station master at one of the larger junctions on the
Northern Railway. Her large, sky-blue eyes seem to shine
with the pure light of innocence. Her nose is straight and
fine, her lips like a budding rose; her cheeks glow like
pippins. Her skin is milk-white with, here and there, an
endearing freckle or two. Her breasts, which she often
covers with her hands, as if in modesty, are perfect
hemispheres of medium size and swansdown-soft with
cherry pink nipples. Her upper torso is slight but she
swells generously about the hips and belly; her derrière is
curvaceous and ample; her thighs are creamy and pneumatic. Her mound is bountiful and soft and shows no sign

of her cleft among its sparse ginger hair. Her quim is a lavish confection of labia, which seem to divide and merge with each other throughout their length. Her hole is like a mouth that has sucked a sour lemon and her vagina is firm and tight, though splendidly juicy.

Although she has been gay two years she still manages to suggest a certain coy innocence that I think may suit your clerical punters very well, Kitten. Whenever I touched her in an erotically exciting place, she gave a little jump and uttered a tiny cry of surprise, somehow suggesting she was enjoying it far more than she knew she ought. Along with this she conveyed the notion that, if I were not such a superbly stimulating lover, she would never overcome her shyness enough to permit these liberties.

15. Wednesday, September 1, 2p.m. – Martha Or——son ('Pippin'): a splendid, no nonsense filly straight off the farm, with strong arms and back, a vigorous body, and a healthy appetite for lusty exercise. She is twenty-four and has long, straight black hair, dense and glossy. Her face is plain but agreeable, with large, dark, cowlike eyes and a snub nose. She has a pretty mouth with strong white teeth. She has a rugged, pale-skinned body with breasts like the udders of a young heifer, with long, cylindrical nipples as big as the tips of one's little finger and silky smooth. Her belly is ample and firm as is her bounteous derrière; she needs no cushion, whichever side you mount her. Her thighs are short and powerful – and delightfully vigorous in engagement. The hair of her bush is also dark and glossy but not dense enough to hide her cleft, which is a luminous creamy pink running well up into her mound. Her quim is straightforward – four chubby, healthy labia making two shield-shaped defences around a loosely lidded hole. Her vagina is muscular and firm.

Her method of pleasing a punter is simplicity itself: Follow him in every detail. If he is lusty and vigorous, give him tenfold lust and vigour in return. If he is slow and stupefied, lie there panting away at the last extremity of languorous ecstasy. Not a bad principle to fall back on when your own fertile invention begins to flag!

And here, now, in its proper chronological place, is the promised text of Rachel's letter to Kitten. It comprised nothing but a fantasy, an erotic daydream. There was no covering note and no attempt at explanation – which is why I assume they had discussed the matter at length when they met at my apartment.

Rachel's Erotic Reverie

I am a seventeen-year-old shopgirl in a large store in Liverpool. Sometimes it's Bristol, sometimes London, or even Falmouth. (It must be a seaport. And, for some odd reason, changing the port from time to time helps keep the erotic power of this reverie fresh, even though the actual sexy bits don't change.) My wages are low and I have a struggle to make ends meet. But my best friend Polly, a very pretty girl of eighteen in haberdashery, seems to have plenty of money and is always smartly turned out. One day I ask her how she manages since she earns very little more than me, and so she lets me into her secret. Once in a while she goes on board one of the ships in the dock and 'obliges' the seamen, who give her money for it. In one night she can earn more than in all the rest of the month at the store, but she doesn't consider herself a prostitute because she doesn't do it every night, or even every week. She asks me if I want to give it a try.

At first, of course, I'm horrified and say no. I'm not quite a virgin but I've never had more than a man's finger (and, of course, my own!) inside me and I've never done more with a man's cock than squeeze and tickle it. However, the more I think about it, the more the idea excites me and so I ask her how she arranges it. She says she leaves all that side of it to a fellow she knows; he takes five shillings in the pound but it's worth it. Will she ask him for me and perhaps we can both go and 'do' a big ship together? With my heart in my mouth I say yes.

The great day comes – or great evening, rather – and I'm just a terrified bundle of nerves. Jock, the pandar, drives us down to the docks in his own carriage, which is sumptuous. I like feeling cosseted and I know it's all on account of that hairy hole between my legs. I have a very special, tingly feeling down there as I snuggle into the upholstery.

It's dark when we arrive. A warm, sultry night. The ship looms vast over us as we draw up and I imagine a hundred crew on board, all waiting to cram their meat inside me and Polly. Jock tells us that there are five officers, including the captain, and twelve crewmen waiting eagerly to screw the two of us. My mind is slightly easier when I work out that means eight for one of us and nine for the other. But then he explains that the officers won't screw the same girl as the crew, so one of us must do five and the other twelve. I'm sick with apprehension again until Polly says bravely that she'll do the crew and leave the officers to me. I'm just blessing her with all my heart when Jock says it's not up to us to decide – that's the captain's privilege. What happens is that we both go to his cabin first and let him undress us and screw both of us, passing from one to the other until he spends. Whichever one he shoots his juice into is the one who will go below decks and do the crewmen. The other girl will go round the four remaining officers' cabins and let herself be screwed by each of them in turn; and finally she'll go back to the captain, who will screw her again and shoot his second load into her.

'Does he know this is my first time?' I ask. 'And that I'm practically a virgin?'

Jock assures me he does and that he's a very humane

man and will almost certainly make sure that Polly gets the crew anyway.

Reassured, I go with him and Polly, all the way up to the captain's cabin. On the way we run a gauntlet of fearsome-looking men, all of whom eye us with unmistakably lascivious leers and make crude gestures relating to fornication. I'm sorry for Polly but glad I won't be spreading my thighs for *them* on my first night out!

The captain is a wily old goat – grey-haired, grey-bearded, and with a wicked twinkle in his eye! His cock isn't too large, thank heavens, but it's very stiff, solid, and workmanlike. He wastes little time on preliminaries because, as he says, he's 'saving most of it for his second fuck with one of us.' His crude language is somehow exciting. He screws both of us pretty hard, passing rapidly from one to the other and changing positions often. I'm so relieved to discover that I'm not going to be sick or burst into tears that I begin to relax.

Next moment, I'm actually starting to enjoy it!

And a moment later I'm gasping, panting, sweating in an almost uncontrollable sexual frenzy. The captain says he's never screwed such a hot little tail as mine – and then lets go of himself completely, too. When he shoots me full of his love-juices I almost pass out in my own ecstasy. Only when I begin to cool down do I realize what's happened. I plead with him but he won't change his mind.

Next moment I'm wearing nothing but a yellow silk dressing-gown and my elegant court shoes and I'm being marched down to the crew's quarters with my elbow in the grip of a massive husky bear of a man who tells me he's the bosun. 'I hope you're feeling fit and full of fuck tonight, kiddie,' he says heartily, 'because we've got twelve animals here who haven't fucked a woman in four months.'

I gasp but he can hear that his crude language is really exciting me – as did the captain's earlier. So he goes on:

'Oh yes, little girl – I hope you slapped plenty of tool oil up that tight young cunt of yours, because these fucksters are hoping to screw your sweet little tail till the steam comes out of your ears!'

'Who are they?' I ask, though I can barely articulate those three simple syllables.

'Let's see now. There's me and the quartermaster. We're the two oldest, and believe me – we know where cute little kiddies like you keep *everything* hidden! We'll turn you inside out, the pair of us! The others are all still damp behind the ears. Not one of them over thirty.'

Of course I nearly wet myself with delight to hear that!

He continues: 'Then there's cook and the laundry wallah – they're both Chinese. Then the three stokers, Indian fellers, small, dark, and wiry. And three black fellers we picked up in Mombasa – giants, they are, and with ramrods to match. If they don't split your clam in two, I'm a Dutchman. And finally there's two cabin boys, both virgins. They have two of the finest pleasuring engines you ever saw on men so young, but they never yet fucked up into a woman's cunt. You're not going to believe it when you see it. You're going to wonder how the women of four continents managed to keep their hands off those pretty young fellers – but it's true. So me and the others had a little whip-round and we got you some extra money to give them a real good time – show them everything you know, kiddy, and let them do it for as long as they want.'

He passes me a gold coin for this extra service but I don't care; by now I'm almost fainting with the randy feelings that are shooting like fire through and through me. I drag him into a passageway and open my silk dressing gown to pull the rough cotton and canvas of his clothing hard against me – and his great bearlike body, of course. His cock is massive, and throbbing with suppressed lust as I pull it out. It's all knobbly and crooked, like a parsnip – a veteran of more cunts than he could count. A moment later he's splitting my belly with it and yet I jump up and down on him in my ecstasy, still not able to get enough of that superb, if lopsided, organ crammed into my gluttonous hole.

The Chinese cook (in my reverie I don't bother with little details like how I get from one place to another!) can hardly speak a word of English. 'Fucky fuck,' is all he can say – with a leer that needs no translation in any language. He bends me roughly forward over the galley table and pins my wrists to the wood with two curious forks, like miniature farmyard pitchforks. (I never saw such things in any real kitchen, but this cook has them, anyway. The forks don't pierce my flesh, of course, but they do immobilize my arms very effectively.) Meanwhile he's thrown up my dressing gown and now he's ramrodding away. His cock is not hard and lumpy like the bosun's but soft and almost squashy. However, in some curious way, it does the job and he has no difficulty in ramming it all the way home each time.

The laundryman, who can speak quite good English, buries us in freshly laundered sheets – sheets of pure silk, which he says he keeps for times when girlies like me come aboard. He doesn't move much and his cock is quite small but just lying there, all tangled up in his body and those wonderful sheets, making tiny movements, is a whole new sexy experience.

The three Indian stokers are just as the bosun described them – like three chattering, adorable, happy little monkeys – those vervet monkeys with the beautiful, downy faces. Their bright eyes gleam when they fondle and explore my charms and their teeth shine like stars when they laugh with pleasure. The three of them screw me in short, hysterical bursts. I don't know how many times they spend inside me, but every time I look I see fresh spunk drooling off their dark, slender cocks.

The three black fellows from Mombasa are waiting for me, stark naked. Their bodies are huge but there's not an ounce of fat on them. Their taut, ebony skin gleams over their rippling muscles – but I am mesmerized by those three *enormous* black liquorice sticks standing up like guardsmen, so stiff they slap their own bellies whenever they move. I grab two of them by these massive piledrivers and drag them behind me to the hold – where, of course, they have improvised a most sumptuous bed for our frolics. Their cocks are so huge that the fingers and thumb of neither hand can meet around them. In fact, they are a hand and a half round at the base – and not much thinner at the top! (That's ten inches circumference, I've measured it since.)

The two with their cocks in my hands get so passionate at the sight of my girlish tail wagging eagerly in front of them that they both get into me the moment I lie down – one behind me and one in front. I don't mean one in Miss Brown and one in Miss Laycock, I mean *both in my hole!* They screw me in counterpoint, one pulling out as the other rams himself home. The third one gets so randy he can't stop, either; he sticks his cock into my mouth from one side and I 'play' him like a mouth organ.

All three of them spend into me at the same time, two right up at the top of my hole and the other into my mouth – and all over my face and neck. The two who were inside me are exhausted but the one who used my mouth wants more.

While writing this down I've been resisting a temptation to embroider the account – in the way I would if I were writing this for one of my father's erotic magazines. You know, things like how I sigh and wriggle my hips, how they caress and lick my nipples, how each new inch of each new cock feels as it vanishes inside my cunt . . . and so forth. But the fact is that, for the most part, such details do not enter into my reverie at all. My thoughts linger far more on the bosun's jocular threats and on the actual situation. The mere *thought* of being led along the deck of that merchantman, wearing nothing but my silk dressing-gown, and knowing that somewhere out there ahead of me are twelve men who have travelled from all corners of the globe in order to screw me 'until the steam comes out of my ears!' – that is far more lascivious to me than heaving bubbies and buttocks and thrusting cocks and tingling cunts.

But one exception is the bit that follows now with Jason – the only one of the blackamoors I bother to name. He now spends about ten minutes arranging my body for his pleasure. First he lies me face-down on the deck, which is of steel plate, covered only by a thin cotton sheet. I relish its hardness because I know what he's going to do; a soft mattress would absorb the impact of his thrusting but the hard metal means I'm going to get all of it.

I'm lying face-down, eyes closed, perfectly relaxed, a dreamy smile playing about my lips as he parts my thighs, moves my legs this way and that, places different pillows in various combinations under my belly and mound. In my mind's eye I am treasuring two different images – the beautifully rounded cheeks of my white-girl's bottom, raised up so invitingly by the pillows underneath me, and his gloriously lean, tight, black-man's buttocks, shining like polished jet, with his powerful muscles trembling just beneath that skin. Trembling to begin. Trembling to drive that mighty ramrod whose hot pink knob keeps brushing the backs of my thighs and tickling my hairy, wet cleft, which is fluttering, too, with my excitement.

The way it happens is like this. He places a pillow under me, and then, with slow, amorous deliberation, he lies on top of me, covering my body completely with his. Then he wriggles himself up my body until his great, hard cock is notched firmly in my cleft. And then those fabulous muscles of his buttocks start to ripple as he lifts his bottom, dragging his cock up the full length of my cleft, coming to rest on my tight little bumhole. After a couple of strokes like that he gets off me and makes some small rearrangement to the pillow, and then repeats the whole sequence. And this goes on many times before he is finally satisfied that my body is perfectly deployed for his thrills.

Then comes that delicious moment when he climbs upon me and I know he's going to begin because, once he's wriggled upward and got his cock nicely tucked in between the lips of my cleft, I feel the top sides of his feet press firmly against my soles, as if I were standing on his feet. Now his sensational ebony body is completely covering mine. We are touching each other all the way up to my head, where I can feel his lips on my left ear. He sticks out his tongue and starts to lick in my earhole – and down there, in my quivering pussy, his mighty piledriver is doing the same with that other hole.

He takes an age to get all the way into me, poking his tool in a little, pulling it out, poking it in a bit more . . . and so on until at last I can feel his massive knob pushing tight against the top of my hole. He rests like that for almost a full minute, soaking in my juices – not pumping me but making it twitch and throb inside me all the same. Then he slowly withdraws it, all the way out, and I almost faint with joy for I know what he's about to do and I can imagine those superb buttocks of his arched right up, and I think of his ramrod poised over my shivering tail like some avenging carnivore.

And then *wham!* Into Miss Brown he thrusts that great baton, so deep and so hard I can imagine he's pushed it right up into my lungs.

'Lie still now, girlie.' His soft low voice makes my ear tingle. 'Relax and don't move a muscle. I'm going to fuck in here for a lo-o-ong time!'

He withdraws so slowly I can feel every fraction of an inch of his cock as he withdraws it from me; then he piledrives it into me as hard and as fast as that first time. And so he goes on for an eternity, during which I lose count of the number of thrills I get.

The quartermaster does me in his own cabin, which has a bed rather than a bunk. He makes me lie on the bed with my legs up in a V, and the height of the bed is such that he can stand on the floor and his tool almost falls inside me. He clasps my feet tight against his ears and fucks me merrily in that one position.

And so finally there are the two virgin cabin boys, with whom I do all the things Freddy and I worked out in his programme for testing the fillies at Lazy Daisy's on a fair and equal basis. In fact, since Freddy has started taking care of my night starvation, these cabin boys are twins, the living likeness of Freddy himself!

And that's the end of my favourite reverie. With its help I can usually manage fifty or sixty orgasms spread over about ninety minutes. There are variations in which, two nights later, Polly and I return to the same ship and this time *she* gets the crew and I am screwed by the officers. The crew do the same to Polly as they did to me and I lead the officers to places where we can watch without being observed. So we see Polly getting the same treatment as I got, and then the officers and I go and repeat the experience.

There's another variation in which one of the cabin boys is so overwhelmed by the power of his lust that he comes to my lodgings and spends the night there with me, screwing me so hard and so many times that he can only crawl back to the ship in the morning.

It took some time for Kitten to digest this amazing effusion. Meanwhile, I was plodding on in my self-sacrificing way, testing the fillies of Lazy Daisy's on Kitten's behalf and reporting back to her. Thus:

16. Friday, September 3, 7p.m. – Harriet Ro——ts ('Babyface'): a short, slightly built filly of twenty-five with straight brown hair, cut to shoulder length. Her parents are on the stage, her father being an actor-manager with his own group of players. Despite her age she is one of the two 'babies' at Lazy Daisy's, the other being 'Kiddy.' But, whereas Kiddy's body is a miniature of a mature woman's, Harriet's seems hardly developed at all. Her face is truly angelic and childlike, with a high forehead, large, innocent eyes, and the Cupid lips of a small child. Her body is spare and skinny with almost no trace of female breasts; only her rather large nipples proclaim her torso as that of a woman. Even her skin has the fine, slightly waxen texture of a child's. Her waist and hips are slight and her derrière indistinguishable from that of a young boy; her thighs are slender and birdlike. Her mound is small and hairless – because she plucks it assiduously every day, not because of any true physical immaturity. Her quim has the soft, chunky quality of a baby girl's, with simple, straight labia. Her hole, however, because of the traffic it has endured over the years, is that of a woman in her twenties. Her vagina is still superbly tight and juicy.

Her manner of exploiting her child-like qualities is pretty well identical with Kiddy's; the happy hour I passed in copulation with her merely confirmed their erotic power.

17. Monday, September 6, 3p.m.– Anne-Marie D——ss ('Tendresse'): a nineteen-year-old Parisienne Jewess with a luxuriance of long, wavy brunette hair. Her parents are cloth importers in a fairly large way of business. She has the prominent nose of her tribe but on her, as on many beautiful women, it is a most seductive ornament; her dark, vivacious eyes and full, sensuous lips are its perfect complement. Her slender, willowy, body is graced with breasts that are round and full, with dark, prominent

nipples. Her belly has a curious bulge at the top but is concave beneath, where her dark, abundant bush reaches almost up to her navel. The lips of her quim gleam coral pink in the depths of this luxuriant forest. When parted they reveal complex folds and whorls of soft, oysterlike flesh that almost conceal the opening of her vagina, which is tight and fine in texture. Her derrière is especially curvaceous while her thighs are slender, graceful, and vigorous in action.

She showed me an interesting position, novel to me, in which she lay on her back with her legs straight up in the air while I lay sideways-on to her – in which position I was able to rut in her furrow or poke her in either hole with surprising facility – and, of course, to indulge in a mixture of all three at will. You'll like it, Kitten, when I show you.

18. Wednesday, September 8, 7p.m. – Hannah O'M——y ('Bridey'): a tall, wild, abandoned nineteen-year-old Irish rose, with fine, wavy red hair, cut to shoulder-length. Her father is a gamekeeper on a large estate in County Fermanagh. Her face wears an air of permanent surprise thanks mainly to her high-arched brows and pale-green eyes. When she smiles, which is often, the surprise shades over into suggestions of mischief-making and naughtiness. Her fine, milk-white skin is adorned with more freckles, of all shapes and sizes, than the Milky Way has stars; when you see her naked for the first time you wonder if a new race has not joined the white, red, yellow, black, and brown peoples of the world. Despite her tallness her build is slight and her limbs are thin to the point of being skeletal; yet her muscles are firm and she is one of the most active of all Lazy Daisy's fillies in an engagement. Her breasts are of medium size, high and firm, with small nipples (which, nonetheless, have their due meed of freckles, too). Her derrière is small and neat. Her sparse red bush is long and wispy and her cleft is so fine it almost

merges with her hair down there. Her labia are thin but deep; their outline is clearly visible in the daylight between her thighs, even when clamped together. The perfume off her quim is breathtakingly sublime. Her hole is small and constricted but her vagina is soft and capacious, doing nothing to hurry the ardent lover along.

19. Friday, September 10, 6p.m. – Katherine St——son ('Gazelle'): a shy and (on the day of our encounter) rather sad little seventeen-year-old with short, straight black hair, severely cut. Her father seems to have no occupation other than fly-fishing in season. This was her first week in the game. Perhaps she will liven to the work in a month or two. I hope so for there are few fillies at Lazy Daisy's who are better equipped for it by bounteous Mother Nature. She has the gamine face of the first young girl with whom every man ever fell hopelessly in love. Her dark eyes gleam with a sad, reflective, far-off light; her adorable, retroussé nose with its finely flared nostrils suggest a fastidious taste whose approval one must strive to earn; her wet, bruised-looking lips just beg to be kissed and comforted. Her breasts are as divinely perfect as humanly possible – soft, firm, and gloriously rounded with engorged nipples that makes one's fingers itch to caress them. Her slender waist swells to broad, beautifully moulded hips and a most delectable derrière. Her bush is dense and glossy on the upper part of her mound but, like a goatee beard on a man's chin, it tapers to a point before it makes the turn round into her fork. At that point her almost hairless cleft begins. Her outer labia are fine and smooth and not yet engorged with the heavy traffic of her new trade. Her thighs are straight from Canova's most graceful sculptures. When she draws them apart they open her labia to reveal a perfect young blossom of a quim, whose intricate flesh is of a pale and most delicate pink. Her hole is long and relaxed, half-hidden among the frills

of her cunny. Its aroma is an enticing blend of fish and some nameless spice, very close to the paste known as 'Gentleman's Relish' – which I shall never again eat without thinking of darling 'Gazelle.' Her vagina is meaty and firm.

20. Monday, September 13, 5p.m. – Marina Di——a ('La Bella'): a medium-tall Italian woman of twenty-two with longish dark-red hair, verging on black. Her father is a cathedral stone mason in Milan. She has a most aristocratic face, with large, serious, limpid eyes, a Roman nose, and firm, chiselled lips that smile in a vaguely dreamy fashion most of the time. She carries her head with great poise on her long, swanlike neck, to which her small, pert breasts form a perfect counterbalance. Her belly is made to appear even more concave than it is by her habit of thrusting forward her mound and clenching in her slim derrière, which gives her ordinary walk a most seductive glide. Her mound is, in any case, prominent – made more so by her outer labia, which are enlarged and tumid with the frequent exercise. Her inner labia are but rudimentary and do not conceal her clitoris. Her slim, graceful thighs show daylight at her fork, which accentuates the swollen appearance of her labia. Her vagina is soft and loose.

21. Wednesday, September 15, 6p.m. – Polly W——m ('Angel'): a quiet, taciturn filly of twenty-three with long, fine, straight hair whose basically fair colour is tinged with auburn. Her father is a cattle dealer in the Vale of York. She has adopted a most amazing manner – suggested to her in the first place, I believe, by her eyes, which are pale grey and hooded by heavy upper lids. This gives her the appearance of living in a permanent stupor – which, I know, is far from being the case. However, she has turned it to her advantage, for, naturally, it attracts to her those

men who do not desire a girl to be too active – the men who prefer to awaken a 'sleeping beauty' rather than find themselves overwhelmed by a sexual Gorgon with an insatiable appetite for carnal pleasure. In short, she spends most of her time during an encounter with a man, lying quite immobile with those eyes of hers still half closed, sighing and moaning with apparent pleasure and goading her partner to give her more and yet more of it. Her body is perfectly formed for this particular style of encounter. Her lips are loose and wanton. Her breasts are of exquisite size and shape, with dark, swollen nipples that look as if they carry a thousand-volt charge even before a man touches them. Her back is slender and willowy, terminating in the splendid, onion-like bulbs of her derrière; she has a snake-like way of moving it that can drive a man (of her self-selecting type) wild in his frenzy to please her. Her mound is prominent and adorned with whorls of bright ginger bush that do nothing to hide a cleft of gratifyingly large, meaty proportions; its perfume is a heady blend of musk and cinnamon – indeed, every inch of her skin exudes a diluted version of the same blissful aroma. Her quim is perfectly fashioned for her particular manner – poke it from whatever direction you please and her labia seem to guide you effortlessly into the warm, juicy depths of a firm passage whose every inch of flesh seems charged with some magical power to excite and thrill her (or so her behaviour suggests!).

22. Friday, September 17, 10p.m. – Cicely D——g ('Flora'): a pleasant, vivacious, Scottish filly of twenty-two with shoulder-length, straight red hair. Her father, a nonconformist preacher, died when she was two. Her mother then married a retired clergyman, who stole Cicely's virginity at the age of seventeen and then cast her out when she accused him of it; she is still in regular, secret touch with her mother, who is now quite proud of

her daughter's wealth and independence. Cicely might not be any man's first choice as a partner for the four-legged frolic, but she would almost certainly be every man's second choice – for, although she has no single feature of outstanding attraction, there is not one unattractive detail to repel a man, either. Her face is pleasingly ordinary, her voice is gentle, her smile warm. Her breasts, neither large nor small, are cutely inviting. Her waist is comfortable and her derrière adequately padded. Her quim is dainty and almost odourless, and her vagina is neat and effective. In an odd way, you might say she is an *ideal* woman – in that she is the sort of female any artist might draw, or any sculptor sculpt, if he did not have a *particular* female before him as a model.

23. Monday, September 20, 4p.m. – Rosa Pl——er ('Satin'): an odd yet delightful young seventeen-year-old, tall for her age, with short, dense, curly brown hair. Her father is a sea captain (though she later claimed she had meant to say he was a doctor on an ocean liner – so who can say what he is?). Her slightly immature body has no remarkable features. Her dark-green eyes are restless and birdlike. Her nose is aquiline and superior. Her thin lipped, rather small mouth is ever ready to smile – not always for any identifiable reason. Her breasts are still those of a child, though her nipples are fully grown and, indeed, seem to occupy most of her bosom. Her waist and hips are splendidly matched and, like her commodious derrière, leave one wishing for no further development. Her mound is small and sparsely forested as yet, with a shallow cleft, barely visible until one bends down to kiss it there. Her labia are small and smooth and her quim is sleek and simple; it has an elusive aroma that reminds me of the small-mammal house at the zoo but I cannot refine it closer than that. It is certainly most attractive to a man. Her vagina is delightfully narrow and gripping, though it

yields well to the intruding gristle. Her oddity, however, lies in the suggestion she conveys that, while you may be enjoying a frolic with her, she is simultaneously conducting some much deeper investigation of *you!* Thus, for example, when I was in the middle of screwing her in one particular (and particularly enjoyable) position, she gave a little wriggle of her derrière, popped Iron Jack out of her, twisted round to a new position, impaled herself on him again, and clamped herself firmly around me, giving me a little sigh of ecstasy to encourage me to continue! No matter that I had been enjoying our former position – and making my enjoyment quite volubly clear to her – something went click in her mind and it was a case of 'All change!'

24. Wednesday, September 22, 5p.m. – H—n Chin See (probably not her right name as I notice it is an anagram of Chinese, too): a slender, willowy Chinese maiden of twenty-four with short, highly lustrous, straight black hair, which is cut in a characteristic Chinese bob. Her gazelle-like eyes are dark and soulful in a face that is the perfect (to Occidental eyes) type of Chinese beauty. Her breasts are diminutive but exquisitely formed, with cherrylike nipples in small, pale aureoles. Her slight body with its creamy-yellow skin is a flawless example of femininity and beauty, with a slim belly and a deliciously rounded derrière. Her mound is a small, almost hairless dome, completely divided by a prim, tight cleft. Her labia are all of equal size, being small and rounded. On parting they reveal a hole of inviting dimensions – my only disappointment being that it did not mimic the shape of her eyes! Screwing her face to face would then have been a totally different experience from screwing her sideways-on. Must not carp, however, she was firm and juicy in action and of more than adequate depth, despite her smallness of stature.

25. Friday, September 24, 8p.m. – Jemima F—y ('Zephire'): a voluptuous young filly of twenty with longish, straight honey-blonde hair. Her father is a canvasser for a national newspaper. Of all the fillies at Lazy Daisy's Jemima looks as if she were designed or intended for the business. To varying degrees the others are girls you might pass on the street; almost all of them have a beauty that would cause heads to turn (that, after all, is why they are so expensive!) but only Jemima would start the drool falling from the dropped jaw at the same time. There is not one curvaceous inch of her that does not make the cry of 'Sex!' ring out through the cavities of a suddenly emptied mind – emptied, that is, of all other thoughts but that of possessing her. Small wonder that I saved her to the last! And she made every weary moment of my labour of love among the other two dozen worthwhile! She has wide, come-to-bed eyes that sparkle with suggestions of naughtiness; a perfect little nose with delicate nostrils; rosy cheeks that promise health and vigour; a mouth on the verge of being *too* generous for the petite and pretty face it adorns. The line of her neck and shoulders is graceful and tender – a perfect complement to the volume of her breasts, which no artist or sculptor could improve upon. They, too, are on the large side for her slender frame, but are amazingly uplifted (and uplifting!) and firm; her nipples are like two flawless cherries. Her skin is creamy white and the odour from her armpits on a hot summer afternoon is the very essence of seduction. Her mound is a mountain of pleasure, split by a crevice of wondrous beauty, plump and soft. Her inner labia unite in her fork and run forward in a single ridge to join her outer labia high in her mound. This ridge, of the tenderest pink flesh, is like the ridge down the midline of a man's organ and seems every bit as sensitive, too. The flavour of her quim is both heady and soporific. Her hole is small and like the trumpet of a lily. The vagina into

which it leads is succulent and sturdy; it has a certain muscular power, which she uses to great effect.

That concluded my Herculean labour on behalf of my darling Kitten. On rereading it now, after more than forty years, I am struck by the one thing on which I did not then think it necessary to comment but which now marks the greatest single difference between the girls of those days and those of the present: the clothes they wore. The modern Utility miss in her modern Utility camiknickers and Utility bra would have raised sneers of derision among the girls of my gilded youth. Even the drabbest scullery maid of those days – nay, even the female prisoner in her penitentiary – knew that the zone between her knee and her navel was a temple of enticement, pleasure, naughtiness, temptation, provocation . . . according to her temperament or to the occasion; and she took pains to adorn, garnish, and beautify it accordingly.

The mere act of undressing her was to plunge one's fingers into an erotic billowing of frills, ruches, furbelows, pleats, and ruffles in every seductive material imaginable. Sheer silk stockings in black, peach, ultramarine, viridian, or alizarine; chenille garters in crimson or lilac; art-silk suspenders in glossy black, embroidered with little scarlet roses; sateen corsets in glossy black shot with purple or deep maroon, or black-and-pink stripes, hugging her glorious form, or flesh pink with tier upon tier of organdy frills, rising in all cases to two snug arbours in which her bubbies lay at rest, free to tremble as nature intended – and free for the roving hand to grope, as nature also intended.

And there in the heart of all this adornment was the most stimulating garment of all, at once provocative and utilitarian to the nth degree: her 'convenient' or 'open' drawers, which both hid and revealed her most private treasure, and both invited and denied the hornified male his entrée. The odd glimpse of naked flesh among this riot of haberdashery and colour could set a man shivering and shaking with passion.

How curious that in an age when women were considered pure and sweet and really rather above the earthy compulsions of sexual desire their undergarments mocked that very notion – whereas today, when all the world acknowledges that women have as healthy a sexual appetite as men, their undergarments proclaim to that same world: 'If you're looking for a bit of fun, you won't find it here!' Ah me!

Shortly after I handed Kitten my final report, she gave me a sealed envelope for Rachel. Unfortunately, this, too, had an accident with a steaming kettle – which explains how I am able to reproduce it here.

Kitten's Erotic Reverie

I have written this on the inspiration of Rachel's erotic reverie. But if anyone reading it is hoping for the same 'high explosive' quality, I fear they will be gravely disappointed. Until I read Rachel's wonderful confession I was not even aware of having such reveries myself; now, thinking it over, I must confess that I have been enjoying them – almost without realizing it – for many years, right back into the days of my innocence.

Let me describe the form it took in those early days, before I knew anything of Venus and her art. I was brought up by strictly religious parents who considered it best for my protection to tell me nothing whatever of the mysteries of sex; my mind was not even polluted with thoughts of pollen and the busy bee. Yet, of course, I was aware that there are profound differences between men and women and I knew it centred on that zone of shame between our thighs.

Curiously enough, thanks to certain inferences I made

from farmyard animals, I was more aware of *male* genitalia than female ones. I never gazed at my own quim in a mirror, for instance; but the merest passing glance at dogs, bulls, and boars in the field enabled me to guess what men might have 'down there.' Not, mind you, that I ever gave it much serious thought.

My reverie concerns an actual day in my life when I, aged fourteen, took my cousin, a little girl of about eight, to the photographer. My mother accompanied us, of course, but she left us at the studio and went off to do some shopping.

My cousin was one of those devastatingly pretty young things with a beautifully supple body, slender waist, and sinuous thighs – the sort of little girl who cannot help stirring men to erotic fancies. The photographs my mother required were of her in her Greek-dancing costume, a diaphanous veil that might just as well not have been there at all. The photographer, a young man in his early twenties, was clearly having trouble with her – or rather with the emotional disturbance she was causing inside him. It is here that my reverie takes over. On the actual day, he controlled himself admirably (as men usually do), finished taking his plates, gave us a cup of tea, talked affably if rather patronizingly to us, and handed us back at last to dear Mamma.

But in my reverie – which, I must stress, I began to enjoy before I had even the smallest degree of sexual enlightenment – things are different. I become aware of his excitement and am fascinated by it. I know it has something to do with that forbidden zone up at the top of my cousin's legs – and mine. So when he bends down to make some small adjustment to the scenery or his camera tripod, I go and stand near him, placing my forbidden zone near his face.

I observe that he lingers over what he is doing, makes unnecessary adjustments, and so on, just to keep his face near that part of me. And thus, even though I know nothing of its function (indeed, until Freddy took my virginity on that memorable Friday afternoon last July, I didn't even know I had a *hole* up there!), I am almost painfully aware that this is a powerful and mystical part of my body. Merely by my possession of it I can hold this young man's attention, change his behaviour, make him sweat, cause his fingers to tremble.

I lose no chance to exploit this power of mine. When he sits down at his desk to make a list of the exposures he took, I sit *on* the desktop, as near to him as I can get – prattling on like an artless young girl about this and that. But all the time I'm swinging my legs and wriggling my bottom – and watching how it chokes his breathing and makes his fingers nerveless.

That's all! I told you it was tameness itself.

Since working at Lazy Daisy's I can now identify the intense feelings of joy these fancies gave me in the days of my innocence; they were, indeed, my first small sexual orgasms, even though they were accompanied by no overt thoughts of a sexual nature. I never wondered what was happening in that same region of the young photographer. I had not the faintest interest in *his* forbidden zone and did not in any way equate it with mine. Mine was the one with all the power; his was a matter of sublime indifference to me!

Postscript: And now that I have taken the trouble to write this little reverie down, I can see it has strong links with my work at Lazy Daisy's. It is all to do with quim-power! I am not being too fanciful if I say that a house of pleasure is a device for amplifying that mysterious quim-power to an almost infinite degree. In that photographer's studio my young-girl's quim, all tucked away inside my drawers and then further hidden between my thighs, and the whole arrangement being covered over in a white, summery frock, was the feeblest of beacons.

Yet it sent out rays of some kind – animal magnetism, or something – commands the young fellow was compelled to obey. He knew he wouldn't get the merest sniff of it under all that freshly laundered clothing – much less a sight of it – much less still the chance of a touch. He knew his hopes in that direction were literally zero. Yet my quim radiated her commands and compelled him to linger close by in all his hopelessness.

But the two dozen quims that lie in waiting, patiently and passively, here at Lazy Daisy's, are a different matter altogether! They send out a combined signal that has ten thousand men's cocks at a stand, all over Yorkshire and Lancashire, every day. These are men who know of our existence but who will never be able to afford a visit here (and would never be admitted even if they could). These unhappy fellows think of our quims and salivate, and shiver, and lose their concentration, and feel a hard bone rising up to throb inside their trousers. What then of those who can afford to come, and do, and are admitted! *You poor creature!* I sometimes think when I see one or other of them enter, bright-eyed and trembling. *You were here only last week. And when you left with your tail between your legs you looked as if you'd had enough starch taken out of you to last a year. And here you are, back again! What a treadmill you are on!*

I think of them now, at their daily business all over the north of England – riding to hounds, sitting as magistrates, pleading as barristers, taking part in parades or military exercises, sitting by their firesides with a rewarding book, lying in their beds . . . It makes no difference what healthy, uplifting, or exhausting labour may consume them. Sooner or later they will heed the call our twenty-four much-loved quims are radiating from this house, day and night, whether we are sleeping or awake. And one by one, like poor slaves whose minds have been taken over by a superior power, they come bowling up our front drive, desperate to obey *our* imperative and free themselves of our magnetic power for another brief respite.

And that, let me confess it now, is one of the greatest pleasures of working here – to feel that animal magnetism radiating out from my little quim, and to see the high and mighty males who answer its call, pay their tribute, and spend their powers, poking it and washing it to a silence that never lasts!

This delightful little effusion of Kitten's was the cause of the next great change in my life, for my own fair copy of it (made before I reglued the letter and passed it on to Rachel) fell into the hands of my father. 'So!' he cried, brandishing it in my face, 'this is what occupies your mind while you are out hunting bugs!'

Put like that, what could I do but agree?

I could hardly tell him the truth! Yet even now it amazes me to think of the conclusion to which he leaped. It was, I grant, a reasonable assumption that I had composed the text since it was in my own hand. But to go on believing that the youth who could dream up such an erotic concoction could at the same time be as fanatically interested in 'bughunting' as I pretended to be leaves the mind rather stunned. Anyway, he told me that if I wished to continue living under his roof I would have to knuckle under to his ideas of right and wrong and cease to write such filth. I took this to mean the same as its corollary – that if I wish to continue writing such filth, I should cease to live under his roof.

I told him so, quite amiably, I thought.

He turned rather pale and said he'd cut me off without a penny.

I asked if that would be the same as disowning me.

He said it certainly would.

I asked him if he was absolutely sure about that.

He foamed at the mouth a bit but I gathered he was, indeed, absolutely sure about it.

So I asked him if I got Sidney Graustein to draw it up in the form of a declaration, would he have the courage of his convictions and sign it?

Put like that, what could he do but agree!

He flung my 'filthy effusion' into my face and stalked out of the room – indeed, out of my life altogether.

A week later I was all alone in the world and the great sexual odyssey of my life was underway.